SEXY BABE

A Hollywood Thriller

James L. Conway

Camel Press has granted permission to publish excerpts from *Dead and Not So Buried* (2012).

ISBN: 9780988549937

For more information contact: www.jameslconway.com
:

Also by James L. Conway

Dead and Not So Buried

In Cold Blonde

For Rebecca

Who will always be my Sexy Babe

We are all of us stars, and we deserve to twinkle.

MARILYN MONROE

.

ONE

The worst day of my life began with an orgasm.

His, not mine. So what else is new?

His name was Jason Settles, an actor who had that bad-boy thing going on. Jason had long sun-bleached hair, brown bedroom eyes, a perpetual three-day beard and these incredibly perfect white teeth, well, caps really, but this was Hollywood and everyone had caps, or wanted them.

Jason was usually typecast as Sexy and Dangerous, and his girlfriend, Grace Taylor, that's me, was usually cast as the cute, perky, blonde, blue-eyed Girl Next Door. Which, I guess I looked but rarely felt like.

Jason lived on Wonderland Drive just off Laurel Canyon in this little blue bungalow with a hot tub in back. It seemed like every house in Laurel Canyon had a hot tub, some kind of weird remnant of the 70s, I think. It was in that hot tub that Jason and I had first made love. And the answer is no, I didn't get off that night either. To be perfectly frank, I generally need a little mechanical help, if you know what I mean. It kind of freaks guys out, though, when you ask them to use a vibrator on you. Makes them feel inadequate or something. So I usually just fake it and take care of myself later.

Okay, that's probably too much information. Anyway, after Jason's wham bam thank you Grace, he climbed out of bed and went into the bathroom. "You want the shower first?" he asked.

"No," I said. "I need to get home and change. I've got an audition at ten." Then I bolted up in bed. Shit! My agent was supposed to fax the scene to me here at Jason's house. I leapt out of bed and raced to Jason's fax machine. Thank God, the scene was there.

It was three pages. Not bad, I thought, walking back to the bathroom. Usually, the more pages the better the scene. Then I read the character name: Sexy Babe.

"Oh, no," I muttered as I joined Jason.

"What is it?" he asked through a mouthful of toothpaste.

"My character. It's Sexy Babe."

"The role's not even big enough for a character name?"

I scanned the material, just two lines in a three-page scene. This was bad. I was supposed to be reading for guest star roles, leads in pilots, break-out parts in edgy independent movies, not two lines as a nameless bimbo on *NCIS*. "I may not have worked in a while," I said, insecurity filling every pore of my being. "But I'm not doing another bit part."

"Hey," Jason said, "look at the bright side; at least it's not Sexy Babe #2."

The bright side, of course. I'm good at looking at the bright side. In fact, I've got a deep well of eternal optimism. I just have to remind myself to tap it.

"No, Jason," I said. "The bright side is realizing that this must be some kind of mistake. Someone must've sent me the wrong sides. I'll just call Lucas when the agency opens and straighten it all out."

I stepped on Jason's medical scale, reached to adjust the weights, and then stopped. "Who weighs 94 pounds?"

"Who, what?"

"Weighs 94 pounds. The scale is set at 94 pounds, it's usually set at either 185ish, your weight, or 105ish, my weight. Hey, I know," I said, trying to be funny. "You're probably banging the model next door. She looks like she weighs 94 pounds."

"Really," Jason said, as he stepped back into the bedroom and started getting dressed. "I hadn't noticed."

Okay, about a hundred things wrong with that answer. First, no man could *not* notice how skinny Melody was. She was five-foot-ten, all legs, tits and ass. Second, she traipsed around the backyard in a band-aid sized bikini doing weird Tai Chi exercises every morning. Third, Jason may be gorgeous, but he's not a very good actor, so he could've definitely used a take two on the "Really, I hadn't noticed," delivery. And now that I thought about it, he looked guilty as hell.

Then it hit me. "You're sleeping with her, aren't you?"

"Don't be ridiculous."

Whoa, that reading was even worse than, "Really, I hadn't noticed." Now I was sure. "Jason, stop lying to me. Why don't you just man up and admit you're sleeping with her."

This was where he was supposed to sweep me up in his arms, tell me how stupid I was being, how much he loved me, and then shut me up with a passionate kiss. Instead, he looked at me and said, "All right, I'm sleeping with Melody."

His words seemed to hang in the air in front of me. I'd asked for the admission, hoping he wasn't sleeping with her. But actually hearing him say the words hurt more than

I could have imagined. I didn't know what to say, what to do next.

"In fact," Jason said, filling the awkward silence. "I think I may be in love with her."

Any confusion I felt was suddenly washed away. "Wait," I said. "You think you're in love with another woman yet you screwed me ten minutes ago?"

"I was trying to find the right time to tell you."

"Yeah, tough decision. Do I dump Grace before I fuck her or wait until I'm done."

"See, I knew you would turn this around on me."

"What?"

"That you'd find a way to blame me."

"I do blame you. Hello! You're fucking another woman!"

"Because..." He trailed off like the rest of his sentence was obvious.

I tried to think of what would come next and drew a blank. "Because, what?"

"Think about it," he said, staring hard at me. "It's all your fault."

"My fault?"

"I'm not the one with intimacy issues."

"So you're saying that if I didn't have intimacy issues, you wouldn't have cheated on me?"

"There you've said it. And I forgive you."

"You forgive *me*?"

"What we had was great, Grace. Awesome, even. But it's time we moved on." He grabbed his keys off the counter. "I'm going to the gym. It might be best for everyone if you were gone when I get back." He walked out the door.

Okay, Jason was a jerk. I knew that. But for the last six months he was *my* gorgeous jerk.

4

And I always knew Jason was just an in-between guy – the guy after my last less-than-perfect boyfriend and before the long-dreamed-about Mr. Right. But still… Ouch.

Oh, and the worst thing – I weighed 109.

I burst out Jason's front door fifteen minutes later. My arms were filled with the detritus of our six months together. A box filled with make-up, tampons, toothbrush – you know, that stuff. I balanced a pile of clothes on top of the box and tried to talk into the cell phone wedged into my shoulder. "Sexy Babe? Come on Lucas, it's got to be some kind of mistake."

Lucas Abrams was my agent. We hooked up when I first got to town — yes we slept together and no, I didn't. Actually it was more a fling than a thing; he came to a showcase where I performed a scene from *Carnal Knowledge*. He'd just been promoted to an agent at Pinnacle Artists after making the "mail room to assistant" odyssey. He liked my work, and signed me. We went out that night to celebrate, had too many Cosmos, and ended up back at his place. We both admitted it was a mistake in the morning, agreed our working together was more important than our sleeping together, and we've been platonic ever since.

"Actually," he said. "The fax was a mistake."

"I knew it." I reached my seven-year old red Miata convertible, dumped my crap in the back seat, and took proper hold of the phone. "I mean, you promised me no more bit parts. So when I saw --"

"Not that kind of mistake," Lucas interrupted. "More like the 'you're not a client anymore so we're not sending you out on auditions' kind of mistake."

"What?"

"Times are tough, Grace. Too many actresses, too few parts. So the partners have decided to trim the client list."

"If this is a joke, it is so not funny."

"No joke. Look, I fought for you, I did. But the partners just looked at the bottom line. Each year you've booked less and less work."

"But we've been so close! I almost landed that Cameron Crowe comedy six months ago. And you said I was the second choice for the CBS pilot."

"I was being nice, Grace. You were a bust in both auditions."

"What?"

"You've got tons of talent, don't get me wrong. But you're just not the same actress I met five years ago. It's like the passion's been sucked out of you."

"Do you have any idea how hard it is to learn two or three parts a day, drive all over town auditioning –- seeing the same actresses trying out for the same roles –- and almost never getting hired?"

"I do. But you used to be excited to have all those auditions. Now you dread them. Does that tell you anything?"

"It's hard not to get discouraged, Lucas. But I'll do better, I promise. Give me another chance; I'll be the new improved Grace Taylor, you'll see."

"I'm sorry, it's out of my hands. Stop by anytime to pick up your head-shots and demo reel."

"Lucas, no, please…"

"Prove us wrong, kiddo. Go out there and become a star." He hung up.

I promised myself I wouldn't cry on the drive home. I made it twenty feet. Tears of anger, frustration and humiliation poured down my face. I was crying so hard

6

traffic was a blur so I turned on the windshield wipers. They scraped uselessly against the bone-dry glass and when I realized how stupid I was, I started laughing.

Then my old optimism came roaring back. Hey, it'll all work out, I told myself. I had tons of actress friends who would be happy to introduce me to their agent. And guys hit on me all the time. So fuck Jason Settles. Grace Taylor was available again and Hollywood was full of hot guys.

It was about a fifteen-minute drive from Jason's house to my apartment in Westwood. Or should I say, apartment about to go condo.

Would you pay $560,000 for a 400 square-foot, one bedroom apartment in a thirty-year-old building? Me neither. Never mind the fact I had no money and lousy credit. The apartment was shabby, the walls were paper-thin, the refrigerator rattled, the toilet ran, and the shower stall smelled like rotten cheese.

My lease was up and, since I wouldn't buy the shithole, they were kicking me out. I had twelve days to vacate the premises. To be honest, I hadn't even started looking. I was kind of hoping Jason would ask me to move in with him.

Idiot!!

I heard the phone ring inside the apartment. I was holding the box in one arm and the armload of clothes in the other, but I managed to dig my keys out of my purse and let myself in. I dumped my stuff on the chair and dove for the phone like a lifeline. "Be someone I know and love."

"Will I do?" I recognized the voice instantly. Madison Stone, one of my best friends. We met at an audition for the TV show, *House*, both reading for a newlywed who's got a brain tumor and only Dr. House's quirky brilliance can save her. If I was the Girl Next Door, Madison was usually cast as the Drop Dead Gorgeous. Madison had incredible red hair, a killer body and this oozing kind of sexuality that usually left guys tripping all over themselves. And, if she'd been a better actress, she could have been a star. But to be honest, and she was the first to admit it, Madison was a little stiff. She always seemed to be "acting," was never able to disappear into the role. But she worked it. She was in two different acting classes, and a cold reading workshop. Madison did book a lot of print work and enough commercials to keep her in a nice apartment, let her shop at Barney's, and treat us to hundred-dollar lunches at the Ivy.

"Oh, thank God, Madison. You won't believe the day I'm having. Jason dumped me and my agent fired me."

"Oh, sweetie, I'm so sorry. I never liked Jason, though. None of us did. But your agent is a different..." Madison tailed off. A beat later her voice was louder, angry. "What the hell are you doing here?" She was talking to someone else in her apartment.

"Madison, who's there? Are you all right?"

"Get away from me." She sounded scared now. Near panic.

"Madison!"

She screamed. Then I heard what sounded like a punch, followed by another scream, shattering glass, the thud of the phone hitting the floor, and then the line went dead.

Oh shit. I quickly called her back, but it just rang. And rang. Not good.

Madison only lived a couple of blocks away, so I thought about running over there and rescuing her, then got real. I'm an actress, not the Bionic Woman. I called 911. It was busy. Ten-fifteen on a Thursday morning and 911 is busy! I called again. Busy. Goddamn L.A. I grabbed my purse and bolted out the door.

I started running. If I cut through the alley and caught the light on Santa Monica Boulevard, I could be at Madison's in a couple of minutes. And while I may not have been the Bionic Woman, Madison and I did take a self-defense class from Charlie Wang's Women Empowerment Academy.

I reviewed Charlie's Five and Five. The five target areas: Eyes, Nose, Throat, Jaw and Groin. The five attacks: Palm Strike, Throat Strike, Head Butt, Elbow Blow, Knee Kick. Charlie was also a huge proponent of mace. We drilled using it when attacked from the front and attacked from the rear. On graduation day, we each got a diploma and a four-ounce can of mace. I'd never fired it in anger, so to speak, but it was in my purse and ready to go.

I looked for help as I bolted out of the alley and raced down Kelton Avenue. No cops, anywhere. No hunky guys standing around who might want to help a lady in distress, either. The light blinked from yellow to red as I got to the intersection. Screw it, I thought, and I darted into the street. Screeching brakes and blaring horns greeted me, but I made it across Santa Monica unscathed and stopped in front of Madison's building. There was an exterior staircase leading to the second floor landing and Madison's apartment.

I pulled out my cell phone, tried 911 one final time and couldn't get a signal. I had a copy of Madison's key, part of Charlie Wang's Buddy System. I grabbed it and started up the stairs. When I reached the apartment, I put my ear to the door, heard nothing. Tried to look in the window, but the drapes were drawn.

I thought about knocking. But if some evildoer was inside, I was afraid they would just shoot me through the door. So I unlocked the door, traded the key for my can of mace and slowly stepped inside.

The living room was empty, but a complete mess. Stuff was tossed everywhere. I inched forward, peeked into the kitchen. Madison was sprawled on the floor. I rushed to her, blood dripped from a gash on her forehead. She was either dead or unconscious.

"Madison!" I whispered urgently. I put two fingers to her carotid artery –- I played a nurse on an episode of *The Mentalist* and the technical advisor had taught me how to do it. The pulse was strong, thank God. "Madison," I whispered again. I looked for something to staunch the bleeding. There was a dishtowel on the counter. I grabbed it, but when I pulled it, I realized it was sitting under a nest of copper measuring cups. They went flying; with a loud clang, they hit the floor.

There was a thud from somewhere in the apartment, then the sound of running footsteps. Crap!

I whirled toward the kitchen door, the mace aimed in front of me. A man burst into the kitchen. Big, mean and ugly. Not him, the gun in his hand. He was short, but all muscle, with a pockmarked face and maniacal eyes.

As he raised the gun, I sprayed him full in the face. He screamed and dropped to his knees, his hands clawing at his eyes. I bent over Madison, tried to get her to her feet, but she was still out and dead weight. No way I could pick her up.

Then the thug, still frantically rubbing his eyes, got to his feet. He was recovering fast. I reached out to spray him again, but he knocked the can out of my hand.

Shit!

He dove at me but I darted to my left and he missed. Then I made a beeline for the door.

I half ran, half fell down the stairs. As I hit the ground, I looked back to see the thug flying out Madison's apartment after me. I hurtled myself into the middle of Santa Monica

Boulevard waving my arms, screaming, "Help! Somebody help me!"

The blare of a horn turned me around and I saw a bus roaring towards me. I heard the brakes scream as I dove out of the way. I could feel a hot wind rush past as the bus just missed me. I tumbled to the pavement. There was the screech of another set of tires and a BMW's bumper rocked to a stop inches from my face. I looked up to see a personalized license plate that read, MNYMKR.

The thug ran up on the other side of the street. I leapt to my feet, sidestepped the BMW and raced down the sidewalk. I heard angry horns, squealing brakes and screamed curses as the thug weaved his way through the traffic behind me.

I barreled around a corner right into a young LAPD cop who was walking out of Starbucks. His latte went flying. "Oh, thank God," I said, pointing behind me. "That man attacked my friend and wants to kill me."

The cop looked. "What man?" I turned and looked. The thug was gone. He must've seen the cop and boogied.

"He was there, I swear. Scary guy with a humongous gun."

Something suddenly clicked behind the cop's eyes. "Wait a minute, I know you, don't I? You're an actress, right?"

Okay, I'll be the first to admit, I loved being recognized. Anyone who acts for a living is lying if they say they don't like the attention. And sure, the paparazzi can make your life hell if you reach a certain perfect storm of fame, celebrity or infamy. None of which applied to me. So, the occasional fan was still a thrill. "Yes," I said. "I'm an actress. Grace Taylor." Then back to the felony at hand. "Now, about my friend?"

"Of course, I'm sorry," he said. "Where is she?"

Did I mention the cop was cute? He was young, early twenties, with a baby face, these crazy hazel eyes and a sweet shyness that was totally endearing. His name was Sean, by the way. Officer Sean Harris. He told me that as we ran back to Madison's apartment and climbed the stairs. When we got to Madison's door, it was open.

We cautiously entered the apartment. Sean had his gun out, and I had my mace out. The living room looked the same. "This way," I said and led Officer Harris into the kitchen. Madison was gone. "Madison?" I called. I ran down the hall to the bedroom. It was trashed just like the living room. "Madison?" I looked in her bathroom. Empty.

Officer Harris joined me. "Where is she?"

"I don't know. She was there in the kitchen." I ran back to the kitchen, he followed. "Look," I pointed to a small smear of blood on the floor. "That's blood. Madison's blood. She had a cut on her forehead. And look around the apartment. It's been wrecked. That creep wrecked Madison's apartment."

He took out his notebook. "What's your friend's name?"

"Madison Stone."

He wrote it down. "And you're Grace Taylor. What's your address and phone number?"

"1615 Veteran, Westwood. 310-555-4968."

Officer Harris's radio squawked to life. A dispatcher said, "251 Adam attention, a 211 now in progress at Beverly Glen and Santa Monica, Half Moon Liquor Store. Shots fired."

Officer Harris keyed his mike. "10-4, I've got a two minute ETA." Then to me, he said, "There's an armed robbery going down two blocks from here. Sorry, but I've got to go."

"What about Madison?"

"She probably woke up while you were gone and went for help. I suggest you go home and wait for her to call. If she doesn't show up in a couple of hours, call me." He handed me his card.

"Okay," I said and he left. But it wasn't okay. Who was that guy with the gun? And where the hell was Madison?

TWO

The guy who attacked Madison and chased Grace watched Officer Sean Harris hurry down Madison Stone's staircase from the front seat of his rented Ford Focus. His name was Joey DeCarlo. DeCarlo knew Madison wasn't in the apartment, he'd checked after he broke off chasing the blonde girl. Where the fuck was she? And who the hell was that blonde bitch? He was tempted to walk back into the apartment and shoot her in the face. But that wouldn't get him Madison back, and that's all that mattered right now.

Joey took out his cell phone, dialed a number, and then let his finger hover above the send key. This wasn't going to be pleasant. With a sigh, Joey pressed send.

Two thousand eight hundred and ten miles away, in a pool hall in Newark, New Jersey, Eddie DeCarlo ate a broiled chicken breast sandwich, with lettuce, tomato, and Dijon mustard on seven grain bread. No cheese, no mayo, no fries, no onion rings. Just healthy shit, since his cholesterol was 236 and his blood pressure was 147 over 96.

Being a mob boss was dangerous enough, what with ambitious rivals always looking to take over your territory, and the Feds wanting to put you in jail. No reason to further muddy the waters with heart trouble. Eddie even quit smoking. Fuck, he should have never gone to the goddamn doctor. But he'd just turned fifty and Christina and Lucy, his fifteen-year-old twins, convinced him he should have a check up. Well, Doctor Campanile scared the shit out of him. "How'd you like a heart attack, or worse, a stroke." That was the image that put Eddie over the top, being helpless, strapped to a wheelchair, drooling like his Uncle Vinnie.

Eddie was a vain man. He was movie star handsome and proud of it. He had thick, jet black hair with a touch of gray at the temples, deep set brown eyes that could inveigle or impale and a tough, square jaw.

Eddie sat at the bar in front of a bank of five 42-inch plasma TVs, each tuned to a different channel: ESPN and ESPN2, FOX NEWS, TVG, the horse racing channel, and CNBC, the financial station. The TVs were new, the result of a Best Buy delivery truck hijacking. Eddie had to pay cash for the high-definition satellite dish, but it was worth it. The picture quality was incredible.

A couple of Eddie's crew were playing 9 ball. Two more sat at the bar with Eddie, one was reading the *Daily Racing Form,* and the other surfed the net for porn on his laptop. But the most important member of his crew was in L.A., and when Eddie's cell phone rang, he knew it was Joey checking in. "Yeah," Eddie said, answering.

"I found her," Joey said.

"How's she look?"

"Hot, Eddie. She's a redhead now."

"Yeah, well, I bet her bush is still black. When I was with her, when she had that platinum blonde hair, her bush was still jet-black. You'd think they'd dye their pubes to match, or shave it off, but fuck it. You get the, uh, thing?"

"Not yet."

"How complicated can it be? Just ask her where it is."

Joey took a deep breath. "That's sort of the problem, Eddie. I lost her."

Eddie's blood pressure spiked. He fought to stay calm. "Joey, you know I love you like a brother."

"I am your brother."

"I know we grew up together, and I remember changing your diapers, but when you screw up like this, I'm convinced Ma must've found you abandoned on the doorstep, or in a dumpster or living with a pack of wolves. Because there is no fucking way someone so stupid could actually be related to me!"

"I'll find her, Eddie. I'll find the tape."

"We're on an open line here," Eddie snapped. Fuck, won't he ever learn, Eddie thought.

"Oh, shit. Sorry. I mean thing, I'll find the thing."

"You better. We're running out of time, Joey."

"I know." Joey noticed the blonde walking out of Madison's apartment. An idea formed and he smiled, "Don't worry, Eddie. I've got a plan." Then Joey hung up before Eddie could scream at him again.

Eddie got off his stool and started pacing. Funny how doing a favor for an old friend could suddenly turn into such a fucking mess. He punched a number into his cell phone and hit send.

One hundred and eighty miles away, in a hotel suite in Washington, D.C., a cell phone rang. A cell phone the owner bought just for conversations with Eddie DeCarlo.

Alan Cross answered on the first ring. "Yeah." No more, no less. That was typical of Cross. He was impatient, aggressive, an alpha male who lived life like he was in competition with everyone. There was a sharpness to Cross, to his features, to the clipped way he spoke that left the impression of a ruthless businessman. Fair enough.

Cross was in real estate, shopping malls to be exact. He owned fifty-six of them, huge malls with hundreds of stores in the world's greatest cities; New York, Chicago, Las Vegas, Los Angeles, Paris, London, Shanghai, Macao. He lived in Atlanta, the site of his first mall, and the local press coverage of his fiftieth birthday party the previous month mentioned that Cross's wealth now passed the billion-dollar mark.

But the reason Cross's birthday was covered at all wasn't the fact that he was rich. It was really because of who he was married to: Margaret Cross, or more precisely, *Attorney General* Margaret Cross of the great state of Georgia. And as Alan Cross stood in front of the picture window of his Watergate suite staring out at the Capital, his wife was getting dressed in the bedroom for the most important meeting of her life.

Alan listened as Eddie said, "This is one of those good news, bad news calls."

"I was hoping for a good news, great news call."

"Yeah, well, I'd like a ten-inch dick but what're you going to do. So, good news first, we found her. But we're having a little trouble with the, uh, package."

"We've only got twelve hours, Eddie. Maybe less."

"Jesus Christ, what's the fucking hurry?"

"The timetable's been moved up. They're meeting in an hour. Announcement is set for nine tomorrow morning, *if* it doesn't leak before then."

"You should've married a teacher, you know that, or a waitress or a fucking ballerina. But no, you pick a bitch with brains and ambition."

"We all make mistakes, Eddie. That was mine. Don't let not recovering the package be yours. Twelve hours." Cross hung up.

Back in New Jersey, from a rented apartment half a block north of Eddie's pool hall, FBI Special Agent Christy Cortez listened to the call between Eddie DeCarlo and Alan Cross. She sat in front of a state-of-the-art computer array. The Justice Department warrant allowed the FBI to tap the pool hall's phones, Eddie DeCarlo's home phones and Eddie's cell phone. Eddie was smart, assumed he was being bugged and was very circumspect in his conversations. But, people make mistakes, and that's what the FBI was counting on.

The door opened and Christy's partner, Special Agent Jerome Stubblefield, walked in with a large Starbucks bag. He pulled out a Grande Latte for himself and a Cinnamon Dolce Latte for her.

"Eddie just got a call from his kid brother," Christy said.

"Joey?" Stubblefield said, handing her the coffee.

"Thanks, sugar free?" Christy was fighting a losing battle with her mother's genome. She ran three miles a day, ate only 1700 calories, yet her ass kept getting bigger.

"Of course," he said. Stubblefield was six foot three, weighed 310 pounds and ate anything he could get his hands on.

"Yeah, Joey," she said. "He's been off the radar since Tuesday. Now we know why."

"You get a location?"

"California." She checked one of the computer screens. "The closest cell transmission tower is Westwood. Eddie sent him to track down a girl."

"What girl?"

"Don't know. But Joey mentioned he was supposed to get a tape from her."

"Audio tape? Videotape?"

"Don't know. But it's important. Eddie was worried. As soon as he hung up Eddie called a cell phone in D.C. The guy he talked to was worried, too. Said they only have twelve hours."

"A deadline, I like that. Whose cell phone?"

"No way of knowing," she said, typing into her keyboard. "It was a throwaway."

"Well, if Eddie wants that tape, we sure as hell want that tape." Stubblefield took a huge blueberry muffin out of his Starbucks bag. Christy eyed it, ravenously.

"You're cruel," she said.

Stubblefield smiled and took a bite, then thought of something. "Is Westwood anywhere near Chatsworth, California?"

"Yeah, it's all L.A."

"Good. I've got just the guy for the job."

Two thousand eight hundred and fifteen miles away, in the Oakwood Memorial Park, a man was reunited with his wife. She'd been dead for two months, buried next to a royal palm tree in the oldest section of the cemetery. He was being buried in the plot next to her. She died of lung cancer, a long, horrible death as the rogue cells feasted on her body. His death was much quicker, a .38 hollow point to the roof of his mouth.

Only a handful of mourners stood in front of the open grave. But they all understood the wracking grief that had finally forced the FBI agent to take his own life, none more so than the man's partner, Ryan Griffin. Ryan was thirty-eight, twenty-five years younger than his partner, and he idolized his mentor.

Dempsey Magee had taken the young Ryan under his wing when Ryan first joined the FBI after seven years on the Chicago Police Department. They'd met at Quantico. Dempsey was one of Ryan's Field Counselors when he was a New Agent in Training. And there was something about the brash young cadet that appealed to Dempsey. He was smart, but that wasn't it. He excelled at Defensive Tactics, but that wasn't it. And he aced the Physical Training test all three times, but that wasn't it, either. It was the mischievous twinkle in Ryan's eye. The cocky SOB would play the part of by-the-book agent, but deep down, he'd never be turned into a FBI automaton. One of Dempsey's jobs was to sniff these rebels out and send them packing. But not Ryan. Ryan reminded Dempsey of his son. Dempsey's only child was killed by a drunk driver when the boy was only eleven. If Billy had lived, he'd have looked a little like Ryan. And been that smart, that athletic, that rebellious. Dempsey decided to protect Ryan, even requesting to go back into the field and partnering up with the newly graduated Special Agent.

Ryan knew all this. And as he stood over Dempsey's grave, his heart ached. His father had run off when he was seven and was never heard from again. Ryan didn't blame him. His mother was a total bitch. He didn't hate his father for leaving. He hated his father for not taking him along.

Dempsey helped fill the void. They never used the words father and son between themselves, but they both knew the roles they were playing, and they both relished it.

Ryan Griffin's cell phone vibrated. The ceremony was over, so he stepped back and quietly answered. "Hello."

"Ryan, it's Jerome," Stubblefield said. "How you doing?"

"A lot better than Dempsey."

"Condolences, man, I know how close you were."

"Thanks."

Like Stubblefield, Dempsey and Ryan were part of the FBI's Organized Crime Division working out of the Manhattan field office. Dempsey had taken a leave of absence to be with his wife during her final few weeks, leaving Ryan odd man out, so he was assigned to Stubblefield and Christy. Dempsey's suicide had forced Ryan to take a few personal days to fly to L.A. for the funeral. "I need your help," Stubblefield said. "We may have a break on the DeCarlo case. Joey's in L.A. and something's about to go down. Interested?"

"Only if I get to punch and shoot people."

Stubblefield laughed. "How fast can you get to Westwood?"

Twenty-eight point five miles away, in Westwood, LAPD officer Sean Harris stood outside the Half Moon Liquor Store as the Coroner wheeled out the first of the dead bodies.

Just a half-hour before, Sean had left the decidedly adorable Grace Madison to respond to the 211. As he ran, he thought about how cute she was. He wondered if an actress like Grace would ever be interested in a cop. She didn't seem too judgmental, he decided. Maybe after the 211 he could stop by and make sure her friend was all right. Sean pulled his gun as he reached the liquor store and looked through the doorway to see a big black guy empty a double-barreled shotgun into a skinny blonde woman.

Harris had been trained for situations like this. They talked about it in class. They drilled the procedures into you at the live-fire range. It was a moment Harris was waiting for, the moment that could give him the opportunity to be a hero, like his dad, a LAPD Homicide detective, or his two uncles, one a SWAT officer, the other a Lieutenant running the Hollywood Division Vice Squad. Each of them had distinguished themselves on the streets.

When Sean was growing up, the Harris brothers filled his head with tales of glory. Like the time his father, while off duty, just happened to be in a Bank of America when three guys wearing ski masks came in to rob the place. Sean's father killed all three and got a bullet in his thigh for his trouble.

Uncle Jack was making a simple traffic stop when he heard a noise in the trunk of the car. When Uncle Jack asked the driver to step out of the vehicle, the man pulled out a pistol and fired three shots through the door. The first two missed but the third hit Uncle Jack in the stomach. In agony, Uncle Jack shot the driver, killing him. He climbed over the dead man, blood gushing from his stomach wound, ripped the keys out of the ignition, opened the trunk of the car and found a bound, gagged, but still alive six-year-old girl.

Uncle Brad was driving past a 7-11 at three-thirty in the morning when he saw an ATM machine with a thick cable wrapped around it, being jerked out the front window by a tow truck. Uncle Brad hit his lights and siren. The two guys in the tow truck opened fire with Uzis. The bullets tore through Uncle Brad's black and white and into his legs. Unable to hit the brakes, Uncle Brad steered his vehicle into the tow truck. Uncle Brad's airbag deployed, almost knocking him out, but he was able to see the tow truck trying to back up and get away. Though in pain from the gunshot wounds, and groggy from the airbag smacking him in the face, Uncle Brad was still able to pull his gun and shoot both perpetrators through the windshield.

The brothers Harris used to get together on holidays and compare scars. And young Sean Harris dreamed that one day he too could get the Medal of Valor, but hopefully, without getting shot.

So, as the roar of the shotgun filled his ears and the bloodied woman crumpled to the ground, Sean was sure this was his moment. He spun into the liquor store, his Glock in firing position. "Drop the weapon," he screamed, trying to keep the fear out of his voice. "Hands in the air."

The black man, looking absolutely terrified, obeyed. "You don't understand."

Sean said nothing as he kicked the shotgun across the room and cuffed the black man's wrists behind him. The black man started crying. "She killed my wife."

It was only then, once the man was safely cuffed, that Sean's tunnel vision cleared and he saw the dead black woman behind the counter. And the handgun gripped in the fingers of the wounded white woman. She was alive, awash in blood, but breathing. And with a shaking hand, she aimed the gun at Sean. He raised his Glock to fire when, suddenly, two shots rang out and the left side of her face disappeared.

Sean jerked his head to the door. Two cops stood there, smoking guns still aimed at the now very dead woman. The cops had killed her. *They* would be getting the Medals of Valor.

The female perpetrator, a strung-out meth head as it turned out, had burst into the store and fired three shots into the ceiling. That's when the dry cleaner next door called 911. The black husband and wife who ran the store were both behind the counter. The husband handed over the money while they begged for their lives. It didn't help. The perp shot the wife, turned the gun on the husband. He dove beneath the counter, came up with his shotgun. That's when Sean arrived.

In the chaotic aftermath, a detective took Sean's statement, gave him a slap on the back and told him he'd done a good job. But not good enough, Sean thought. That doped-up speed freak could've killed him. He could've shot the black guy thinking he was the perp. If he wasn't careful, he realized, trying to be a hero could get him killed.

The second body was carried out, the wife. The grief-stricken husband followed, his hands on the body bag, not wanting to let her go. There was nothing Sean could have done to save her life, she was dead by the time he got there, but still, oddly, he felt responsible. That somehow he hadn't done enough.

And that made him think of Grace Taylor and her missing friend. Had he done all he could to help them? He reached into his pocket, to make sure he hadn't lost his notebook in the melee. No, it was there. He opened to the page with Grace's address, and smiled.

THREE

I was worried sick. I ran back to my car and drove around the neighborhood, my cell phone to my ear, multi-tasking my search for Madison. I called the local hospital, drove to Urgent Care, called a bunch of friends who lived nearby. I even cruised by Cozy Time, Madison's favorite coffee spot. Nothing.

As I drove back to my building, I had this funny feeling I was being followed. I checked my mirror, couldn't really tell. But it freaked me out. What if that thug was still after me? I parked, ran into my apartment, tossed my purse on the couch and threw the dead bolt.

"That won't keep him out."

I spun, saw Madison standing in my kitchen doorway, a blood-stained towel pressed to her forehead. She said, "Nothing will keep him out if he knows I'm here."

I threw my arms around her. "Thank God you're all right. When I saw you on the kitchen floor, I thought you were dead."

"I came to when Joey chased you out the door. I ran around for a while, not sure what to do, then I used my copy of your key to hide out here."

"Thank God for Charlie Wang! Oh, you should've seen this really cute cop I brought back to your apartment. He thought I was a total nut case."

Madison took the bloodied towel from her head. "I could use some more ice."

"Of course." I grabbed a fresh dishtowel, dug some ice out of the freezer as I asked, "So, who was he?"

"An old boyfriend. Color him obsessed."

"What old boyfriend? You told me you moved to L.A. because you couldn't find a boyfriend."

"Look, Grace," she said. "I haven't been completely honest with you. I left New York because of this guy. He used to beat me. I was afraid he'd kill me, so I split."

I handed her the dishtowel. "And now he's found you."

Madison nodded, tears in her eyes. The look on her face broke my heart. Madison was always so together, the girl with beauty, brains and a plan. Now all I saw was fear.

"Don't worry," I said. "We'll figure this out."

Crash! The front door suddenly splintered open and the thug charged into the apartment. I screamed as he raised that big frickin' gun, but Madison was cooler; she grabbed a frying pan and slammed it into his face. She broke his nose and blood went flying, and so did the gun. It thudded to the floor in the corner of the living room. Madison swung the pan again, but the thug blocked the blow, and then smacked Madison across the face with a vicious backhand. She hit the wall hard and went down. He turned on me, blood on his face, fury in his eyes. "Where's your mace, now, bitch?" he hissed, and threw a punch. I ducked, dove toward the gun. I landed just short, stretched out, was about to wrap my fingertips around the grip when I felt two hands grab my legs and yank me back. He hauled me to my feet, and then hurled me into the kitchen. I slammed into the counter. Utensils went flying as I flipped over and tumbled to the floor. I desperately scanned the debris for something to defend myself, but he was on me in an instant. He grabbed me by the hair and pulled. As I came to my feet, my right hand found the handle of my butcher knife. I wrapped my fingers around it and, as he turned me around, I jammed it into his chest. It scraped past some bone then sunk up to the hilt.

His eyes went wide with shock, then a switch seemed to go off and he fell to the floor. His body twitched a couple of times then went still.

Really still.

Not breathing still.

Dead still.

Madison slowly got to her feet. "Oh, my God, you killed him."

"I didn't mean to. I just grabbed the knife to protect myself and..."

Madison stood over the body, stared at it, horror-struck. "Now we're really in trouble."

"How could we be in trouble, he was trying to kill us."

"We may have been better off if he had."

"What?"

"I haven't been completely honest with you," Madison said, moving to the broken front door. She forced it shut. "This guy wasn't an old boyfriend. He was the brother of my old boyfriend."

"So?"

She picked the gun off the floor and put it on the kitchen counter. "His brother is Eddie DeCarlo."

"Why does that name sound familiar?"

"Because Eddie DeCarlo's name is on the news a lot, usually preceded by words like reputed mob boss, Mafia kingpin or Godfather."

"So we call the cops or the FBI or whoever and --"

"No, no, no," Madison interrupted. "If Eddie finds out we killed his brother he'll put a contract out on us. He won't rest until we're both dead."

Now I looked horror-struck. "So what do we do?"

Madison searched through Joey's clothes. "We make sure Eddie never finds out Joey's dead. We make sure *no one* ever finds out he's dead." She pulled out a set of car keys. I could see a Hertz Rent-a-Car logo on the key chain. "So, here's the plan," Madison said. "We get his body into the car, drive him to the desert, dig a hole and --"

The buzz of the doorbell interrupted her. Madison and I exchanged panicked looks. I snuck a peak through the drapes. "Oh, shit," I whispered. "It's that young cop from your apartment. What do we do?"

Madison picked up one of DeCarlo's legs. "Let's get him to the bedroom." I grabbed the other leg and we dragged him, knife still sticking out of his chest, into the bedroom.

"What about the knife?" I asked. The door buzzed again.

"Forget about it, just get rid of the cop," Madison said, shoving me into the hallway and closing the door.

Another buzz. I took a deep cleansing breath – an acting trick I learned which *never* seemed to work – and opened the door, nonchalantly trying to block as much of his view of inside the apartment as possible. "Officer, hi," I said. "What a nice surprise."

He smiled, a bit nervously I thought. Then he noticed the broken door jam. "What happened to your door?"

I was so tempted to tell him the truth. He looked honest and accessible and, well, helpful. But Madison had sufficiently scared me, so I said, "Oh, a drunken boyfriend who wouldn't take no for an answer broke it. But don't worry, he's history."

"Good," he said, then caught himself. "I mean, I'm glad it was nothing more serious."

"So, Officer…"

"Sean. Please, call me Sean."

"Sean. What can I do for you?"

"Well, I felt bad about having to run off with the 211 and all, and I just wondered if you'd heard from your friend?"

"Madison, yes, yes I did. And she's just fine. Turns out the guy in her apartment was an old boyfriend, too. But she's fine now, he's apologized and everything's hunky dory." Hunky dory? What the hell was the matter with me?

"Great. Glad to hear it." There was an awkward beat as Sean just stood there looking at me. I could tell he wanted to say more. He had that, *I want to ask you out but I'm too nervous to*, look on his face. And under normal circumstances I might have helped him along. He was awfully cute. Of course, my mother would have been horrified. She wanted me to think of my life as a movie starring Grace Taylor, and everyone else in the world was either a supporting character or an extra. And when it came to boyfriends it was essential that you cast them well: movie stars, producers, directors, studio executives – the movers and shakers. And under no circumstance date anyone who wore coveralls or a uniform to work.

I didn't always follow my mother's advice, but since I had a dead body in the bedroom, blood all over the kitchen floor and a Mafia contract hanging over my head, I figured the sooner he left the better.

"So, thanks for stopping by," I said. "I really appreciate it."

"Yeah," he said. "Okay. As long as you're okay, and she's okay, I guess I'm okay."

"Okay. Bye now." And I backed into the apartment and closed the door. I looked out the peephole. Sean just stood there, thinking. Then he started to leave, suddenly stopped, turned back to the door and reached for the doorbell, then stopped again, gave this embarrassed smile, shook his head and finally left.

Madison joined me. "What'd he want?"

"To make sure you were okay. And to ask me on a date, I think. But he chickened out."

"Good. You've already got a date and his name's Joey DeCarlo." She dangled the rental keys. "I'm going to find his car." Madison walked out and I leaned against the door, overwhelmed. It wasn't even noon yet and I'd been dumped, fired, evicted and killed a man.

My cell phone rang. I didn't want to talk to anybody, and then it occurred to me that it might be Jason calling to say he'd made a terrible mistake and he wanted to stay with me. Or Luke, my agent, wanting to tell me the agency's reconsidered and they wanted me back. Pathetic, I know. I checked the caller ID: Mom.

Perfect, I thought. Because this was all my mother's fault. The acting thing, I mean.

Mom grew up in Pasadena. She starred in all the school plays, was actually one of the Rose Bowl Princesses in 1974 and just naturally matriculated into Hollywood. A brunette who reminded everyone of Kate Jackson, she did TV guest shots on shows like *Mannix, Barnaby Jones* and *Hawaii Five-O.* She had dreams of becoming a movie star, a dream she gave up for Daddy.

They met at the Roxy, a rock club still in business today. Marianne Faithful was performing the night they met. Mom was touching up her make-up in the very crowded ladies room when the door burst open and this guy blustered in with his hand over his eyes. "Sorry, ladies, I'm so sorry. I won't look, I promise, but half the toilets in the men's room are backed up, there are a million guys waiting in line and I just can't hold it any longer. You got any room?" There were a few giggles as Mom led the man to an empty stall. As he stepped inside he lowered his hand and looked at her.

"It was love at first sight," Daddy would say. "Even though I'd never seen her before, it was like I'd known her my whole life. Like the missing piece of a puzzle."

You think its easy growing up with that kind of romantic baggage? I will admit I've gone to the Roxy a few times, and when I'm in the bathroom, I sort of hope the door will open and my Mr. Right will bluster in with his hands over his eyes.

Anyway, Daddy worked for an insurance company in Tampa and loved Florida. Mom was an L.A. actress and loved California. They tried the long distance thing for a while. Disaster. They were both miserable. So Mom put love ahead of career and moved to Florida.

After a couple of years of marriage, along comes baby Grace. And like it or not, Mom was determined to make me the star she never became. My first role was at nine weeks old. I played Baby Jesus in a local Christmas pageant. Then came the dancing lessons, singing lessons, beauty pageants, school plays.

I finally rebelled my senior year at Hillsborough High School. I went goth, dyed my hair jet black, and got five lip-piercings and the tattoo of a black cat on my ankle. I thought my mother would have a nervous breakdown. "You look like a slut. Is that what you want? Is this why we've worked so hard for so many years? So you can ruin your face with those things in your lip? And that clown make-up and who knows what drugs you're taking."

Grass was the answer I never gave my mother. I smoked grass every day. You think it's easy being a slacker? Hey, I was cute and perky, remember, so it took a lot of effort and major chemicals to suppress all that natural enthusiasm.

Now it didn't take Dr. Phil to understand why I rebelled. Daddy got it instantly. He told Mom she'd been using me as a surrogate for the life she never had. I had to make my own decisions. Don't worry, he told her, the goth thing was a phase and I'd grow out of it.

And I might have. But I never got the chance. Daddy died a week later. A heart attack when he was cleaning up after dinner. Mom was a wreck but managed to call 911. We cradled him in our arms while we waited for the ambulance. That's where he died. No last words. No goodbyes. Just a final ragged breath and he was gone.

That night, I washed off the make-up, took out the piercings and dyed my hair blonde. I'll never forget the surprised, relieved and grateful look on my mother's face when I came downstairs for breakfast.

The next few months were tough. Mom was devastated by Daddy's death. He had been her whole life. So Mom's friends gathered around her, me included. It was all about making Mom feel better. I even rejoined the drama club for her and starred in the spring musical as Roxie Hart in *Chicago*. I actually enjoyed myself; so much so, I majored in theater at the University of Florida

My college years were a blur of classes, plays, parties and boyfriends. I had three boyfriends to be exact, two actors in the theater department and one professor. So cliché, I know, but Professor Paul was hot. He was also married. He'd told me he was separated, so I figured it was all right. Until his wife walked in on us one night, and I found out that they were only separated because she'd been on teaching sabbatical in Florence, Italy.

And no, I didn't get off with any of them. But Professor Paul did spend one night trying to find my G spot. He must've found my F spot or my H spot, because he came close, sooooo close – but alas, no cigar.

The day after graduation I jumped in my Miata and headed for L.A. Once I signed with Lucas, the work came quickly. I guest starred on a bunch of shows like *CSI, Bones,* and *Gray's Anatomy.* I drifted in and out of a few relationships, made a couple of really good friends and was living the life Mom had always envisioned for me.

All of which brings us back to the worst day of my life.

I thought about letting the call go to voicemail, but I was so freaked out I thought hearing Mom's voice might calm me down, so I answered. "Hi, Mom."

"Grace, honey, I just got the new issue of *TV GUIDE,*" my mother said. "What shows should I circle?"

"Nothing this week, Mom."

"But you haven't been on anything in almost four months, Grace. And that last job was just those two crappy lines on *Two and a Half Men.* You're never going to get your own series at this rate."

I didn't usually unburden myself to Mom, because, frankly, she didn't want to hear my problems. She only wanted to hear good news. However, today seemed like a good day to make an exception. "Mom, I --"

"Are you working with Cliff Osmond like I asked?" she interrupted. "He's the best coach in town. He's the one that taught me to take that little extra beat before a punch line."

"Mom, something terrible has happened."

"You didn't break up with Jason, did you? He's such a nice boy. Just apologize for whatever you did and beg him to take you back."

That punched about a hundred buttons. "Why do you assume it was something *I* did? It just so happens that -- "

BUZZ. Great, now the doorbell interrupted me.

"Hello, anybody home? Ms. Taylor?" a voice called. Then the door was shoved open and my landlady, Adele Finch, walked in with a young couple.

Oh, shit!

"Mom, I've got to go," I blurted as I hung up and rushed to the door. Adele Finch was older than my dead grandmother and a crotchety bitch to boot. She'd been giving me grief from the moment I moved in -- my stereo was too loud, I had too many parties, I parked too close to her precious twenty-year-old Lincoln -- and she was thrilled when I opted not to buy the apartment.

"What have you done to the door, Grace?" Mrs. Finch asked, "It's a mess." She turned to the young couple. "Don't worry, I'll have it fixed before you move in." She turned back to me, "Grace, this is Ken and Bridgette Kern, they'd like to see the condo." Ken and Bridgette looked nice enough, early twenties, eager smiles, a newlywed feel about them, but now was so not the time. "The bedroom's right down the hall," Mrs. Finch said. "Why don't you take a look?"

"No!" I said. "You can't. The, uh… the bed's not made."

Mrs. Finch laughed. "I'm sure they've seen an unmade bed before." Then she noticed Joey's gun on the kitchen counter. "Is that a gun?" She picked it up. "What're you doing with a gun?"

I lurched after her, grabbing the weapon. "It's just a prop." Then I noticed Ken and Bridgette disappearing into the bedroom. "No," I called, but too late. A beat later we heard a scream, followed by Ken and Bridgette running out of the bedroom.

"There's a body in there," Ken said.

"That a prop, too?" Mrs. Finch asked sarcastically. "I'm calling the police."

As she crossed to the phone, I turned, unwittingly aiming the gun at her. "Don't touch that phone," I said.

Mrs. Finch leapt back as she stared at the gun. Ken and Bridgette tried to sneak out the front door. I spun towards them, the barrel now pointed in their direction. "I'm sorry, you can't leave." I followed their terrified eyes to the gun in my hand. "Oh, no, you don't understand," I said. "I'm not going to shoot you. This is all a big misunderstanding."

"You didn't kill that guy?" Ken asked.

"Well, I sort of killed that guy."

A gasp from Mrs. Finch, her hands shot to her chest, her knees buckled and she dropped to the floor.

"Heart attack," Ken said, rushed to her side and began CPR.

"Now you've killed *her*," cried Bridgette.

I didn't know what to do, but I knew I had to get out of the apartment. I grabbed my purse and draped a sweater over the gun. "Call 911," I said to Bridgette, "I've got to go."

I sprinted out the door and as I turned the corner onto the sidewalk, I ran right into Officer Harris. "Hi," he said, a surprised smile on his face. I was just coming back to see you."

"This isn't a great time." I tried to get around him but he blocked my way.

"It's just that, well, I'd love to take you out for a cup of coffee, or a drink, or even dinner."

Talk about bad timing; if I'd just met him one murder earlier. "I'd love to but-- "

A car horn interrupted me. I turned to see Madison pull to the curb in Joey's rental. When she saw me talking to the cop, she honked again.

"Sorry," I said, "I've got to go."

Bridgette suddenly burst out of the apartment building and pointed at me. "Murderer! She's a murderer!"

Sean looked from Bridgette to me.

"Looks like Bridgette's off her meds again," I said. "Well, see ya…"

I started for the car but Sean grabbed my arm and spun me back to him. I pulled back the sweater and aimed the gun at him. "Let go of me." He did. Shock and disappointment filled his face as I unsnapped his holster and took his weapon. "This isn't what it looks like," I said.

"It looks like you're aiming a gun at me and taking my weapon."

"Okay, it is what it looks like, but…" Madison honked again. I so wanted to explain everything to him, I knew he'd understand, but things were unraveling so quickly, I was freaked. I had to get out of there. "I'm sorry," I said backing toward the car, keeping Joey's gun aimed at Sean.

I hopped in and handed Sean's gun to Madison. "He asked me out," I said.

Madison pulled out. "And that's why you pointed a gun at him?"

"No! The landlady showed up with prospective buyers, they found the body, the landlady had a heart attack and the shit hit the fan."

"Guess we go to Plan B."

"Oh, thank God. I didn't know there was a Plan B."

"Well, there isn't yet. But when Eddie finds out we killed his brother, there better be. So part one of Plan B is to get out of town. And since your police friend probably just radioed in our license plate number…" Madison slammed on the brakes. "Part two of Plan B is to get out of this car."

The car rocked to a stop. We leapt out of the rental car onto Wilshire Boulevard. I followed Madison to the sidewalk and we starting walking, fast, just short of a trot. "And part three of Plan B?" I asked.

"Finding someone to help us." She took out her cell phone, dialed. "Hi, Suzie, it's Madison Stone. I need to see Eric right away. Great, thanks." She hung up. "Next stop, Sunset Boulevard."

"How we going to get there?"

"Oh, I don't know, two beautiful women on a crowded street," Madison stepped to the curb. "How about this?" She stuck out her thumb.

Three cars screeched to a stop. "Works every time," she said. We hopped into a BMW and drove away.

FOUR

"I can't believe it," Special Agent Ryan Griffin said into his cell phone. He was talking to Stubblefield and Cortez in New Jersey. They listened on a speakerphone from the surveillance apartment while Ryan sat at a stoplight in his rented Chevy Equinox.

"There are these two hot chicks, a redhead and a blonde, hitchhiking on Wilshire Boulevard," Ryan said. "Oh, shit, look out. Jesus, three guys pulled over at once, almost hitting each other. Smart girls though, they got in the most expensive car."

"I'm surprised you didn't pull over," Christy said. "Two on one action sounds right up your alley."

"Very funny," Ryan said as the light changed. "So I just got to Westwood, what kind of car am I looking for?" Finding a car in the middle of the L.A. haystack was not as impossible as it might sound. Joey DeCarlo's phone call to his brother Eddie had come from a Verizon cell phone tower at Latitude 34.066139, Longitude -118.44000, more commonly known as 801 Hilgard Ave. That's Westwood. The next closest cell tower was only 1.8 miles away, thus narrowing the search to a couple of square miles.

Stubblefield checked one of the computer screens. "According to the Hertz main frame, Joey DeCarlo rented a 2011 tan Ford Focus, California license plate Frank 346 Zebra."

"Tan, huh. Couldn't have rented a red or green car, I see nothing but tan cars."

"I spoke to LAPD," Christy said. They've got a BOLO out on the car." BOLO, be on the lookout, the modern day version of an all points bulletin.

"Not sure that'll be necessary," Ryan said, noticing a tan Ford Focus parked seventy-five yards down Westwood Boulevard with both the driver and passenger's door wide open.

Ryan turned down Westwood, pulled to a stop next to the car. He checked the license plate, F346Z. "Weird. I found the car abandoned on the side of the road." Ryan looked around. "No sign of Joey."

Sirens suddenly pierced the air. Ryan turned to see a LAPD cruiser roar past, followed by an ambulance, two news vans, then three more black and whites.

"Are those sirens?" Stubblefield asked.

"Yep. And when Joey's around, trouble's never far behind. I'll call you back." Ryan jumped into his Chevy and squealed after them.

Three helicopters hovered above Grace Taylor's apartment building. Six news vans clogged the street, their portable satellite dishes cranked skyward. Four black and whites, the coroner's van, an ambulance, and two unmarked Crown Vic's and a SID unit – Scientific Investigation Division, LAPD's version of CSI – completed the vehicular circus.

Police tape crisscrossed the front of the building, and a crowd had gathered. Ken and Bridgette were giving press interviews, so was Adele Finch from the back of the ambulance. She was fine, it was more a panic attack than a heart attack, so she refused to go to the hospital just yet; she wanted each second of her fifteen minutes of fame.

Inside the apartment, Ryan badged his way to the detective in charge of the investigation, Jaime Rodriquez. Once upon a time Rodriguez may have been a good cop, but he'd been to too many horrific crime scenes, seen too many cases thrown out of court, ingested too much Jack Daniels and paid too much alimony to three ex-wives. He was a bitter, miserable man, inside and out. Rodriquez looked at the FBI credentials then at Ryan. "This picture doesn't do you justice," Rodriquez said, handing Ryan back his ID. "You look like a much bigger prick in person."

"Easy, Detective, I'm only here to help."

"I know how you guys help. Last year one of your comrades barged in on one of my cases, a serial rapist. He claimed the guy was a confidential informant vital to the national security. You guys love pulling the homeland security card, don't you? So he talks the D.A. into dropping charges. Two weeks later, that perverted fuckwad vital to our national security raped someone else, only this time, he killed her. Suddenly the FBI is all, I'm sorry, our mistake, you better prosecute that SOB before he strikes again."

Ryan was used to local resentment toward the FBI; hell when he was a Chicago cop, he hated the Bureau's storm trooper tactics, too. It was a lot different when you were the guy wearing the jackboots, though. It was a lot more fun.

"I'm not here to pick your pocket, Detective," Ryan said. "But I might be able to shed some light on your victim."

Rodriguez held up an evidence bag containing a bloodstained wallet. "New Jersey driver's license says Joseph DeCarlo."

"That's right. I'm part of a FBI task force investigating Joey's brother, Eddie DeCarlo."

40

Recognition creased Rodriquez's forehead. "Don Eddie DeCarlo?"

"Yep."

" So what, this some kind of mob hit? Hey, Harris, get over here."

A very chagrined looking Sean Harris joined Rodriquez and Ryan. There was nothing more humiliating for a cop than to have his or her weapon taken from them. And Sean's had been stolen by a *girl*.

"The suspect is a woman," Rodriquez said. "She confessed to the landlady and a young couple. Admitted she killed him."

"It was self defense," Harris said. "It had to be."

"This is Officer Harris. He insists on defending the girl, even though she stole his service weapon."

"She was scared," Harris said. "She didn't know what she was doing."

"See what I mean," Rodriquez said.

Ryan looked at Sean. The kid was obviously a rookie, and embarrassed. But there was a bright-eyed intensity Ryan liked. "Tell me what happened," Ryan said.

"At approximately ten-thirty this morning I encountered a young woman named Grace Taylor, an actress by the way, you'd probably recognize her." Sean picked up a picture of Grace from the coffee table. It was a shot of her standing next to Marg Helgenberger, one of the stars of *CSI*, taken when Grace guest-starred on the TV series.

"She's got an axe in her head," Ryan said.

"She was probably the victim in that week's episode," Sean said. "Here, this is a better shot." Sean picked up one of Grace Taylor's headshots from a stack on the bookcase. A headshot was just that, an 8x10 picture of the talent, with a list of their credits stapled to the back. Grace was smiling at the camera looking very sweet and innocent.

41

"She that cute in person?" Ryan asked.

"Cuter. Anyway, she came running up to me saying she was being chased by a man with a gun and that the man had attacked her friend. When I looked, though, there was no one chasing her, and when we went to her friend's apartment —"

"There was no friend, either," Rodriguez interrupted.

"The apartment had been searched," Sean insisted. "And there were signs of a struggle. I suggested to Ms. Taylor that her friend might have recovered and gone for help. Then I was called away on a 211."

"During which he almost shot an innocent store owner," Rodriguez said. "Then he runs back here, bumps into the actress lady as she's fleeing the scene, and gives up his weapon without a fight."

Sean's cheeks flushed red. Ryan wasn't sure if it was from anger or embarrassment, but he was sure he didn't like Rodriguez. Time to throw the kid a bone. "Detective Rodriguez," Ryan said. "The FBI knows that Joey DeCarlo came to L.A. to find a woman. Sounds to me like Grace Taylor's friend may be that woman." No reason to mention the tape, not yet, at least.

Sean smiled, flashed a look at Rodriguez who just scowled at him. The smile vanished.

"I've got your statement, Officer Harris. Why don't you go outside and give them a hand with crowd control?"

"But, I --"

"Now," Rodriguez snapped. Sean slinked off. "That kid's a disaster waiting to happen."

"We were all rookies once."

"If you say so." Rodriguez looked at his interview notes. "The other woman's name was Madison Stone. After Grace Taylor took the douche bag's gun, she jumped into a tan Ford Focus with a redhead. We're assuming that was Madison Stone."

Ryan remembered the two girls he saw hitchhiking, the blonde and a redhead, and Joey's car abandoned half a block away. I'll be god damned, he thought. Now the missing tape really started to intrigue Ryan. And who was Madison Stone? Why'd she mean so much to the DeCarlos? "Detective Rodriguez, you find anything else when you searched Joey?"

"Like what?"

"I don't know. Plane ticket? Itinerary? Drugs?"

"No, just his wallet, cell phone and a money clip with twenty-two hundred bucks in it. You ever wonder why so many of these scumbags carry thousands of dollars around with them and all we've got is maxed out credit cards and a pocketful of nickels."

Ryan knew there was nothing else to learn here. If he wanted answers, he was in the wrong apartment. He handed Rodriguez a business card. "That's it for me, then," Ryan said. "I'll get out of your hair, as promised."

"You're kidding?"

"Nope. Eddie DeCarlo's the target of our investigation, not Joey. He was just a foot soldier. I'm guessing he came to L.A. to track down an old girlfriend and got killed for his trouble. Not a federal concern. But I would appreciate a call when you wrap it up, love to know what actually went down here."

"Yeah, sure," Rodriguez said, planning to throw the card away the minute the FBI fuck was out of the room. "You take care."

Ryan shook his hand and walked out the door. The news crews were everywhere, waiting to hear just how big the story would be. If it was a simple stabbing, no one famous, just another dead schmuck, they'd pack their trucks and go to the next calamity. But if celebrity was involved, or sex, or any hint of scandal, they'd devour the story like a flesh-eating virus. And from what Ryan knew so far, they better be hungry.

Ryan spotted Officer Harris standing by a police barricade, his back to the press, trying not to get noticed. Ryan walked up to him. "You must feel terrible."

Sean looked at the FBI man. He'd been warned about getting too friendly with the Bureau. His dad and uncles all had horror stories of the Feds screwing up their cases. But this guy seemed sincere. He'd been nice to Sean inside the apartment, defended him to that prick Rodriguez. And Sean really felt a need to open up to someone.

"I do," Sean said. "And not just because she took my weapon. I really feel like if I hadn't left Grace Taylor alone to respond to the 211, none of this would have happened."

"Sure," Ryan said. "You would have been there when DeCarlo showed up, so, no fight, no knife, no murder."

"Exactly."

"You can still help her, you know. By helping me. I think there may be a lot more going on than meets the eye. And Grace Taylor may be in much more trouble than you could ever imagine."

"Really, what can I do?"

"Grace Taylor's friend was attacked at her apartment?"

"That's right."

"Take me there."

"But I'm supposed to help with crowd control."

"The crowd seems pretty controlled to me."

Sean looked around, there were a lot of press and spectators but they were all respecting the police lines.

"You want to help Grace or not?" Ryan asked.

Sean didn't want to disobey orders, but he did want to help. And Madison's apartment was so close he could take the FBI agent there and be back before anyone noticed he was gone. "Ok," he said. "Let's go."

FIVE

Hope springs eternal. How do I know? Well, my life was collapsing around me, but when Madison told me where we were going, I actually got excited.

"My manager's a great guy. Resourceful," Madison said as we got out of the BMW at 9200 Sunset Boulevard and walked into the prestigious high rise. "If anyone can help us, Eric can."

A manager! Of course, that's what I needed to turn my career around. I'll meet Madison's manager, he'll love me, sign me, make a few calls, get me signed by CAA or WME, I'll have a movie or a TV series before you know it.

That is, if I lived long enough. But Madison could be a drama queen, so deep down I was also hoping all her Mafia blood oath blather was exaggeration.

We got out of the elevator on the twenty-third floor. Madison led me down the corridor. "So how long has this guy been your manager?" I asked.

"Two years. I signed with Eric just after I moved to town."

"Who else does he represent? Any big stars?"

Madison seemed to think about that for a moment, then, "No superstars, but his clients work all the time." We reached the end of the hall, a large bronze plaque proclaimed AAA ENTERTAINMENT. I followed Madison through large oak doors into a small reception area. A beautiful Asian girl sat behind a desk. She said, "Madison, go right in, Eric's waiting for you."

"Thanks, Suzie," Madison said. Without breaking stride, Madison opened the office door and we swept into Eric's office. It was spectacular; huge desk, gigantic couch, ginormous flat screen TV. Eric stood in front of floor-to-ceiling windows, Beverly Hills framed behind him.

"Madison, come to poppa." He held out his arms and she folded into them. Eric was tall, six two or three, with slicked back hair, long, lean face, salon tan, and oversized smile. As he hugged Madison, his eyes rummaged over my face and body. He asked, "Who's your friend?"

"Grace Taylor," Madison said as they parted. "Grace, meet Eric Andrews."

He shook my hand. "You must be an actress, too."

"All my life. Well, almost, all my life. I had my first role at nine weeks. Baby Jesus."

"I was never religious, until now." Okay, that was a bit smarmy, but it was Hollywood. "Do you have a manager?" he asked. "I have a feeling we could make a lot of money together."

"Forget it, Eric," Madison snapped. "She's not interested."

Not so fast, I thought. "Not so fast," I said. "Actually, I recently decided to seek new representation."

Madison shot me a stern look. "That's not why we're here."

What was her problem? "Madison, maybe a manager's what I need to jump start my career."

"Maybe, but not Eric."

"Why not?"

"Eric has a... specialized client list."

"And I'm not good enough?"

"On the contrary," Eric said. "I could do a lot with that girl next door thing you've got going."

"Really?" I said, smiling. I couldn't resist shooting Madison a "so there" look. "Thank you, Eric." Finally, some good news, maybe the day wouldn't turn out to be a complete disaster, after all.

"Grace," Madison said. "Eric could do a lot with your girl next door thing as an escort."

"What?"

"A call girl, sweetie. A hooker. Eric is a pimp."

"Pimp is such a pejorative word," Eric said. "I prefer facilitator. I'm simply providing my clients an alternative way to make money until their acting careers take off."

I shot Madison a totally confused look.

"You know all the times I flew out of town to shoot commercials?" Madison asked me. "Ever wonder why they never aired? I wasn't making commercials, Grace, but I was working."

"For the world's richest men in the world's most beautiful places," Eric said.

I was floored. "You're a hooker?"

"It's a long story which I'll tell you later, I promise, but right now we need to get out of town. Eric, you have any parties booked?"

"Matter of fact, I've got one in Vegas. Sheik Khalid's Gulfstream takes off in two hours."

"Room for two more?"

"I'm sure he'd be delighted."

Madison looked at me. "Ever been on a private jet?"

I had a hard time processing the question. I was still wrestling with the Madison's revelation. "A hooker?" I mumbled.

"I'll take that as a 'no'." She turned to Eric. "Count us in."

"Great. Pack for five days. Be there at three o'clock, Van Nuys airport, executive jet terminal."

"I know it well. Oh, and can we borrow your car, we've got a few stops to make first."

He tossed her his keys. "Sure, but you mind telling me what the crisis is?"

"Oh, just an old boyfriend who won't take 'drop dead' for an answer." She kissed Eric on the cheek. "I'll leave your keys at the terminal." She grabbed me by the hand. "Let's boogie."

Eric's car was a bright red Porsche convertible. Madison drove expertly, weaving in and out of the crowded Sunset Boulevard traffic. "We need to swing by my apartment for a minute," she said. "I've got some money stashed away."

"Sure fine," I said. "Whatever." My surprise had turned to anger. I felt, well, belittled by Madison's secret, like I wasn't a close enough friend to trust with the truth.

Madison sensed my mood. "I'm sorry."

"You could have told me, you know. I'm your friend, I wouldn't have judged you."

"I tried to tell you so many times, but…"

"What? You thought if you told me you're a hooker I'd what, freak out? Call the cops? Run home to Florida?"

"Worse. I thought I'd lose you. Look, I've been lying my whole life. I've had to, to survive. Christ, practically every conversation I have begins with a lie. My name's not even Madison. But when we met at that audition, I felt so comfortable with you. You were funny, and optimistic, and oozed this positive energy. I wanted to be more like you. And just for the record, I wasn't an escort when I moved to L.A. I mean, I had been an escort in New York, but when I moved to L.A. it was to start over. I didn't start hooking until a few months later when the money was running out and the auditions were few and far between."

"Your name's not even Madison? What is it?"

"Anne. But I buried her long ago. I've been Allison, Amber, Holly, and now, Madison."

Talk about your backstory. I was dying to hear Madison's. One secret piled on top of another.

Secrets. I suddenly felt like a total hypocrite. I had my own collection of secrets I'd never told Madison. Secrets I was afraid to tell anyone. Secrets I'd buried so deep sometimes I wonder if they ever really happened. For an instant I thought about telling Madison. Then I realized I couldn't. I was too ashamed.

We pulled to a stop in front of a Best Buy. A display of TVs filled one of the windows. Small ones, big ones, there must have been ten different screens all showing the same thing, an aerial shot of a neighborhood street. "Why does that look familiar?" I asked.

Madison glanced at the screen just as the picture changed to a reporter interviewing an attractive young couple, Ken and Bridgette.

"Oh, my, God," I said. "It's them, that couple from my apartment."

"I'm getting a bad feeling about this," Madison said.

The picture switched again, this time to a close-up of me.

"Yeah," Madison said. "Bad feeling doesn't begin to cover it."

It was my headshot. The cops must've gotten it from my apartment. "I hate that picture," I said. "It just screams Girl Next Door. I am so sick of being everyone's Girl Next Door."

"Bright side, being wanted for murder will do wonders for your squeaky clean image."

A police car pulled next to us. "Yikes," I muttered under my breath.

"Stay cool," Madison whispered.

The cops were young, a white guy and a black guy, burly sorts who appreciated the sight of two pretty girls in a red convertible. Madison dazzled them with a smoky smile. "Afternoon, officers."

It almost wasn't fair. Men just melted in front of Madison. The two cops straightened up in their seats and turned on their most charming smiles. "Afternoon," the black guy in the passenger seat said. "How are you ladies today?"

"Fine," Madison said.

His eyes drifted from Madison to me. "Just dandy," I said. Then his eyes drifted past me to the window full of TV sets. I had no idea what was on the screens right now, I was afraid to look so I just prayed it wasn't little old me.

The light changed. "Have a great day," Madison purred and pulled out.

I so wanted to turn around and look, but I didn't dare. "Are they following us?"

Madison checked her rear view mirror. "No, they're just sitting there."

"That's good, right?"

The whoop of a police siren pierced the air. "No, not so good."

I turned to see the police car, lights now flashing, roaring up behind us. I slumped in my seat, deflated, expecting Madison to pull over so we could face the music. Instead, she screamed, "Hang on!" and floored the Porsche.

I was pinned to the back of my seat by the acceleration. Madison spun the wheel hard and we did a 180-degree skid across three lanes of traffic, narrowly avoiding a delivery truck and sending a Mini Cooper over the curb, inches from a fire hydrant.

The cop car did a 180 behind us, just missing a double-decker tour bus full of wide-eyed vacationers who must've thought they had driven into some kind of action movie.

"You can't think this is a good idea," I said.

"No. But it's the only one I've got."

The traffic light cycled from yellow to red but Madison kept going. Pedal to the metal, speedometer zooming past 70, Madison blasted into the intersection. I closed my eyes waiting for the inevitable crash, pain and agonizing death. I heard horns, screeching tires, a shouted "fucking asshole!" but no sickening jolt, plaintive screams or white light. I opened my eyes. We zoomed down La Cienega. I looked back, the cop car was still there, and as we barreled through Santa Monica Boulevard, another black and white joined the chase.

"Great," I said, "more cops." Then I looked up. A helicopter was heading our way. "And here comes the helicopter. I've seen these high speed chases on TV. The cops always win."

Madison noticed something up ahead and smiled. "They may know the streets, but I know the malls." Madison yanked the wheel right. We fishtailed across another three lanes of horrified traffic and into the Beverly Center parking structure. Madison spun the wheel. We bounced over a few speed bumps then slid to a stop in a handicapped parking spot.

"You can't park here," I said. "It's a --" Madison withered me with a look. "Right," I said, "never mind." We leapt out of the car and raced into Nordstrom's.

I started to run but Madison grabbed me by the blouse, slowing me down. "Don't run, you'll attract security." She grabbed brunette wigs off two mannequins. "Follow me."

We slipped into a dressing room, stood side by side at the mirror and put the wigs on. Neither fit very well, but they would do the trick. "Amazing," Madison said. "This changes your look completely."

It was true. Perky was out, serious was in. "I actually am a brunette," I said. "Born a brunette, I mean. But my mother said blondes stand out more so she started dying my hair when I was six years old."

"Mine's brown, a god-awful mousey brown. But over the years I've been everything; blonde, black, platinum, frosted, even streaked it purple once."

As I looked in the mirror I realized I had no memory of my natural hair color. Weird, huh? I had no memory of what I *really* looked like?

I suddenly wondered what my life would have been like if my mother had never colored my hair, never pushed me onto the stage. What would I be doing? Who would I be? Then an epiphany hit me like the proverbial freight train. Forget who you would be – *who the hell are you now*?

But before I could contemplate it, Madison shoved me out the dressing room door and we started walking through the store.

"Think of this as an acting exercise," Madison said. "We're just a couple of bored housewives spending our husbands' hard earned money." We got on the escalator, heading up. I looked back to see four cops spreading out beneath us. As one of the cops looked in our direction, I stared right at him. My heart was beating a million times a minute, but I acted calm, not scared. His eyes held mine for a moment, I smiled, he smiled back then looked away, continuing his search for a blonde and a redhead.

We got off the escalator on the second floor, actually street level in this mall, and headed for the Beverly Boulevard exit.

"Ever wonder what you'd be like if you never dyed your hair?" I asked Madison.

"No. Why?"

"I don't know. Random thought, never mind."

We spun through the revolving door and got spit onto the sidewalk. "Now what," I asked.

"We can't go to my apartment for the money anymore. The cops will probably be there by now. So, Plan C," Madison said and stuck out her thumb. Three cars screeched to a stop. Madison chose a Lexus. We hopped in the back seat and zoomed off.

SIX

Ryan kicked open the door to Madison's apartment. Ryan and Sean entered, guns drawn. They didn't think anyone would be in the apartment, but it was always safer to never assume.

Ryan went left, searched the hallway, bathroom and bedroom. Sean went right, checked the living room and kitchen. "All clear," Ryan said.

"Clear, here," Sean said.

Ryan joined him in the living room. "First things first," Ryan said. "We need to find a picture of Madison Stone."

Sean spotted a stack of headshots in a corner bookshelf. He grabbed one, looked at it. "Yeah, this is her. This is the woman who was driving the getaway car."

Ryan took the head shot. It was a color picture of a beautiful, very sexy redhead. A smile touched her lips and her smoldering green eyes seemed to know something you didn't. Eyes Ryan remembered well. He glanced at the acting credits on the back, just a couple of TV shows and a few commercials. He flipped the picture over and looked at her again.

"You recognize her?" Sean asked.

Ryan nodded. "Her name may be Madison Stone today. But two years ago she was known as Amber Stanley. She was a thousand dollar a night escort who worked for a well-known Manhattan madam, Lucinda Krusenko."

"A call girl?"

"We're not sure how or why, but Eddie DeCarlo bought Lucinda's business and shortly after that Amber Stanley, aka Madison Stone, became Eddie's girlfriend. He took her to the track, Yankee games, nightclubs, trips to Atlantic City. Eddie's married, by the way, wife, twin daughters, the whole *Soprano's* lifestyle. But all these goombas have girlfriends, and Amber belonged to Eddie.

"Then about a year ago she disappeared. We figured she strayed and was given a Sicilian divorce," Ryan drew a finger across his throat. "Or maybe Eddie had gotten bored. Either way, she was out and another babe, a hot little Thai number, was in. To be honest, we didn't give it much thought."

"But obviously Eddie DeCarlo did," Sean said. "You think he's been looking for her and, once he found her, he sent his brother to bring her back?"

"You're close," Ryan said, starting a methodical search of the apartment. "Joey called Eddie this morning, said he'd found Madison but hadn't gotten the tape yet."

"Tape? What tape?"

"We don't know. Audio. Video. But look at this place, Joey was desperate to find it." Ryan lifted a picture off the wall, checked behind it for a hiding place. Nothing but wall. "And since the tape wasn't on him, I'm guessing he never found it. But I will. So thanks for your help, I'll take it from here."

"What?"

"You've got crowds to control, and I've got a tape to find, so run along, I'll be fine."

Sean didn't move. The last thing in the world he wanted to do was go back to the chaos at Grace Taylor's apartment building. It was only a matter of time before the press found out the part Sean played in the murder and its aftermath, and he had a feeling that prick, Detective Rodriguez, was going to throw him to the wolves. Instead of being the hero he, his dad and uncles had dreamt about, he'd be a goat.

More importantly, Sean had a feeling Ryan was going to find Grace and Madison. And he'd like to be part of that. First of all, if he were able to find them and bring them in, he'd find some redemption. Second, he still felt partly responsible for the mess Grace found herself in. And lastly, well, he just wanted to see Grace again.

"I've got an idea," Sean said. "I'll stay and help you. Like you said, the crime scene's secure enough, and that tape could be anywhere; let me help you look." Sean moved into the kitchen, started digging through the cabinets.

Ryan watched him. Sean's eagerness bordered on desperation and Ryan knew why. He'd been humiliated by Grace Taylor. And, in spite of it, Ryan guessed Sean had a crush on her, too. Every instinct Ryan had told him to kick the kid to the curb. But a plan was simmering in the back of Ryan's brain, and having some help from someone *outside* the FBI might come in handy.

Still, the kid was awfully green. He might be more trouble than he was worth. Ryan decided he'd be better off without him. "Sorry, kid, no can do. Go back to the crime scene."

"But I can help. Look, I know I'm a rookie, and you probably figure I'll just get in the way. But my dad's a cop, his two brothers are cops. All I heard growing up was shop talk. I've lived and breathed police work since I was born."

The kid was actually starting to grow on Ryan. Still... "No. You're slowing me down already. Instead of looking for the tape, I'm standing here arguing with you."

Sean didn't want to leave! He couldn't leave. He had to find a way to convince Agent Griffin to let him stay –- then Sean remembered something that changed everything. "If you really want to find out where the tape is, why don't you just ask Madison where it is?"

"How am I supposed to do that?"

Sean took out his notebook. "She's with Grace Taylor, right?" Sean flipped to his notes from his interview with Grace. He'd gotten her address and number. Sean handed it to Ryan. "Grace Taylor's cell phone number."

Ryan smiled, impressed.

SEVEN

The Lexus dropped us off at the Bank of America at the corner of Sunset and Vine. We still had the wigs on. Since it was too dangerous to go to Madison's apartment to get the money she had hidden there, Madison brought us to the other place she had some cash stashed, her safe deposit box.

"Thanks, Tony," she said to the personal injury attorney who had picked us up. "Have fun in Hawaii." Tony was taking his wife to Kauai for their tenth anniversary. Madison recommended a couple of restaurants on Poipu Beach and a surfing spot in Hanapepe. It amazed me how guys opened up to Madison. As hot as she was, she was accessible. She made every guy she talked to feel like he was the most important guy in the world. She'd look them in the eye, touch their arm, hang on every word. And it wasn't an act. She genuinely liked people. She was actually the most honest person I knew – or at least I thought she was. Now that I realized our whole relationship was built on a mountain of lies, I didn't quite know what to make of her.

"This shouldn't take long," she said as we walked into the bank. "I'll be right back." Madison left me by the door and walked over to the customer service desk.

My cell phone rang. I took it out of my purse. What should I do? Answer it? Turn it off? Throw it away? It rang again. I checked the Caller ID, it said: Madison.

Madison? I looked at Madison now being escorted into the vault. She wasn't calling me. But someone was from her apartment. Another ring.

"Excuse me, Miss…" a voice behind me said. I spun to find myself staring at a security guard, and seeing anyone with a badge at this point sent my heart into overdrive. "No cell phone calls inside the bank. You'll have to step outside."

"Sure, sorry, officer, I mean your guardship, whatever." I backed out of the door and tentatively answered the phone. "Hello."

"Hi, Grace, how you doing?"

A friendly voice, I thought, vaguely familiar. "Who is this?"

"It's Sean, Grace. Sean Harris. Officer Sean Harris."

"Yikes!"

"Don't panic, Grace. I've got you on speakerphone. I'm here with someone who wants to help you. His name is Ryan."

"Hi, Grace," another voice said. It was a little deeper than Sean's, but full of confidence and authority. "My name is Ryan Griffin. I'm a Special Agent with the FBI."

"The FBI!"

"It's okay, Grace," the FBI guys said. "Don't hang up. We want to help you."

Then it all came out in a rush of words. "This is all some terrible mistake," I said. "It was an accident. I didn't mean to kill anybody. I didn't mean to point my gun at anybody or give them a heart attack or steal your gun, Officer Harris. Or get in a high speed chase. I mean, I've

60

never even had a parking ticket! One thing just led to another and -- ”

“Grace,” the FBI guy interrupted. “It’s all right. Slow down. I believe you.”

“You do?”

“I do. And I want to help you.”

Oh, thank God, I thought. “Oh, thank God,” I said.

“And so does Officer Harris.”

“I believe you, too,” Officer Harris said.

“I’m sorry about your gun,” I said.

“No problem, Grace,” Officer Harris said.

Then the FBI guy took over. “Now Grace, for me to help you, you need to help me.”

“Sure, anything, what can I do?”

“Give me the tape.”

Tape? What the hell was he talking about? “What tape?”

“I don’t have time for games, Grace. Give me the tape and I can make the police problem go away.”

“I don’t know anything about a tape, really. You’ve got to believe me.”

“Well, Madison does. Is she there? Can I talk to her?”

“No.”

“The tape is why Joey DeCarlo came after her. The tape is why you are now wanted for murder. The tape is why you’re going to spend the rest of your life in jail unless you cooperate with me.”

A steel edge had come into his voice. It scared me. “You don’t sound very much like someone who wants to help me.”

“Make no mistake. Madison got you into this trouble. I can get you out. But you need to get me that tape.”

Madison walked out of the bank. Her eyes went right to the cell phone. “Who’re you talking to?”

"Somebody from the FBI."

"What!" Madison grabbed the phone, shut it off and stuck it in her purse. "They can trace a cell phone." She grabbed me by the elbow, steered me toward the street.

"He says he wants to help us," I said.

"He's a cop. All cops lie."

"He said all we had to do was give him some tape and he'd get us out of trouble."

"Tape? What tape? Audio tape? Videotape? Scotch tape?"

"He said you knew all about it."

"He's lying. I don't know anything about a tape. Now, come on, we've got a plane to catch."

Madison stuck out her thumb. Four cars screeched to a stop. She picked a Bentley this time. We got in and drove off.

EIGHT

In Eddie DeCarlo's pool hall, all eyes were on the bank of plasma TVs. Fox News, MSNBC, and CNN were carrying the story. Only the sound from Fox News was on. "To repeat, the victim, Joseph DeCarlo, a reputed member of a New York crime family was found murdered in a Hollywood apartment building." The picture cut to a close-up of a body bag being wheeled to the coroner's van. "Sources tell Fox News that DeCarlo was stabbed to death with a butcher knife."

"A butcher knife," Eddie repeated, in a harsh, hateful whisper.

"Police are looking for an actress, Grace Taylor, in connection with the murder." Grace's headshot appeared on the screen.

"That's not Amber," Frankie the Fish said. Frankie was one of Eddie's top lieutenants, his favorite caporegime. In his early forties, Frankie got his nickname from his huge eyes, accentuated by black framed glasses with Coke bottle thick lenses. But he was street smart, loyal and an unapologetic sociopath. "Who the hell is she?"

The Fox News broadcast now cut to an aerial shot of the high speed chase between the two black and whites and Eric's red Porsche convertible. The camera zoomed in on the two women, a blonde and a redhead.

"There she is," Eddie said. "The redhead."

"She still looks good," Frankie said.

The Fox News reporter continued. "The police have tentatively identified the other woman in the car as another actress, Madison Stone."

"Actress, my ass," Eddie mumbled.

"If you have any information as to the whereabouts of these two individuals, please contact the Los Angeles Police Department."

"And I wouldn't mind a phone call either," Eddie growled, and the room burst into nervous laughter. Then all eyes settled on Eddie. No one was sure how he would react. His temper was legendary. And now someone had killed his brother.

This whole fucked up mess had started a week ago. Alan Cross called Eddie and said they had to find Amber ASAP. Cross told Eddie why it was so important and Eddie sent out his own version of "Be On the Lookout" for the hooker formerly known as Amber.

The Family had a database of every major madam and pimp in the country, another Eddie DeCarlo innovation, and each one was emailed a picture of Amber. The reward was $100,000. Three days later a Hollywood manager responded – Eric Andrews. He emailed Madison Stone's headshot and his cell phone number.

Eric wasn't convinced that Madison was the woman they were looking for. The emailed picture of Amber was blond, and she wore a lot more make up. But the similarities were too obvious to ignore, the shape of her face, eyes, mouth. It sure as hell looked like Madison.

God damn it, Eric thought. He liked Madison. She was a total pro, not a spoiled, drug-addled bitch like so many of his girls. And she was serious about her acting ambitions. But Eddie DeCarlo was looking for her. If Eric lied, didn't respond to Eddie's email, and it ever came out that Madison/Amber was working for him, Eric was as good as dead. Not to mention the hundred grand reward and the value of having a marker with Eddie DeCarlo. And hey, Eric finally rationalized to himself, it's not his fault Madison got herself involved with the mob. So Eric sent them Madison's headshot.

When Frankie the Fish got Madison's picture, he was encouraged. The girl looked a lot like Amber. Then Frankie had the nerds in the tech room Photoshop the picture of Madison, turning her red hair blonde.

No doubt about it, Amber. Frankie took the picture to Eddie.

"I think we found her," Frankie said.

Eddie stared at the picture with a tight smile. "Call him."

Frankie dialed Eric Andrews on his cell phone. Since Frankie the Fish used his phone and not Eddie's, the FBI had no record of the call. That was one of the flaws with the court-ordered wiretaps. It just covered Eddie's work phones and his cell phone. If he happened to take a call on anyone else's phone, the FBI had no way of knowing. "Mr. Andrews," Frankie said. "I've got Eddie DeCarlo calling."

"Good afternoon, Mr. DeCarlo," Eric said, surprised by how nervous he was. He wondered if the nervousness was from talking to someone as powerful as Eddie DeCarlo, or from betraying a friend. "I take it you've got my email."

"Yeah. It looks like Amber. When did she get to L.A.?"

"Two years ago, she's only worked for me the last eighteen months."

"The timing fits, she left New York two years ago. What's her address?"

"Madison's a nice kid, Mr. DeCarlo, I hope she's not in any trouble." There was a long beat and Eric knew he'd said too much. "Not that it's any of my business," he added quickly.

"She's not in trouble, I assure you, and you're right. It's not any of your business. Now," Eddie said, a little more edge in his voice, "her address, please." Eric told him and Eddie wrote it down. "Thanks, Eric, I won't forget this." Eddie hung up.

Eddie sent his brother Joey to L.A. with one simple instruction. Get the videotape from Madison. Do whatever it takes. But Joey had failed, so for the second time in a week, Frankie the Fish called Eric Andrews, again using his cell phone, then handed the phone to Eddie.

Eric Andrews sat at his desk watching the news reports on his 60-inch plasma screen TV. If he was nervous talking to Eddie before, he was petrified now. "I'm so sorry for your loss," Eric said.

"Where is she?" Eddie demanded.

"I don't know, I swear. Madison and a friend of hers, this Grace Taylor they're showing pictures of on TV, came to my office a couple of hours ago. They wouldn't tell me what had happened just that they needed to leave town, fast."

"And you didn't assume it had something to do with my looking for her?"

"I did, of course. I thought they might be running, trying to get away from you. I never imagined they'd killed anyone."

"Even so, I'd expect a phone call alerting me to the situation."

Eric felt the bottom drop out of his stomach. He'd thought about calling, even picked up the phone after she left, but he felt like such a heel, and he liked Madison so much, he'd set the phone back in its cradle. No good deed goes unpunished, he thought. Well, time for a little damage control. "I was going to call, I swear, but there was no hurry. She's running around town now preparing for a trip, I have no idea where she is right now. But I know where she'll be tonight."

"Where?"

"Las Vegas. A Saudi sheik is flying in a load of party girls. Madison and Grace will be with them. They'll be staying at the Paradise Hotel."

"Thank you. Oh, and Mr. Andrews, next time, tell me what you know when you know it."

"Or else…" Eric said, finishing the thought.

"I'm glad we understand each other." Eddie hung up, handed the phone back to Frankie. "We've got them." Eddie said. "Book us a plane to Vegas."

NINE

Officer Sean Harris sat among a small pile of videotapes in Madison's living room. He'd stuck each one in the VCR to make sure it was the movie advertised on the box and not the missing tape. Madison had an even bigger collection of DVDs but since all the phone conversations specified tape, Ryan said not to bother with the DVDs. "Okay, that's it," Sean said pulling the last tape out of the VCR, "*Pretty Woman* was really *Pretty Woman,* and I'm officially out of videotapes."

Ryan walked into the room with what looked like a brick wrapped in a black plastic bag and covered in white powder. "Look what I found hidden in a sack of flour."

"Is that the tape?" Sean asked.

"Doesn't feel quite right," Ryan said. He ripped the plastic, pealed it away to reveal a thick stack of hundred dollar bills. He riffled through the bills, counting. "Twenty-five thousand dollars," Ryan said.

"You'd think she'd come back for the money."

"I'm sure she wanted to but was afraid someone would be waiting for her." Ryan looked at the money, shook his head. "You know, your friend, Detective Rodriguez, had a point. All the bad guys have money, and what do we get for our trouble? Squat. I got shot at three times last year, all she had to do was suck a few cocks."

"More than a few, I suspect," Sean said.

Ryan laughed. "You got that right." He dropped the money on the living room table. "But this was all I found. She's got to have the tape with her."

Sean stared at the money, a depressing possibility dawning on him. He almost didn't want to ask the next question. "Do you think Grace Taylor's a hooker, too?"

"They tend to stick together."

That's what he was afraid of. He was heartsick. "Man, she could've fooled me."

"Listen, kid, don't be a sap. That girl is trouble. She's probably a call girl; we know she killed a man, fled the scene of a crime and stole your gun. You want to get her back and save a bit of your dignity, I get it. But flush any fantasies about walking off into the sunset with her. Trust me, her side of this story is going to have a very sad ending. Speaking of which..." Ryan hit send on his cell phone, "Let's see if Grace has turned her phone back on yet." He got a busy signal, snapped the phone closed. "Nope." Then he realized, "But Madison's got to have a phone, too, right?" He spotted a stack of bills tucked next to an appointment book on a small corner desk. He rifled through the papers, held up a Verizon bill. "Bingo." He found Madison's number on the bill, dialed. Busy. "Turned off, too," he said. Then he dialed a new number into his phone and hit send. "But if she used the phone earlier today we can trace the number and find out who she talked to... Hey, Christy, it's Ryan."

In the FBI surveillance apartment in Newark, Christy smiled. "Looks like you got yourself a situation out in Hollyweird." Christy and Stubblefield had been watching developments on TV. I'm putting you on the box." She hit the speakerphone button.

"Can't do anything the easy way, can you Ryan?" Stubblefield asked through a mouthful of Pad Thai. He'd ordered the noodles, spicy catfish, Thai fried rice and a double order of the Thai golden wings. Christy picked at her tofu salad.

"What fun would that be?" Ryan said. "Listen, I need a favor. I've got Madison Stone's cell phone number. I need to know if she made any phone calls after…" Ryan turned to Sean. "What time did she flee the apartment?"

"Twelve fifteen give or take."

"Twelve fifteen," Ryan said into the phone.

Christy's fingers flew across the keys as she accessed the necessary data bases.

"How's Eddie taking the news?" Ryan asked.

Stubblefield checked the monitor for the camera trained at the pool hall entrance. A few of Eddie's boys were outside smoking. "Can't be sure," Stubblefield said. "We haven't picked up any phone calls. But you know he's gotta be pissed." A black Mercedes 600 pulled to a stop in front of the pool hall. "Hold on, that's Eddie's car." Stubblefield picked up a walkie-talkie, keyed the mike. "Kenny, Gail, you see that?"

Special Agents Ken Patterson and Gail Miller were stationed in a Crown Vic a block north of the pool hall. Their job was to follow Eddie wherever he went. "Ten four," Kenny said. "About time he went somewhere, I was getting bored."

Eddie and Frankie came out of the pool hall, got in the back of the Mercedes.

"And away we go," Kenny said. The Crown Vic pulled out.

Back in the apartment, Christy looked up from her keyboard. "Ryan, she's only made one phone call. It was at twelve twenty-one, to 323-555-8947. Number belongs to

AAA Management, 9200 Sunset Boulevard." Her fingers flew over the keys again. "According to the Internet Movie Database, it's run by a guy named Eric Andrews."

Ryan picked up Madison's headshot, checked the back. "Yeah, he's listed as her manager. I'm on my way there now. Could you run a check on Andrews and call me with the results?"

"You got it."

Ryan hung up, eyed Sean. "Where do you live?"

"What? Uh, Studio City, it's not too far, why?"

"If you want to stay with me, you're going to have to ditch the uniform. And you might want to call in sick for the rest of the shift so they don't come looking for you. After what you've been through today, I'm sure they'll understand."

"Great," Sean said, excited. "So, what, I'm going to be like your partner?"

"I'm not really sure. We'll figure it out as we go."

"Cool." Sean followed Ryan out the door. Then Ryan stopped. "I'm going to hit the head. I'll meet you in the car."

"Okay," Sean said and trotted off. Ryan walked back into the apartment, closed the door, and then turned to the money on the living room table. He picked up the stack of bills, stared at the cash for a long moment – he was thinking about taking it.

His partner, Dempsey, would be so disappointed. Dempsey had been a throwback. He'd believed in God and Country, service and sacrifice. He'd actually believed virtue was its own reward.

Dempsey worked for the FBI for twenty-eight years. At thirty years, he was going to retire, and then he and Barbara would buy an RV and travel the country Dempsey loved so much. Barbara's cancer wasn't part of the plan. But undaunted, Dempsey prayed every day. God would save his precious wife. But just to be sure, Dempsey spent every penny he had on medical treatments. Still, she died.

Most believed grief killed Dempsey, drove him to suicide. The truth was, it was so much more than grief. It was Dempsey's realization that everything he believed in was a lie. God didn't save Barbara. And Dempsey's reward for a virtuous life? He was left a broken-hearted, penniless widower.

So Ryan wondered: if Dempsey was standing where he was now, with all that money in his fist, knowing that every platitude Dempsey had believed in betrayed him, would Dempsey take the money?

The answer was no. No question, Ryan realized. Dempsey lived by a rigid code of conduct. The world may have betrayed Dempsey, but he'd never betray himself.

But Dempsey had also taught Ryan his Rule Number One. Never make the same mistake twice. Ryan was convinced that Dempsey's blind trust in justice, a higher power and a greater good were wrong. He wasn't going to make the same mistake as his mentor.

Ryan had a plan, and it began here and now. Ryan shoved the twenty-five thousand dollars into his pocket.

TEN

It wasn't easy to talk Victor into driving us to the Van Nuys Executive Terminal. That was the name, by the way, of the guy who picked us up in the Bentley, Victor Carrero. He was Colombian, maybe thirty-five years old, bald, but it looked good on him, and he had a pencil-thin moustache that didn't. He was covered in gold; earrings, ID bracelets, three necklaces, two gold rings on each hand. The bling didn't surprise me, I mean, it was a $250,000 car. He told us he was in the import/export business, translation: drug dealer.

"You girls are beautiful," he said in a lilting, Spanish accent, "but I'm driving to Santa Monica not Van Nuys. I'm not even sure Bentleys are allowed in the Valley."

"I'm sure they'll make an exception for you, Victor," Madison said. Then she leaned across the backseat, her lips inches from his ear. "Please take us to Van Nuys," she whispered.

Like I said, it almost wasn't fair. Men always melted. Well, almost always. "I'll take you anywhere you want to go for a blowjob," Victor said. Madison met his eyes in the rearview mirror. He had a knowing smile on his face. "Oh, come on, baby, don't look so surprised. You are out on the street with no car, no luggage and you want a ride to a private jet terminal. I know all about girls like you. I *hire* girls like you. So, I feel reasonable today, make me happy and I'll make you happy."

I expected Madison to tell him to stop the car. I expected Madison to slap him. I expected Madison to do anything but what she did next. She climbed into the front seat, unzipped his pants, and started giving him head –– while we were driving!

Madison was a total pro. I mean, she totally got into it. She moaned like she was having the time of her life; she told him how beautiful his cock was, he told her how beautiful she was, she kissed him tenderly on the neck then went back to work on his penis. The Bentley had tinted windows so nobody could see what was happening as we got on the 101 and headed west. But I couldn't take my eyes off the real life porno scene. I was swept up in a part-shock, part-voyeur fascination.

Soon, Victor was the one doing most of the moaning, he started muttering in Spanish, then, "Yes, baby, oh, yeah, just like that!" Then an all too familiar grunt and groan, grunt and groan, grunt and groan. Finally it was over. He took a few deep breaths then said, "Mucho gracias."

Madison rose out of his lap, kissed him gently on the cheek. "No, thank *you*."

Victor laughed. "And my mother told me never to pick up hitchhikers."

Twenty minutes later we pulled into the Van Nuys Executive Terminal. I couldn't wait to get out of the car and bolted out of my seat the moment we came to a stop. I expected Madison to do the same, but she stayed in the front seat with Victor. They talked for a minute, he laughed, she laughed, she handed him something and he handed her something, then she kissed him on the lips and got out of the car.

I wanted to ask her about the blowjob. Ask why she'd done it. Ask *how* she'd done it so casually. Didn't she feel cheap? Demeaned? But the questions seemed well, rude. However, I was so fascinated by the little chat fest once we parked, I had to ask, "What were you two talking about?"

"Insurance policy. When Victor gets home and turns on the television he's going to see our pictures plastered everywhere. We can't have him calling the police and telling them he dropped us of here, can we? So I flirted him up, gave him my card and promised a reward for his silence."

"What'd he give you?"

Madison held up a gram bottle of cocaine. "A going away present." I eyed it hungrily as she dropped the brown vial into her purse. I never did coke in Florida. Grass and Ecstasy was as wild as we got at school. But coke was big in Hollywood and lately I've been partying a little harder. Drinking a bit more, sometimes too much more but that's another story. And I've started using coke a bit. The idea of snorting something is a bit gross, but coke does deliver this invincible sort of buzz that makes you feel so much better about life.

I followed Madison into the terminal. "This is a first name business," she said. "So you need to pick a name."

"What's wrong with Grace? It's one thing I actually like about myself."

"The name Grace is getting a little too much airtime at the moment. Pick something else."

We reached the counter, a pretty receptionist with the nametag, MARY, smiled at us. "Can I help you?"

"Yes," Madison said. "We're looking for Sheik Khalid's plane."

Mary pointed out the window. "The silver G-5, they're boarding now."

"Thank you."

I followed Madison onto the tarmac. "Her name was Mary. Could I be Mary?"

"Sure, if we were going undercover as a couple of nuns. You want something evocative. Misty, Destiny, Cheyenne. You know, a porn star name."

We reached the plane, a big, beautiful jet that glistened under the sun. A handsome, uniformed pilot greeted us with a smile. He held a clipboard. "Good afternoon," he said.

"Hi," Madison said. "Eric Andrews should have called. We've been added to the trip."

"He did and you are. Any bags?"

"No. We'll pick up what we need at the hotel."

"Great. Climb aboard."

We did, and, as I stepped inside, the first thing that hit me was the smell of fine leather. The cabin was luxurious; thick beige carpets, huge brown leather lounge chairs, a bar at one end, a conference table at the other.

"Wow," I said.

Madison smiled. "The only way to fly."

Four girls were already on board, gathered at the bar. I was surprised how young and beautiful they were. They were dressed casually, showing lots of skin, but still tasteful. Could they possibly be hookers, too? Behind the bar, a uniformed flight attendant, also attractive but totally corporate, was mixing drinks.

"Hi," an Asian girl said, "I'm Jade." She indicated the others. "And this is Tiffany, Cassandra and Savannah."

Savannah was melt in your mouth beautiful. A light-skinned black woman who looked like Halle Berry, her hair was an intricate tangle of cornrows. She smiled when she saw Madison, glided into her arms and they kissed. And I don't mean a friendly peck-on- the-cheek kind of kiss.

This was a deep, passionate tongue-dancing kind of kiss. Let me tell you, Madison was one surprise after another. The kiss also stirred something in me, a memory I thought I'd tucked safely away.

When they broke, Savannah lovingly stroked Madison's cheek. "Nice to see you, sweetie."

"You, too."

"Who's your friend?"

"Ah... Destiny," I said.

"Hi," they all said. Then the flight attendant asked, "Can I get you a drink?"

"I'd love one," I said, making a beeline for the bar. "Vodka tonic, lots of lime and lots of vodka." I used to drink gin but switched to vodka a few months ago. The hangovers weren't nearly as bad.

"How about you?" the Flight Attendant asked Madison.

"No, thank you." She shot me a hard look. "It's a little too early for me."

I got her message –- we've got too much to worry about right now, don't have that drink – but ignored it. So far that day I'd been dumped, fired, attacked by a mobster, stabbed the aforementioned mobster, stolen a cop's gun, fled a crime scene, survived a high speed chase and hung up on a FBI agent. I needed that drink.

ELEVEN

"Are we being followed?" Eddie asked his driver, Enrico.

Enrico, Eddie's second cousin on his mother's side and a Marine vet who'd been wounded in Baghdad, glanced in his rear view mirror. "Yeah, about three cars back. Same brown Crown Vic, same two Feds inside."

"Good." Eddie sat next to Frankie the Fish in the back of his Mercedes. The FBI followed Eddie everywhere he went and did nothing to hide their presence. They did it more to piss off and annoy Eddie than to trap him, but sometimes annoyed pissed-off people made stupid mistakes.

Eddie didn't make stupid mistakes. That's how he'd survived this long.

Death had always been a part of Eddie's life. His father was gunned down in front of him when he was nine years old. Eddie and his dad were playing catch on the front lawn while four-year-old Joey watched. A Buick drove up, the front and rear passenger windows rolled down, two Uzis stuck out. His dad yelled, "Get Down!" Eddie threw himself over Joey's body, protecting his young brother, then turned to see the cavalcade of bullets rip his father to shreds.

As the car drove off, young Eddie ran after the Buick. Screaming, cursing, throwing rocks until it disappeared.

As the sound of sirens filled the air, Eddie ran back to his father's bullet-ridden body, and with tears running down his face, he made an oath that one day he'd avenge his father's murder.

The hit had been ordered by Tommy Provenzano, head of a rival family, as warning to Eddie's father's Don to stay away from the landfill business on the eastern shore. Eddie's father's Don, Angelo Liggio, an old relic with emphysema, didn't want a gang war and backed off.

But not Eddie. He hung around his dad's friends, on the street corners, in the baristas. He heard them bitch about not being able to avenge his father's murder. He learned the name of the two shooters, the name of the driver. Names he would never forget.

His father had taught him the Sicilian proverb: Revenge is a dish best served cold. Nine-year-old Eddie knew his limitations, so he was patient.

He convinced his mother that they should move out of the neighborhood. Maybe go to Queens where Aunt Esther lived. His mother was more than happy to move Eddie and little Joey away from the Family's influence –- she wanted her sons to become a doctor and a lawyer, not two more Mafioso.

What Eddie didn't tell his mother was that Tommy Provenzano's family ran Queens, and the driver and two button men lived nearby.

When Eddie was fourteen, he killed the first one, a punk named Frank Greco. Greco used to drink himself silly at a titty bar three blocks from his apartment, then stagger home about midnight. Eddie knew it had to look like an accident; if anyone suspected a hit, the shit would hit the fan and his plans would be ruined. So Eddie stole a pick-up truck and, as Greco weaved his way home on a hot August night, Eddie flattened him. It was dismissed as a hit and run.

On Eddie's fifteenth birthday, he treated himself to his second murder. The driver this time, a weasel-faced son of a bitch named Marco Agostino. Agostino was divorced and lived alone in a shabby studio apartment in Jackson Heights. On September twenty-sixth, Eddie followed Agostino home from La Finestra, a local restaurant. He jumped Agostino in an alley, sticking a stiletto in his neck. Agostino flopped to the ground squirting blood. Eddie watched him die, then stole Agostino's watch, ring and wallet. It was written off as a mugging.

Two down, one to go, and again, Eddie took his time. Nine months to be exact. The last hit man, Paul Santino, had moved up in the organization, and was now one of Provenzano's capos. Along with the promotion came more money and Santino bought a nice four-bedroom house with a pool in the backyard. Santino's nickname was Ironman. He was a fitness freak. He pumped iron, ran marathons and swam laps every morning at seven-thirty.

On the last morning of his life, Santino dove in and started swimming, his muscled arms gliding through the water. As he flipped to make his turn at the deep end of the pool, a hand reached into the water and grabbed him by the ankle. Eddie held his leg in the air forcing Santino's head underwater. Santino's legs flailed, trying to kick free of his attacker, but Eddie held on. Soon, the kicking weakened then finally stopped as Eddie savored every twitch of Santino's dying body.

The body was found face down an hour later by Santino's wife. The coroner ruled it an accident, case closed.

Eddie's revenge was complete and he was sure no one would ever figure out what he'd done. He was wrong. A few weeks later, as he was walking home from school, a black limo pulled to a stop in front of him. The rear window rolled down revealing the pockmarked face of Tito Navarra. Tito had been old Don Liggio's underboss, and had taken over the Family a couple of years earlier. A cold-blooded killer, he'd risen through the ranks not because of his cruelty, but because of his brains. Tito respected the past, but kept his eyes on the future.

"Get in," Tito said.

Eddie's first thought was to run. He'd murdered three made men. He knew what was going to happen next. You get in the backseat, they deposit a couple of .22 slugs to the back of your head, and they dump you out.

"Don't worry," Tito said, as if reading his mind. "You're in no danger." Eddie got in. Tito closed the door. They were alone in the back of the limo. It started moving. "I knew your father," Tito said. "We came up together. He was a smart man. Respected. If he had lived, he might have been the one sitting in this limo."

Pride swelled Eddie's chest. He idolized his father. "Thank you, Don Tito."

"You remind me of your father. You're handsome, like him, smart, too. I checked with the high school. Honor role, no less."

"Good grades mean a lot to Mom."

"To me, too." Tito looked into the boy's eyes, a look so penetrating Eddie felt naked. "I know what you did. A perfect revenge. Three deaths spread over six years. The Provenzano Family will never connect the dots. But I did. The Family needs men with your kind of dedication, patience and fearlessness. But most of all, we need men with your kind of brains. It's 1974. The future is business and technology, not hookers and hijacks. After graduation, what college are you going to?"

"I was thinking of joining Uncle Marty's gang. It's always been understood I'd go to work for him as a soldier once I finished school."

"You're too smart for Marty's gang. You'll be working directly for me. And your first assignment is four years at NYU. Business school. It's all arranged and paid for. Capisce?"

College and a place at the foot of the throne; it was a dream come true. "Capisce," he said.

Eddie excelled at NYU. He fought on the wrestling team; the desperate, sweat-filled, one-on-one struggle of a wrestling match appealed to him. You needed speed, muscle and brains to win. An excellent metaphor for life, Eddie thought.

Eddie became friends with one of his teammates, Alan Cross. The two couldn't have been any more different. Eddie was a tough New York street kid. Cross was the son of an Atlanta, Georgia millionaire, born with the proverbial silver spoon in his mouth. But Cross was no spoiled brat living off his father's money. He was ambitious, a fierce competitor and the only one on the team to ever beat Eddie. That had gotten Eddie's attention, and respect. The two were soon fast friends.

Eddie was fascinated as Cross told him how his father had amassed his real estate fortune. Cross was equally fascinated by Eddie's real life stories of the Mafia.

After graduation, the friendship continued, and much of Cross's early success as a developer was due to lucrative terms Eddie was able to convince the New York labor unions to give Cross's construction projects. Not to mention using the Family's influence to grant Cross advantageous zoning exceptions. Cross repaid Eddie by giving him a small piece of each development, which Eddie in-turn gifted to Don Tito.

Eddie also brought the fiscal sophistication and diversification to the Family that Don Tito had hoped for. While not abandoning the traditional "hookers and hijacking," Eddie expanded the Family into every new venture the growing technology revolution spawned; pornography in the eighties, bank fraud in the nineties, stock fraud during the internet bubble at the turn of the century, and loan fraud during the subsequent housing boom. And now he had rooms filled with computer geeks phishing through the Internet to supply his vast identity-theft business.

Eddie's influence grew quickly. Within five years he was Don Tito's underboss, and after a stroke killed the Don in 1997, Eddie took over the Family.

After Eddie's ascension, a couple of the other Families decided to take a shot at the young, college-educated Don. They didn't think Eddie had the guts to stand up to a show of force. Eddie's bloody counterattack silenced any doubts and cemented his position.

For the next few years the other Dons saw how Eddie's financial genius was enriching his Family, and wanted in. Eddie soon became the de facto banker for all five Families. As their bank accounts grew, so did their respect.

Back in the limo, Eddie turned to Frankie. "Get me Vincenzo." Frankie dialed, handed his cell phone to Eddie.

Two thousand, four hundred and fifty-five miles away, in Las Vegas, Nevada, Vincenzo Sica answered his cell phone. Vincenzo was thin, gaunt, really, with sunken cheeks and a Roman nose that supported a pair of Maui Jim sunglasses.

The Family, through one of its many subsidiaries, owned a slot machine assembly plant in Las Vegas, and

Vincenzo ran the operation. It was totally legit, employed 23 people who worked in the ten thousand square foot warehouse, and made a small but dependable profit. But Vincenzo's real job was to lay off the East Coast's bookmaking action with the Vegas casinos. Each week the Family booked over fifteen million dollars in bets, everything from horses to basketball, golf to football. The ten percent vig was enough profit for Eddie so, whenever the bets became lopsided, Vincenzo would visit a few of his favorite sports books and level the action.

Vincenzo went to high school with Eddie's brother, Joey. They were on the football team together; linebackers, both ferocious, both feared by every running back in Division A football.

While Joey was a bit of a thug who used brute force to crush his opponents, Vincenzo was smart and quick, he out-thought the running backs and was always there to close a hole. The coach wanted to make Vincenzo a running back, but Vincenzo liked hitting people too much.

After graduation, they both went to work as soldiers for Uncle Marty's gang. They made a good team and, with Joey's brawn and Vincenzo's brains, they became Uncle Marty's top enforcers.

When Eddie graduated NYU and went to work for Don Tito, he recognized Vincenzo's talents and felt he was wasted on the street. He moved Vincenzo into the backrooms, where Vincenzo's quick mind and head for numbers made him a natural for the gambling operation. But he missed hurting people, so Eddie also let him break the occasional leg when a gambler wouldn't pay up.

Three years ago, Eddie moved him to Las Vegas, and Vincenzo had flourished in the desert. A lifelong bachelor, Vincenzo loved Asian hookers. There were barely enough in Jersey to keep him happy, but Las Vegas was crawling with beautiful Asian ass, and he was determined to fuck every one of them.

"Hello," Vincenzo said from his office overlooking the warehouse.

"It's Eddie."

"Jesus, Eddie, I'm so sorry about Joey."

"Thank you."

"I saw those cunts on TV. Can you believe it?"

"You remember Amber? I was with her about two years ago."

"Yeah, sure, the blonde."

"She's a redhead now." Eddie let the words hang in the air. Realization dawned on Vincenzo.

"You don't mean…"

"I do. The redhead is Amber. She and that blonde are on the run but I know where they're going. Las Vegas."

"Good."

"She'll be checking into the Paradise Hotel in about an hour. She's got something I want. Something I have to have. So go to the hotel, find her, and keep an eye on her. Make sure nothing happens to her until I get there. I should be there by midnight."

"Done and done."

"Thanks." Eddie hung up, turned to Enrico. "How much further?"

"Next block."

"If we get that tape back," Eddie said to Frankie. "Our FBI worries will be over, forever."

The Mercedes turned left, passing an alley. About thirty seconds later the FBI Crown Vic followed. As it passed by the mouth of the alley, a garbage truck suddenly burst from the alley and broadsided the Crown Vic. In a shower of glass and sparks the FBI car flipped over once, twice, three times, before finally coming to rest on its roof.

Eddie and Frankie watched through the Mercedes rear window. "And that," Eddie said, "takes care of that. Get us to the airport, Enrico. I'm feeling lucky."

TWELVE

"I understand your financial concerns. L.A. is expensive and work for specialty acts can be streaky." Eric Andrews looked at the two potential clients sitting on his couch, two beautiful blondes. But more than that, oh so much more – they were identical twins.

They had moved to town from Montana about nine months ago hoping to turn their unique genetic disposition into a little Hollywood gold. But God usually only gives with one hand, and though beautiful, they couldn't act. So they booked some print work, did a gum commercial and a few specialty extra jobs on TV shows, but they could barely pay their bills and were thinking of moving back to Bozeman.

If Eric could convince them to work as escorts *as a team,* the money would be huge. Twins, every guy's ultimate fantasy. And if they'd do pornos *together*, well, they could write their own ticket.

So now came the interesting part, finding out how far someone was willing to go to get famous. "But there are lucrative alternatives for the adventurous."

Eric's office door suddenly slammed open. He spun as Ryan stormed in followed by Sean and Eric's assistant, Suzie. "I'm sorry Eric, they wouldn't -- "

"FBI," Ryan interrupted, flashing his ID. "We're here on official business."

Fuck, thought Eric. It's got to be Madison. Shit.

"Sorry ladies," Ryan said. "But Mr. Andrews is going to have to postpone the meeting."

The confused twins turned to Eric. "If you guys would just wait for me in the lobby, this should only take a few minutes."

Sean's eyes almost popped out of his head as he rubbernecked the twins out the door. He couldn't help but wonder if they were hookers, too, and the erotic possibilities caressed his brain.

Sean was dressed in a blue suit, his only suit, which his mom had bought him for his sister Julia's wedding. She'd married a cop. Ryan told Sean to put it on when they stopped at Sean's apartment. The suit would imply that Sean was Ryan's partner, though he looked way too young to be in the FBI. Sean also slipped his back-up Glock into a shoulder holster and put it on.

Special Agent Ryan Griffin watched the twins leave Eric's office with a fantasy similar to Sean's running through his brain. Only, in Ryan's fantasy, the twins wore cheerleader's outfits. Oh, well, Ryan thought. Back to work. He turned to Eric. "You got a phone call from Madison Stone at twelve twenty-one this afternoon. Then, according to your assistant, you met with her and another woman who matches the description of Grace Taylor. These two women are wanted by the police for murder. But I'm sure you already know that. And I'm sure you're familiar with the penalties for aiding and abetting fugitives."

"You should think about a career in acting," Eric said. "That was a terrific performance, nuanced with just the right amount of sincerity and intimidation. But it's wasted on me. If you want to interrogate me, fine. I'm represented by counsel and I won't speak to you until my lawyer is present." Eric hit his intercom. "Suzie, would you get me Mark Glass, please?"

Eric looked at the two cops and waited for their next move. He wasn't nearly as confident as he appeared; fact is, he'd been dreading this day from the moment he first started pimping his girls.

Eric had come to L.A. full of ambition. He'd graduated Yale with an English major and a business minor, and moved to L.A. hoping to become a writer. His dad, a Westchester cardiologist, knew a doctor at Cedars Sinai who knew this big muckity-muck at WFT Talent Agency. That got Eric a meeting and a job in the mailroom. He discovered he loved the agency business and soon found himself a junior literary agent. The agency represented Hugh Hefner and one night Eric was invited to the Mansion for one of the Friday night movie screenings. He chatted up Hefner and they became friends. Eric became a regular at the Mansion, signing a bunch of the playmates to the agency's roster. Eric also recruited models from the other skin magazines, *Hustler* and *Penthouse*. He fell in love with one of them, Miss August, and married her. The marriage lasted six years, ending abruptly when he walked in on her fucking her personal trainer.

They divorced, but she was awarded the four million dollar house and ten thousand dollars a month for the next six years.

Eric was suddenly living in a two-bedroom condo in Sherman Oaks and maxing out his credit cards to keep his head above water.

Then one of the other agents joked to Eric that he'd pay a thousand bucks to fuck one of his centerfold clients.

"Really," Eric said, the wheels spinning. What guy wouldn't want to fuck a centerfold, for bragging rights alone, Eric thought. And Eric knew these girls; some of them were party animals, giving it away for free to anyone who caught their eye. He was sure he could talk a few of them into making a little extra money. "For two thousand," Eric told the agent. "I just might be able to arrange that."

And that's how it started. Soon, the one agent became three agents, and they told their friends and clients and they told their friends and, well, Eric had a very profitable business.

Unfortunately, when the agency's partners found out what Eric was doing, they asked him to leave. Eric understood and, since he was making far more money on the side than with his commissions, he resigned and opened AAA Management.

Eric booked enough legitimate business with his clients to make a decent living, but with the alimony and his life style he was always broke, so he continued peddling flesh.

And as much as Eric liked the money, there were aspects of it he hated. Like having to deal with hard cases like Eddie DeCarlo, and the nagging fear that one day he'd get arrested.

Now the cops were here. But they didn't want to bust him. They just wanted Madison. But so did Eddie, so Eric had to be very careful. And keeping his mouth shut seemed like the perfect solution.

Special Agent Ryan Griffin looked at Eric Andrews and smiled. Christy had called Ryan after she ran a check of the manager. He was clean, no arrests, but the local FBI office suspected some of his clients worked as high-priced call girls. Since he represented Madison, it made perfect sense. But a lawyered-up suspect who refused to talk wasn't going to help Ryan right now, so he needed a way to loosen Eric Andrews' tongue. Ryan said, "Eric, I'm told perception is everything in Hollywood."

"Absolutely," Eric said. "You are what *they* think you are."

"And what would *they* think if I called all the TV stations, told them I was making an arrest in the Joey DeCarlo murder, then dragged you out the door in handcuffs?"

"*They* would think you were a fool when I sued for false arrest."

"Madison Stone and Grace Taylor were involved in a high speed chase this afternoon. They were driving a red Porsche. They abandoned the Porsche in the Beverly Center parking lot. Guess who the car is registered to?"

Eric confidence evaporated. Fuck. Another good deed goes unpunished. "Me. So I loaned them my car, big deal," he said with hollow confidence.

"It is a big deal. It's called aiding and abetting. And when I leak your clients' extra curricular activities, reveal you as her pimp, what would *they* think of you then?"

The intercom crackled to life. "Mark Glass on one."

"You're a handsome guy, Eric," Ryan said. "You'll look good on those TV shows like *Entertainment Tonight* and *Access Hollywood,* I can hear the lead now, 'the best little whorehouse in Hollywood.' And don't forget the tabloids. I see your face on the cover of *The National Enquirer* with the headline, HOLLYWOOD'S BIGGEST PIMP, beneath it. Not to mention Leno and Letterman; you'll be the butt of jokes coast to coast."

Suzie's voice came over the intercom. "Mr. Glass is still waiting."

Eric and Ryan locked eyes. Eric blinked first. "Never mind, Suzie," he said. "Tell Mark I'll call him back later."

Ryan said, "Tell me about Madison."

"We're dealing with very dangerous people here. It could get me killed."

"Eddie DeCarlo, I know. I'll keep your name out of it."

Eric sighed, sat heavily. "I like Madison, I really do. I'm so sorry I got her into this mess."

"You got her in trouble?"

"Yes and no. I mean, I had no idea why Eddie DeCarlo was looking for her. She must've done something to really piss him off. I got an email about a week ago. A picture of Madison with blonde hair, and trashier make-up was attached. And a reward was being offered, a hundred grand."

"That's real money," Ryan said. "And no matter how much you liked Madison, that hundred grand got your attention."

"That's right. And when I talked to Eddie I tried to make sure he wasn't going to hurt her or anything."

"And he assured you he wasn't."

"That's right."

"And a mobster like Eddie DeCarlo wouldn't lie, would he?"

"Fuck you. If I hadn't called Eddie and he found out I represented Madison, got his email and ignored it, he would have killed me."

"Hey, Sean," Ryan said. "You feeling sorry for Eric?"

"Nope," Sean said, happy to get to finally play a part.

"Me neither. Now Eric, just so we're clear, if Eddie gets to Madison before I do, she's dead."

"I know."

"So tell me where she is and you'll save her life."

"But if Eddie finds out I told you, I'm dead."

"I'm not going to tell him. Sean?"

"My lips are sealed."

"Eric, you're the only chance Madison's got," Ryan said. "Tell me where she is."

Eric sighed, thought of the saying, "the truth shall set you free." He was about to find out. "They're on a Sheik Khalad's jet to Las Vegas. They'll be staying at the Paradise Hotel." As soon as Eric said it, he did feel better. Wow, amazing.

"Thanks, Eric," Ryan said. "Now one final question, have you told Eddie DeCarlo that Madison is on her way to Las Vegas?"

"No," Eric said, instantly feeling shitty again.

Ryan sensed the lie. "When we leave here, I'm going to check your phone records. See if you made or received a call from Newark, New Jersey once Madison left your office. So let me ask you again, have you told Eddie DeCarlo that Madison is on her way to Las Vegas?"

Eric felt ashamed. Not because he'd lied, but because they were about to find out how thoroughly he'd betrayed Madison. "Yes," he said. "But he called me, I didn't call him."

"And that makes it okay?"

A humiliated beat, then, "No."

Ryan turned to Sean, "You have any other questions for this scumbag?"

Actually, I do, Sean thought. Is Grace Taylor one of his clients? Is she a hooker, too? And just how much would it cost for an hour with those twins? But Sean knew his part in this play and said, "No."

"Good, now if you'll excuse us," Ryan said to Eric. "We've got work to do."

THIRTEEN

The jet catapulted us into the air. I looked out the window. Saw the tarmac falling away beneath us. Goodbye L.A., hello, what? My carefully scripted life had taken a jarring left hand turn and the gin and tonic had done little to alleviate my panic.

"What do we do now?" I asked Madison. She sat next to me, her eyes closed, looking cool, calm and in total control. We sat at the front of the cabin, the rest of the girls were in the back of the plane so we had a bit of privacy.

"About what?"

"The rest of our lives. We don't have clothes, money, a place to live, a job, a car; hell, I don't even have a name anymore."

"One thing at a time. First, money, I got two thousand out of my safe deposit box. That's a start. Plus we can each make about five grand this weekend, maybe more, depending."

"Depending on what?"

"How much the Sheik likes you."

"I hope he's into platonic relationships because I have no intention of actually becoming a hooker."

Madison's look hardened. "Why don't you just tell me what you *are* willing to do to save your life?" she snapped. "Because right now, it's all about survival, and when you're running for your life, you can't do what you *want* to do, you do what you *have* to do. Like sucking off that scumbag drug dealer so we could get to this airplane, like fucking a rich Arab to get some working capital. You don't have to like it to do it. It's just sex, Grace, and I will gladly trade it to keep on breathing."

I hate being lectured, and when attacked, I attack back. "Well, it sounds to me like you've been trading it for a lot longer than this afternoon, and for a lot less than life or death stakes."

Blood rushed to Madison's cheeks. "I don't have to explain myself to you," she said. "You have no idea who I am, what I've been through or what I've had to do to survive. So don't you dare judge me."

"I'm not judging you, I swear. But in the last three hours I've found out you're a hooker, sat helpless as you eluded the police in a high speed chase, I watched you give a guy a blow job and you just made out with a gorgeous black chick. I'm a little confused, okay? We're on the run from a Mafia boss, the cops and the FBI. I'd just love to know why. Why did Eddie DeCarlo send his brother after you? That FBI guys said it was a tape. You said there is no tape. Someone's lying. Who? At least tell me that."

Madison fixed me with a fierce gaze, her green eyes digging into my face. And I thought, God, she's beautiful when she's mad. And then, just like that, I saw her eyes soften, almost like a light being turned down on a rheostat. She'd made a decision, I realized. I could almost feel a protective layer drop away from her. "Don't be mad," she said. "But I haven't been totally honest with you. There is a tape, a videotape. That's what I picked up at the bank. It was with the money in my safe deposit box. It was supposed to be my insurance policy." Madison leaned back in her chair, shook her head. "But what I don't understand is, why *now*? We had an agreement, goddamn it."

"We had an agreement?"

"No, not with you, sweetie, I had an agreement with Eddie DeCarlo. And he's let me be for over two years. What the hell has changed his mind?"

I had to know. "What's on the tape?"

Madison started to answer, stopped herself, then said, "Don't freak out. Me, having sex, with a woman."

If Madison was going to be honest, I figured I might as well open up, too. "Been there, done that."

"What?"

"I've made love to a woman. Only one, mind you. But we did it. A lot."

"Shut up!"

"I was in high school. She was my best friend, Ellen Chapman. I was going through this goth phase. Black clothes, black hair, black make-up, piercings and…" I kicked out my foot, pointed to my ankle, "a tattoo."

Madison was stunned. "You? Girl next door, squeaky clean Grace Taylor?"

"Much to my mother's dismay. I'm not sure whether she ever even knew about the sex or drugs for that matter, but the wardrobe and Morticia Addams hair was enough to freak her out."

"Was Ellen your first?"

"Not my first sex. That honor went to Johnny Detmer, Hillsborough High star quarterback."

"That sounds more like it."

"I was a junior, he was a senior and the hottest guy in school. We did it the first time on our first date, in the back of his mother's Dodge Caravan. I was so star-stuck. I mean, going out with Johnny was like this huge badge of honor. He said all the right things, called me his one true soul mate from heaven, and I was this gooey – I'm so embarrassed about it now – romantic mess. We dated for about four months, then he found another one true soul mate from heaven, a sophomore this time, and dumped me."

"Sorry."

I shrugged. "No worries. A few weeks later I fell in love with Raul Garcia, my co-star in the spring production of *Bye Bye Birdie*. He was Cuban-American, very passionate, and insatiable. We used to do it four, five times a day, backstage, his car, my car, the movie theater, Starbucks's rest room. He couldn't get enough."

"And what about you?"

"What do you mean?"

"Did you want it as much as he did?"

I thought about that. "Actually, no. I just did it because he wanted to do it. Anyway, we dated through the summer, then broke up right after Homecoming."

"Why?"

Okay, this did hurt and I never really told anyone the story. But somehow I'd opened this box of secrets so I might as well pull everything out.

"I caught him fucking Mrs. McDermott, our drama teacher. She was early thirties, and sexy in a Susan Sarandon kind of way. All the guys used to joke about her being this incredible MILF. How they'd like to do her. Well, in Raul's case, I guess the feeling was mutual. I walked into the scene dock one afternoon and they were going at it in the 'Telephone Hour' set."

"Did she get fired?"

"I never told anyone, so, no. But I broke up with Raul. He begged me to take him back. Said Mrs. McDermott had put a voodoo spell on him. But I wasn't buying it. Of course, I could hardly look Mrs. McDermott in the eye after that, so I quit the drama department. And that same week, Ellen's dad committed suicide. Her world had just come unhinged, mine was already in turmoil, so we went off the deep end together. The goth thing was Ellen's idea, but the hair and clothes were almost like make-up and wardrobe. Looking back, I think I was playing a role in my own life, hiding out as this goth girl, without ever really believing any of it."

"And the sex?"

And the sex, indeed. I'd never talked about this with anyone, and suddenly got cold feet. "Wait, how'd we get from your telling me about the tape to my deep dark secrets."

"You brought it up. And don't worry, we've got forty five minutes of flight time. I'll tell you all about the tape, I promise." Madison turned up the intensity on those green eyes. "Now, tell me about Ellen."

"We grew up next door to one another. Our parents were best friends, so we became best friends. But we were so different. I was into dance, and singing and acting –– my mom had me signed up for all these classes as a kid. And Ellen came along. But she had zero talent, a total klutz. When she about eight, she realized how dreadful she was and stopped coming, and became this bookaholic. I mean, she was *always* reading, everything from Harry Potter to Sylvia Plath, even comic books and graphic novels. Then she got into computers and became a total geek. She started her own website about J.R.R. Tolkien and started hanging out with all the brainiacs and smoking a lot of dope. So, though still best friends, we had less and less in common with one another. We even looked like polar opposites. I was a blue-eyed blonde. Ellen was a brown-eyed brunette, very pretty in a Christina Ricci sort of way. She was short, barely five-one, but she was intense, passionate about everything, from politics to her favorite ice cream. Every idea she embraced became like a religion to her. And when she went goth she told me how wonderful the Wiccan Way could be and I was vulnerable and dove into the caldron with her."

"Who seduced who?" Madison asked.

"Oh, she definitely seduced me. See, there was one thing I didn't know about Ellen, that *nobody* knew. She was gay. She'd realized it when she was something like thirteen, but did nothing about it except read every book she could get her hands on, especially poetry, watch lesbian porn on the internet and masturbate. So she was a virgin, but dying to have real sex.

"So, one night, after smoking grass and drinking a bottle of wine, Ellen starts reciting poems by Amy Lowell. They are very erotic, and I assume she's writing about a man and woman. Ellen says no. She's writing about another woman, Ada, an actress Amy Lowell met in 1909 and lived with for years. 'You are my Ada,' Ellen said and kissed me gently on the lips. Now I'm stoned, drunk and incredibly turned on. I look at Ellen and she's practically oozing desire. She kisses my neck, my cheek, my eyes, and then back to my lips. I open my mouth, we start frenching, then next thing I know she's going down on me, I'm going down on her, then she pulls out this vibrator and I have the most unbelievable orgasm..."

"God bless Amy Lowell," Madison said.

"Yeah, I guess. But after that night, Ellen became obsessed with me. She was as bad as Raul, wanting to fuck all the time. But I wasn't in love with her. And I never really enjoyed sex with her after that first night. I still thought about guys and realized I wasn't gay."

"There is nothing wrong with being bi-sexual, trust me."

"If you say so, but I was getting freaked out by Ellen and the whole goth lesbian thing and then my dad died and it sort of shocked me back to reality. I bleached my hair, plucked out the piercings and became mommy's little girl again."

"What happened to Ellen?"

"She teaches poetry at Wellesley, lives with a lovely woman named Abby, they have two adopted children and a wonderful life."

"How nice for her."

It was, I realized. And then it hit me. "It's kind of ironic," I said. "Ellen, the lesbian rebel, ends up with a perfect little life while I, the normal one, has had one failed relationship after another and a career that's on life support."

"Not to mention the murder, the mob and the FBI."

"Ah, nice segue, Madison. Now tell me about the tape."

"Three years ago I had a pretty good life. I was one of Manhattan's highest paid escorts, working for Madam Lucinda, this crazy Russian émigré, who ran one of the classiest black books in the city. She'd come to the country twenty years earlier as a ballet dancer but was hit by a cab crossing the street and confined to a wheelchair. She lived in an apartment with four other Russian girls, all wannabe models. When work was scarce and the rent was due, the girls would hang around hotel bars, meet a decent looking out-of-town businessman, negotiate a price and sleep with him. They weren't professional hookers, just girls who chipped at the edge to make a few bucks. But they were all beautiful, and since Lucinda now had no job, no disability insurance and no way to make a living, she decided to turn her roommates' freelancing into a full-time career.

"Lucinda had a cousin with the Russian diplomatic corps. He dealt with American companies wanting to do business in the Soviet Union –- yes, when Lucinda started, there was still a Soviet Union. He mentioned the availability of beautiful companions to the visiting executives and gave them Madam Lucinda's number. She charged more than anyone else in the city with the promise that her girls were the most beautiful. Business was soon booming."

"With just four girls?" I asked.

"Hardly. As word spread, other escorts called Lucinda wanting to get into her book. There's a pecking order in any business; and, since Madam Lucinda used only the most beautiful women, every high-priced call girl in the city wanted to be represented by her. It was a badge of honor."

"She was the CAA of Madams."

"Exactly. And she was even pickier with her clients. They had to be rich, respectful to the girls, oh, and did I mention rich? She had CEOs, CFOs, UN Ambassadors, actors, athletes, writers, directors, the crème de la crème. She also made nice with high-ranking city government and police officials so they'd leave her alone."

"How did you meet her?"

"A friend introduced us, Madam Lucinda took me under her wing and I blossomed. I'd wanted to be an actress, but soon I was making so much money I sort of forgot about acting and just started partying full-time.

"Then along came Eddie. See, the mob ran most of the prostitution in New York. For years, Madam Lucinda had a deal with the old mob boss, Tito something or other, and he left her alone. Then Tito dies and Eddie takes over. He sees the quality of Madam Lucinda's girls, but more than that, he sees the quality of her clients. If the mob could get close to these movers and shakers, get a little dirt on them, they could exert a little 'horse head on your pillow' intimidation, and Eddie would be able to truly integrate the Family into corporate America. So, as they say, he made Madam Lucinda an offer she couldn't refuse."

"He killed her?"

"God, no. The girls loved Lucinda, none of them would have stayed if he'd tried the strong arm stuff. No, he paid her three million dollars, enough for her to move to Florida, buy a South Beach condo and retire.

"We had a going away party for her. There were speeches, gifts, tears. And sitting at a corner table were three guys. All dressed up, looking for all the world like business executives, but it was Eddie, his brother Joey --"

"Him, I met."

"Indeed. And a guy named Frankie the Fish."

"Not too many businessmen with that nickname," I interrupted.

"No," Madison laughed. "His name's actually Frank Cardino, he got the nickname because of these thick glasses he wears, makes his eyes bug out. So after the speeches Eddie wheels Madam Lucinda from table to table, she thanks each girl and introduces them to Eddie. And here's where it gets a little corny," Madison said. "When Eddie introduced himself and I looked into his eyes, I felt this weird connection. It was like looking into the eyes of a lover or a best friend, someone who knows all your secrets. Someone you've known your whole life."

"Jeez."

"He felt it, too. I could tell. Something changed in his face; he tilted his head, curious. 'Do I know you,' he asked. 'No,' I said. 'Then it's time I did,' he said and invited me to dinner."

"Love at first sight, the same thing happened to my parents."

"At dinner we talked about music, movies, tropical fish of all things, he's a nut for tropical fish, knows all the different species. I think he felt safe with me. We both had something to hide from the world, but not from each other. For the first time in a long time, I felt like I was actually on a date. We made love that night and that's what it felt like, making love. Not fucking for fun, or for money. But tender, caring, sweet. I'd known him less than twenty-four hours and I was head over heels in love. *We* were head over heels in love.

"He moved me into an apartment in Newark, this dreamy old brownstone, told me I wasn't a hooker anymore, I was his girlfriend. Deep down all call girls have the same fantasy, the *Pretty Woman* scenario. You meet a rich john who falls in love with you, takes you off the streets and marries you. Of course that was a little more complicated with Eddie. He was already married."

"And he wouldn't get a divorce?"

"He couldn't. He'd married Don Tito's daughter, a political move, he said, meant to help secure his place as Tito's heir. And even though Tito was now dead, it would be dangerous for him to disrespect the man's memory by divorcing his daughter. But he said his heart belonged to me, promised he'd always take care of me and I believed him."

"A sucker for love."

She nodded. "The first six months were heaven. Eddie would take me out two or three nights a week – all these Mafia guys were married but had girlfriends. The wives knew about it but since it was a tradition for the man to have a wife *and* a girlfriend, they couldn't do anything about it. He even took me on a couple of trips to Las Vegas.

"I'd been around a lot of rich and powerful men in my professional life, and I'd seen how people used to kowtow to them. But it was nothing compared to the way people treated Eddie. They fawned over him. The reason was simple, he told me. If they pissed off some rich guy, they might not get a tip. They piss off Eddie, and he could have them killed. I think that's why there is such a popular culture fascination with the mob, from *The Godfather* to the *Sopranos.* Here's a secret society moving freely among us that routinely uses violence, beatings and murder in the course of everyday business. Everyone knows who they are, the cops, the press, you, me, everybody, yet they are allowed to walk around pretty much unmolested. Sure, the FBI arrests some kingpin every so often, but it's rare. Take Eddie, for example. He's famous, for goodness sakes, his picture is in the paper all the time, *60 Minutes* even did a profile of him. But Eddie's smart, he gives away a lot of money to homeless shelters, orphanages, the Red Cross. So he's created this image as a modern day Robin Hood and turned himself into a folk hero. The press loves it and I can only imagine how much the cops hate it.

"Anyway, for six months I'm in heaven, then he comes home one night, in a foul mood, and tells me he's booked me on a flight to Chicago. 'What for,' I asked, surprised but not suspicious, not worried. I mean, I trust him by now, totally. 'You're going to fuck someone,' he said. I laughed thinking he was joking. 'What's so funny?' he snapped and I suddenly realize he wasn't joking. 'I need someone I can trust,' he said. 'Someone who won't ask questions.' I was getting mad now, at his tone, at his presumption. 'And just who am I supposed to fuck?' I asked. 'That's a question,' he said, and he gave me this hard look I'd seen him give the goombas who worked for him. An imperious glare that meant just shut up and do it.

"I could feel my world beginning to crack. I'd had this wall around me, around my heart. I'd been hurt before, so deeply, I promised I'd never get hurt again. But Eddie had swept me off my feet. He'd brushed aside all of my carefully constructed barriers, so I stood there exposed, emotionally naked, broken-hearted. 'But you told me I was out of the business,' I said, hating my weak pathetic tone. Eddie said, 'I took you out of the business and I'm putting you back it in.' 'No,' I said, 'I won't do it.' His eyes caught fire and he hit me, slapped me across the face. I crumpled to the floor, started crying. He glared down at me, nobody ever said no to Eddie, so I think he lashed out without thinking. He knelt down next to me, took my hands in his. 'Look, baby. I'm sorry, but this is a favor for a friend of mine, a very important friend. His wife has needs he can't fulfill.'"

"His wife?" I asked, surprised.

"His wife," Madison said. "Grace, a lot of call girls are bisexual. Guys love three ways, and pay a lot for them. Why men love to watch two women make love is beyond me, but it's turn-on number one. So I've slept with a lot of women."

I looked at Savannah, the beautiful black girl Madison had kissed when we got on the plane. "Did you work with Savannah."

"Once or twice," Madison said, smiling. "And we've partied ourselves a few times. She's special." Madison's eyes met Savannah's, and even though Savannah couldn't know what we were talking about, she flashed a knowing smile at Madison, and then went back to her friends.

"Go on," I said.

"I told Eddie to tell her I'm taken. 'Tell her what you've told me,' I said. 'You love me.' Eddie shook his head. 'Eddie,' I pleaded, 'a man doesn't share the woman he loves with his friends.' He stood up then, turned his back to me. 'He does when she's a hooker.' He might as well have hit me again. I curled up in the corner, fighting back tears. 'And if I don't?' I asked. He turned back to me then and said, 'I'll kill you.'"

"What a bastard," I said.

Madison nodded. "Numb now, practically in shock, I asked Eddie who the woman was but he wouldn't tell me. 'That's the whole point,' he said. 'She's very important. He's very important. So privacy, confidentiality, is a must. She wants to meet a beautiful woman she can absolutely trust, and that, babe, is you.'

"So I fly to Chicago, go to room 635 at the Ambassador East Hotel and knock on the door. It swings open and this woman stands there. She's tall, almost five-nine, attractive in a no-nonsense, business-like way. She's got dirty blonde hair flecked with gray, pale blue eyes, a nose just a little too big for her face and thin lips. She's had work, a face-lift, I can tell, the skin was just a little too taut. She appraises me, head to toe, nods and asks me to come in. I start to introduce myself but she stops me. 'No names,' she says with just the touch of a southern accent. 'No questions. Understood?' she asks. 'Understood,' I say.

"The first time it was very business-like. I was there to service her, nothing more. No kisses on the mouth, she was very specific about that. Germaphobe, I thought. But kiss her breasts yes, and pussy definitely. She had a very hard time coming, but I'd brought a few toys and before long she was curling her toes.

"We met again two weeks later; the sex was easier, she was much more relaxed. But when she came, she started to cry. She apologized, told me her lover of many years had just died and she happened to think of her as we were making love. She told me about her lover, a girl who worked for her, and how much she missed her. As much as I hated having to make love to this woman, I was starting to like her.

"She brought me a gift the next time we met, a pair of diamond earrings. And she ordered a bottle of champagne. I could tell she was getting comfortable with me, was hoping somehow we could develop a personal relationship. She talked about trips with her husband to Paris, China, India. You name it, she'd been there in their private G-5. I started wondering, who was this woman? The curiosity was killing me. So, after we finish making love, she goes to take a shower and I look in her purse. I find a Georgia driver's license with her picture and the name Margaret Cross. When I got home I checked her out on the Internet. She's married to this rich dude, Alan Cross, who builds shopping malls. He's a billionaire. But she's no slouch herself. She's a lawyer, no, more like a super-lawyer. She's the Attorney General for the State of Georgia."

"That's like the chief prosecutor of something, isn't it," I asked.

"Exactly," Madison said. "And it wouldn't look very good if the people of Georgia found out their happily married attorney general was cheating on her husband with a woman. As you can imagine, I was desperate to leave Eddie by now, but too scared to do anything about it. He'd come after me, I was sure. Maybe even have me killed. But I realized Margaret Cross could actually provide me with a way out. So next time we met, I hid a video camera in my purse, set my purse on the bedroom bureau, aimed the camera at the bed and taped everything.

"When I got home, I put the tape in the machine and played it for Eddie. He turned beet red, furious. He ripped the tape out of the machine; I told him go ahead, it's only a copy and if anything happened to me, the original goes to *Fox News*. He grabbed a kitchen knife, pinned me to the wall, stuck the point under my chin. He broke the skin; I felt blood dripping onto my chest. 'You dare betray me,' he hissed. 'Betray you?' I said. 'You betrayed me. I gave you my heart and you pimped me out like a two-bit whore. Well, here's what this whore wants for that tape. My life back. I'm leaving. Leaving you, leaving New York. If anything happens to me, that tape goes to the press. Capisce?' I asked, sounding tougher than I felt. He just looked at me but something changed. The rage was replaced by, I don't know how to say it, almost admiration, I guess. He lowered the knife, grabbed a napkin and stuck it under my chin to stop the bleeding. 'Capisce,' he said, and walked out of the apartment.

"I told a few friends I was moving to Miami, but that was just to throw Eddie off if he came looking for me. I changed my name, my look and moved to L.A. It was exciting, actually. I was getting a chance to reinvent myself, to stop hooking and start over, finally become an actress."

"Okay, hold on," I said. "How'd you start hooking in the first place?"

"When I was in third grade, a coke whore came to class on career day and gave this incredible speech."

"Funny."

"Not really."

"You don't have to tell me if you don't want to."

"No," Madison said. "It's okay. Remember when I said my dad was a dentist, my mom was a teacher and I grew up in a love-filled house in Scarsdale? What I didn't tell you is they died when I was twelve, plane crash, and I moved in with my Uncle Phil."

The hate-filled way Madison said his name told me all I needed to know. "He molested you?"

"Right up until the day I ran away at seventeen."

"Oh, Madison, I'm so sorry."

"I took the train to the city, totally delusional. I actually thought I'd meet some cute guy on the street, he'd take me in, we'd fall in love and, oh my God, I was such an idiot. I met a guy all right, this rocker with a Jim Morrison complex. He wrote these really depressing songs when he wasn't wigged out on heroin. He lived with four other guys in this tiny two bedroom in the East Village. They were all in the same band, Blood Relatives, and while Trevor, that was my guy's name, didn't work – supposedly so he could write music during the day – the other guys all had jobs to pay the bills. Trevor and I had one bedroom, the other three made do with the second bedroom and living room couch. Trevor loved to fuck, and was noisy as hell, so the other three always knew what we were doing. And when I walked around the apartment, I could feel them staring at me, wanting me."

"How did that make you feel?" I asked.

"Sexy. In fact, God I was such a tease, I'd walk around in nothing but a T-shirt and underpants loving the way they'd drool after me. Anyway, like I said, Trevor used heroin, and soon, so did I. We'd lay around the apartment all day in this blissful daze, which meant he wasn't writing, which meant his roommates were getting pissed. Finally, they cut him off financially. He couldn't pay for the drugs but we both needed them. So Trevor made a deal with the boys. They could each fuck me for fifty bucks."

"That son of a bitch."

"Yeah, well, I wasn't exactly saying, no, don't touch me. I wanted the drugs as much as Trevor did. So I started fucking all of them. Sometimes one at a time, sometimes one big old gangbang."

"Unbelievable."

"And a big mistake. Because it made Trevor incredibly jealous, and one night he came home with a gun instead of a nickel bag and tried to kill his roommates. He wounded two of them and ended up going to jail."

"This is like some bad Movie of the Week."

"And I hit the streets again; I'm homeless, broke, a junkie and desperate. I see this sign for a teenage homeless shelter stapled to a telephone pole, so I go there. Turns out the poster was a scam, a way to attract young girls to this pimp named Nathaniel. Black dude, very slick, and he's got a string of like six girls all living in this Soho loft. He's also got dope so I move right in. Nathaniel got this huge crush on me, said I was different from the other girls; he wanted to take care of me. Oh, he still sent me out every day – Nathaniel got most of his business from escort ads in the yellow pages –- but he wanted me off the needle. And I'm crazy in love with him. I mean, he was a father figure slash boyfriend and I was desperate for both. So I go cold turkey, suffer through three days of absolute hell, but Nathaniel's at my side for every agonizing second.

"You know how you're in an airplane sometimes, flying through a storm and it gets real bumpy. The plane shakes, makes these horrible dips, then suddenly shudders and you burst out of the clouds into blue sky and calm air. That's what it was like. I felt like I burst free. I was barely eighteen but I felt like I was leaving a lifetime of suffering behind me and was reborn.

"Only Nathaniel was a pimp and I was still a hooker, so it's all relative. He still sent me out every day, and I began to wonder, if he's so crazy about me, how can he stand to know all these guys are fucking me? Then a wonderful thing happened. One of the girls got busted, rolled over on Nathaniel and he got arrested. And they throw the book at him; two of the girls were minors, so they pile on the charges and Nathaniel goes down for twelve to fifteen and I'm alone again."

"How was that wonderful?"

"I was free. Of the drugs, of Nathaniel. I had a little money saved and for the first time in my life, I actually thought about what I'd like to be when I grow up. I loved movies and TV, actually had a knack for acting in my brief high school career, so I thought I'd give it a shot. But how to start? Then I saw this ad looking for extras for this big Nick Cooper movie. I apply and get hired. I was hit on by everyone – the extra coordinator, assistant director, other extras, an associate producer, but I politely say no. I'm trying to take this acting thing seriously. Then Nick Cooper himself hits on me and I'm thinking, oh my God, I'm talking to Nick Cooper and before you know it I'm in his trailer and doing a lot more than talking."

"You tramp," I said, laughing.

"Later Nick took me to dinner and we started talking. Suddenly I'm pouring out my life story. He seemed genuinely interested, and said he could help me. I'm thinking he's going to set me up with an acting coach or something, but no, he set up a meeting with Madam Lucinda. Turns out Nick and a bunch of his Hollywood friends are clients. Madam Lucinda liked what she saw and told me she was going to take me under her wing, turn me into New York's number one escort. I was hesitant, not really ready to go back to hooking, but she told me how I'd travel the world, meet fabulous people and make tons of money. In a way, she kind of swept me off my feet. But she didn't lie. It was a wonderful life, until Eddie."

"Until, Eddie," I repeated. "So, back to question number one, what do we do now?"

"Make as much money from the Sheik as your conscience will allow, then hide out, buy ourselves a little breathing room, a little *thinking* room. There has to be a reason Eddie suddenly wants the video, and when we can figure out why, we're going to trade the tape for our freedom."

FOURTEEN

Alan Cross watched CNN in the living room of his Watergate Hotel suite. The windows offered a spectacular view of our nation's marble monuments, but Cross's eyes were riveted on the TV, on the coverage of the murder, car chase and manhunt underway in Los Angeles.

Behind him, in the suite's bedroom, his wife, Margaret, sat with two of her aides, going over the speech she was about to give, blithely unaware of the potential A-bomb about to go off in their lives.

Margaret was never told Madison had videotaped one of their trysts. She was told Madison had been killed in a car accident. Margaret had no emotional ties to the hooker she met in Chicago, she just asked Alan to see if he could find her another companion. Another companion meant another chance at exposure and blackmail. Alan finally did what he should have done years before. He sat Margaret down and told her she had to choose: a public life in politics or her lesbian lovers, because if word of her sexual predilection leaked out, they would be ruined. Margaret's ambition got the best of her, and she reluctantly took a vow of lesbian abstinence, but not before reminding Alan that her "predilection" was all his fault. And in a way, he had to admit, it was.

Alan met Margaret in Atlanta. She was working her way through John Marshall Law School as a waitress at the trendy Park 75 Lounge and Terrace bar at the Four Seasons Hotel and he was well on his way to building his shopping mall empire. She was a tall, confident woman, with intelligent eyes, a quick smile and a charming Southern accent. She was attractive but not beautiful, her nose was a bit too big for her long face. A plastic surgeon could have easily fixed the genetic mistake, but Margaret, Maggie in those days, loved her nose, was proud of it. It was her father's nose and she would joke it was the only thing of value she inherited from him. Poppa was a Greek immigrant who ran a falafel stand in Chandler Park; Momma worked at his side. They barely made enough money to get by, but had big dreams for their only daughter, Maggie. Maggie shared their dreams; she excelled at school and earned a full ride to Emory University for her B.A. and another scholarship for law school. Maggie was ambitious. Hillary Clinton was her idol, and like Hillary, Maggie was going to use law as her political stepping-stone.

The tips were good at Park 75. The bar's clientele were some of Atlanta's most elite businessmen. And the horniest, Maggie thought, since almost all of them hit on her. But Maggie was expert at flirting just enough to get a big tip while still parrying any serious advances without pissing anyone off. Not that she wouldn't have minded dating a few of the well-heeled customers; but, between work and school, Maggie had no time for romance, so she'd decided to postpone dating until after graduation.

Then she met Alan Cross. He just wouldn't take no for an answer. He was rich and women generally found that irresistible. Maggie didn't seem to give a shit, and that fascinated him. He also loved her looks, her elegance, her accent and the fact that she was two inches taller than he was. He left her huge tips, sent flowers, champagne, even a twelve hundred dollar pair of Manolo Blahnik shoes. All he got back was a polite thank you and a glimpse of her dazzling smile.

But the truth was, she was falling hard for Cross. It wasn't his money that appealed to her, though she realized his cash would be a huge help if she ever ran for elected office. It wasn't his looks; the searing intensity of his pale blue eyes actually scared her a little bit. It was his persistence. The more she rebuffed him the harder he tried. It made her feel desired, a very heady feeling for a woman who always felt smart but never beautiful.

She began thinking about him. Looking for him every night, worried he wouldn't come in, relieved when he'd finally arrive. And one night when he ordered his Glenlivet single malt scotch, neat, and asked her out she said, "Yes."

"Turn me down all you want," Cross said, so used to her saying no that he hadn't really listened to her answer. "But one day you'll beg me to…" he trailed off as what she said finally took hold. "Wait, did you just say, yes?"

"Yes."

"Yes, as in you'll actually go out with me, yes?"

"Yes," she said, and laughed.

"But why, what changed your mind?"

"I realized that if I kept saying 'no,' one day you'd finally give up and I might never see you again. And that made me sad."

"You'll never regret it, I promise."

It was a whirlwind romance powered by Cross's Gulfstream; dinner in Paris, a weekend in Aruba, skiing in Aspen, all squeezed around Maggie's school schedule, of course. After graduation, Maggie spent the summer in Cross's summer house on Martha's Vineyard, studying for the bar. She passed, and though offered jobs at a number of Atlanta's top law firms, she kept her eye on the political ball and took a job in the Atlanta District Attorney's office. They were married in the fall at a lavish ceremony at the Four Seasons Hotel – it was, after all, where they met – and they honeymooned in Paris. That's where it happened, the event that would change both of their lives forever.

They were staying at the George V, sitting in the Le Bar at one in the morning, drunk from too much champagne and two bottles of La Tache Pinot Noir. They were sipping Hennessy XO, listening to Jacques on the piano, when Maggie noticed a woman sitting alone at the bar. She looked like a fashion model, tall and elegant.

"She's beautiful, isn't she?" Maggie asked Cross.

"Not compared to you," he said and kissed her. As they kissed Maggie kept her eyes on the woman.

"Why is she sitting alone? It's so late. Is she waiting for someone?"

Cross looked at the woman who looked back at him and smiled. "As a matter of fact, she is," Cross said. "She's waiting for someone to pay her a few thousand francs for the pleasure of her company."

Maggie was shocked. "She's a call girl? But she's so beautiful."

"Many of them are."

"You say that with just a little too much certainty for my liking."

Normally, Cross would have laughed off the line and changed the subject. But he was drunk, in love and a little more honest than usual. "Darling, in my pre-Maggie days, I would occasionally use the services of a beautiful woman in exchange for the local currency."

"Oh my God," Maggie said, surprised but not disgusted, and a little intrigued. "Girls as pretty as that one?" she asked.

Cross studied the woman a little closer, the soft blonde hair, perfect patrician features. "No," Cross said, "I have to say she is exquisite."

"I think so, too."

Cross stared at his new wife. "Okay, I feel stupid asking this question now, but have you ever been with a woman?"

Normally, Maggie would have laughed off the line and changed the subject. But she was also drunk, in love and a little more honest than usual. "No, but I've thought about it."

"Really," Cross said. "You do know that every man's fantasy is a ménage a trois?"

Maggie's eyes drifted back to the woman, to her lips as she puffed her cigarette, to the swell of her ivory breasts atop her silk blouse, to her long, shapely legs. "Let's buy her," Maggie said.

Her name was Camille. Back in the suite, Cross sat in an armchair and watched as Camille led a clearly nervous Maggie to the bed. "Have you ever kissed a woman?" Camille asked in gently accented English.

"No."

"Then I envy you." Camille's voice was soothing, almost a purr. "This is a moment you will never forget." Camille kissed Maggie on the left side of her neck. "And I am honored to be a woman you will never forget." Camille kissed Maggie on the right side of her neck. "The first lover you've ever had who truly knows a woman's body." She kissed Maggie's left eyelid. "The first lover you've ever had who understands a woman's needs." She kissed

Maggie's right eyelid. "I promise you a night of many delights."

Maggie stared into Camille's beautiful face and her nervousness vanished. A serenity filled her. She was flush with desire to kiss this woman, to touch this woman, to taste this woman. Camille leaned forward, their lips met, parted and two tongues became one.

It was the most erotic night of Alan Cross's life. He watched the two women make love, watched his wife orgasm as Camille's tongue caressed her clitoris, watched Maggie kiss Camille's pink nipples, her stomach, then settle between the French courtesan's legs. As Maggie devoured Camille, Camille looked at Alan and crooked a finger at him, come join us. Alan slipped out of his clothes and climbed onto the bed. He kissed Camille, and she melted in his mouth.

He made love to his wife as she made love to Camille. He made love to Camille as she made love to Maggie. Camille and Maggie gave Alan head, together, sucking him, kissing each other. Finally sated, they feel asleep as the rising sun bathed the room in golden light.

When they woke, Camille was gone. They were hung over and oddly self-conscious with each other. Both regretted what they'd done the night before but neither Cross nor Maggie could bring themselves to even talk about it. They went on with their day, and the rest of their lives without even mentioning Camille or the night that changed everything.

And change everything it did, for it awoke in Maggie a need for female companionship. Oh, she still loved Allan and even enjoyed making love to him, but she also never forgot Camille's soft, sweet embrace and the knowing touch of a woman's tongue. So as she built her career, parlaying her Assistant D.A. job into a successful run as

Atlanta's first female District Attorney, Maggie would often fantasize about making love to another woman. A few times she almost asked Allan for another ménage a trois, but always chickened out. If word of any sexual impropriety ever leaked out, her political career would be over. And her political fortunes were looking good, indeed. After eight years as District Attorney, Maggie was her party's nominee for State Attorney General. Alan called on his rich friends and Maggie soon had a multi-million-dollar war chest. The airwaves were bombarded with ads showing the attractive candidate spelling out her dream for Georgia. "Justice for All" was her campaign slogan. She was passionate, articulate and charming. She won in a squeaker, just beating out the Democratic incumbent.

It was during the campaign for attorney general that Maggie met Susan Warren. Susan was a former TV reporter, a pretty blonde with green eyes and dimples. She was hired as assistant Press Secretary and traveled with Maggie as they crisscrossed the state campaigning.

Susan was gay, that was why she was a *former* TV reporter. Someone had shot a picture of Susan kissing her girlfriend in the back of a bar on their cell phone and sold it to a competing TV station. When the scandal broke, Susan resigned to spare her station embarrassment. She was hired by Maggie's campaign as Communications Director a few weeks later.

Maggie liked Susan; she was smart, funny, hard working, and dependable. She was also sexy. And more than once Maggie found herself wondering what it would be like to kiss this woman, to make love to this woman.

And late one night in a hotel suite in Savannah, Georgia, after a grueling day of campaigning and two vodka martinis to help them relax, Maggie told Susan about the night she spent with Alan and Camille. Told Susan how much she liked the smell of a woman, the gentle touch of a woman, how surprised she was by the depth of her orgasm. The conversation was like an aphrodisiac to them both. "Why are you telling me this?" asked a very turned-on Susan.

"I think you know," Maggie said, and kissed her.

The affair lasted five years, through Maggie's extremely popular first term and right through her reelection. And though they cared for each other very much, it was about sex, not love. Maggie was married and intended to stay that way. Susan had a life partner and loved her very much. They were always very careful when and where they'd meet, and the affair might have remained a secret if Susan hadn't gotten breast cancer. It was stage three by the time they found it and she was dead within six months. And on the night Susan died, a tearful Maggie confessed all to her husband.

He'd actually suspected something might be going on, the odd looks he caught passing between them, the many nights they'd spend together out of town. And he wasn't jealous. He understood. He'd had a few affairs along the way, but it was always about sex, never love. And that's what Maggie tearfully told him. Sex with Susan was just that, sex. She fulfilled a physical desire in her that Alan, or any man, could never reach. And, as much as she cared for Susan, she only truly loved Alan.

If anything, Maggie's confession brought them closer together. For the next couple of years they redoubled their efforts to have a baby, while both worked insane hours at their jobs. After a barrage of tests, it was determined that Maggie had PCOS, Polysystic ovary syndrome, and would never be able to conceive.

She took the news badly, went into a brief depression, and then tried to lose herself in her work. But slowly, the itch returned, she began to crave a woman's touch. Her profile as a prominent politician had risen every year, though, and Maggie was aware that any sexual indiscretion could ruin her career. So she turned to Allan for help. Maggie suggested another ménage a trois; Allan worried that it was too risky, and put her off with a "let me think about it."

The solution, Alan realized, was simple – Eddie DeCarlo. On a few occasions when Alan was in Manhattan on business, Eddie would provide him with female companionship, expensive, but first-rate. Running girls was one of Eddie's many enterprises. So who better to provide Maggie with what she needed? Alan called his old friend and Eddie came to the rescue.

Now it was all coming back to haunt them at the worst possible time. Cross's cell phone rang. He answered. "Cross."

Two hundred and twenty seven miles away, hustling across the tarmac of the Newark International Airport toward a chartered Cessna Citation jet, Eddie DeCarlo spoke into Frankie the Fish's cell phone. "Hey, Alan, it's me."

Alan kept his voice low so Maggie wouldn't hear him. "Tell me it's over, Eddie. Tell me you've got it back."

"Not yet."

"This thing has gotten way out of control. Have you seen the TV? Now the cops are looking for her, the FBI's involved; Eddie, this could ruin us!"

"Don't worry about the cops. I know something they don't, where Amber's going. I'm getting on a plane right now, I'll be there in four hours."

"Well, I hope you enjoy your flight because in *one* hour the President is making the announcement."

"I thought we had until tomorrow morning."

"Somebody leaked. The President had to move up the timetable."

"Fuck!" Eddie considered his options, picked one. "Look, I might be four hours away but I've got someone there now. We're cool."

Cross hated being out of control, something he never let happen in business. But now, he had no choice. "I'm counting on you, Eddie."

"Have I ever let you down?"

There's a first time for everything, Cross thought. "No," Cross said.

"I'll take care of it, Alan, I promise."

Eddie snapped the phone closed, handed it to Frankie as they climbed into the Citation and Eddie settled into one of the tan leather seats. He wished he were as confident as he sounded to Alan. Eddie hated being out of control, too, and with Joey dead, the tape missing and Amber/Madison on the run, this was about as fucked up as things get.

"We lost Eddie," Stubblefield said into the speakerphone as he flossed his teeth.

"Don't flick that shit at me," Christy Cortez said, flinching as a piece of food sailed over her head. "His tail was hit by a garbage truck," Christy said into the speakerphone. "Broadsided in an alley."

"How're Kenny and Gail?" Ryan asked from an Exxon gas station in Long Beach, California. Ryan and Sean had pulled off the freeway to fill up Ryan's rental car. Sean was inside buying snacks and soda while Ryan filled the car. They were planning to take the 210 to the 15, and then take the 15 all the way to Vegas. It was only a five-hour drive so Ryan figured driving was almost as fast as flying, between airport security, waiting for the flight and the hassle of renting another car. Besides, Ryan had twenty-five thousand dollars of Madison's money in his pockets, and he didn't want to risk having to explain himself to airport security.

"Both in the hospital," Stubblefield said. "Gail's got a broken arm and leg, Kenny's got broken ribs and his left wrist bent all sorts of directions God never intended. But they'll both fully recover."

"The garbage truck was stolen and the driver fled the scene after the accident," Christy said.

"So it was no accident," Ryan said.

"No," Christy answered. "Obviously Eddie's on the move and he doesn't want us to know where he going."

"No worries," Ryan said. "I think I know."

"Where?" Stubblefield and Christy asked together.

Ryan watched Sean pay the cashier through the minimart window. "Las Vegas. Madison Stone's manager told us Madison Stone and Grace Taylor hopped a ride on a private jet and they're on their way to the Paradise Hotel. I'm on my way there now."

"Does the manager have a relationship with Eddie DeCarlo?" Christy asked.

"Good guess, Christy," Ryan said. "Eddie knows she's on her way to Vegas. Which means Eddie's on his way to Vegas."

"Great," Stubblefield said. "You want some help from the local field office?"

Under normal circumstances, absolutely, thought Ryan. But this situation was far from normal. "No," he said. "I think I got it covered. I brought one of the LAPD cops with me; he's met Grace Taylor, has some sort of relationship with her. I've got a feeling this case needs finesse, not brute force."

"You got it, if things change let me know."

"I will."

Inside the minimart, Sean looked through the window at Ryan pocketing his cell phone. This is so cool, Sean thought. I'm on the road with a FBI agent, *working* with a FBI agent. A few hours ago Sean thought his career in law enforcement was over; humiliated and disgraced, Ryan was sure his father and uncles would disown him. Now he had a chance to ingratiate himself with Ryan, which might be his ticket into the FBI and redemption.

Sean's father had told him to look for a mentor in the department, someone with a few stripes who liked him and would look out for him. Sean hadn't found one in the LAPD yet, but now, he might never have to. If Ryan would be his rabbi in the FBI, he could write a whole new chapter in the Harris family history, from police officer to federal agent.

The secret was to keep impressing Ryan. Sean had picked up his cues quickly during the Eric Andrews interrogation, and Sean could tell that Ryan was pleased. So all Sean had to do was stay on Ryan's good side, do whatever he told him and maybe, just maybe, Sean could finally make his dad proud.

Sean walked outside. Ryan was pulling the gas nozzle out of the Chevy. "Hey, good news," Ryan said. "I was talking to the office, told them I'd drafted a smart local cop to help me out and they blessed the idea."

"That's great," Sean said handing Ryan his soda. "Are we going to hook up with other agents in Las Vegas?"

Ryan shook his head. "Don't think we'll need them. I got a feeling you and I can handle this just fine."

Sean smiled, thrilled at Ryan's vote of confidence. "Want me to drive?" Sean asked

"No, driving helps me think. Get in the car," Ryan said. "Our destiny awaits."

FIFTEEN

I love Vegas. It, well, sparkles. During the day the sun glints off the humongous hotels and the trillion or so cars jammed onto the strip. At night, neon signs blast away, diamonds bling on the fingers and necks of the rich and beautiful, champagne bubbles, dice tumble, laughs cascade in the cavernous, glitzy casinos.

Vegas is all about fun, sex and money. Not a bad combination if you ask me. I'd only been there twice since I'd moved to L.A. First time was just after I booked my first job, a guest shot on *Criminal Minds* – I played the cute girl next door who gets murdered at the end of Act 2. The guy who killed me on the show, this totally hot surfer dude named Randy, swept me off my feet and into a junior suite at the Bellagio hotel for a weekend of champagne, sex (no, not with him, either) and Ecstasy (the drug, not the state of mind). To be honest, I don't remember very much, but I did win three hundred dollars at roulette on my favorite number, 15, and Randy won over a thousand dollars at craps. Randy dropped me at my apartment when we got back to L.A. Monday morning, and never called me again. You always wonder when that happens, even if you're not crazy about the guy, which I wasn't. But you can't help but wonder; was it something I said, the way I look, the sex, does he already have a girlfriend, a wife, commitment issues, what was it?

My second trip was with Jason. He had a guest shot on *Entourage*. The episode was shot on location at the Palms Hotel and Casino, and Jason brought me along. We hung out with stars Adrian Grenier and Kevin Connely, who were surrounded by *their* entourage and a gaggle of other celebrities. Adrian hit on me when Jason was flirting with Paris Hilton. But like an idiot, I stayed with Jason. Later in bed, while making love, I suspect Jason was fantasizing about Paris Hilton, which was fine with me, because I was all about Adrian.

We drove from the airport to the Paradise Hotel in the world's biggest Hummer limousine. It was a party in there. Cassandra poured champagne from the bar. I had two glasses, Madison, still trying to stay in control, had none. Jade sparked up a joint. I had two hits, Madison had none. The girls were swapping war stories. Cassandra talked about the movie producer who wanted her to piss on him. Jade talked about the Australian billionaire who wanted to watch her fuck his dog (she said no), Cassandra told us about the seventy-six-year old Japanese businessman who liked to dress up like Elvis and fuck her while he sang "It's Now or Never." And Jade topped them all with her story about the night she went to a suite at the Beverly Wilshire and found out the client was actually four horny midgets. Yes, she did them all.

By the time we piled out of the limo at the Paradise, I was really starting to like these girls. I felt strangely empowered as the six of us walked into the hotel. You know that slow motion shot you've seen in movies – hot chicks doing a power walk, heads turn to watch them, men filled with desire, even women stare appreciatively –- well, that was us. Six girls buzzed on the bubbly and grass bursting into the extravagant elegance of the Paradise Hotel's lobby.

Suddenly this guy, wearing traditional Arab robes and headdress, came running up to us. "Welcome, ladies, welcome, my name is Omar al-Domaini, I'm here to make sure you and the Sheik have a memorable weekend." Omar was forty-something, tall, elegant with a thick moustache and even thicker jet-black eyebrows. He spoke with a slight accent and was very polite. "I've taken the liberty of checking you all in, so if you'd be kind enough to follow me to the elevator, I'll show you to your rooms."

"Lead the way, handsome," Savannah said slipping her arm through his right arm. As we started walking, Tiffany slipped her arm through his left arm.

"You're awfully cute," Tiffany said. "Do you get to party, too?"

"I'm afraid my duties are strictly business in nature."

"Dude, you're not a eunuch or something, are you?" Cassandra asked.

"No. My testicles are intact and in fine working order as my three wives and seventeen children will attest." We followed Omar onto an elevator. He pressed the button for the twenty-seventh floor. "The Sheik is anxious to meet you but he understands you may need some time to unpack and freshen up."

"Destiny and I didn't get a chance to pack," Madison said. "I wonder if -- "

Omar stopped her with a raised hand. He had perfectly manicured fingernails. "Eric warned us you'd need a few basics. You'll find them in your suite."

"Suite?" I whispered to Madison.

"I told you. In this business, it's first class all the way."

"Where is it?" Tiffany asked, her eyes searching the roof of the elevator. "There," she said, pointing at a tiny lens in the corner. "The eye in the sky." She suddenly pulled her top down exposing her huge breasts. "Here you go, boys," she squealed, jiggling them. "Take a gander!"

"Please," Omar said, covering her breasts with his hands. "A little decorum, please."

Tiffany pressed her breasts into Omar's palms. "What do you know, a perfect fit. You sure you don't want to party, sweetie?"

"Positive," Omar said pulling her blouse back into place. "Though your breasts are lovely."

"The best that money can buy," Savannah snapped and everyone laughed.

The elevator dinged and the door opened. Omar led us down the plush hallway. "We've arranged for three two-bedroom suites," Omar said handing out electronic key cards. "I trust you'll find everything you need; if not, just contact the desk and they will attend to your every need."

"Thank you," Madison said as she slipped our key into the electronic lock and opened the door. I walked in and stopped, staring in awe. It was the most beautiful hotel room, er, suite, I'd ever seen. Las Vegas decadence at its best. The living room was bursting with flowers, a fire crackled in a marble, a flat screen TV tuned to CNN, with the sound muted, hung from the wall, and a chilled bucket of champagne sat next to a five ounce tin of Beluga caviar with all the trimmings.

"Jeez," I said.

"I tried to tell you," Madison said crossing to a rack of clothes next to the wet bar.

I joined her and we started thumbing through the hangers. I couldn't believe it. "Prada, Armani, Gucci," I said. "These clothes must've cost a fortune. And look at the shoes! Can we keep them?"

"That depends on how much fun the Sheik has. We can't just take them, but he's been known to give the girls some pretty incredible gifts."

Madison walked into one of the bedrooms. "I'll take this one. And with any luck..." She opened the mirrored closet wall. "Bingo, a safe." Madison opened the safe, took a videotape out of her purse and stuck it inside.

"That's it, huh? The reason we're on the FBI's 10 most wanted."

"I wish I never made it. I wish I'd just had the guts, or self respect, to run away from Eddie when he first asked me to sleep with her." Madison closed the safe, entered a four digit combination.

"0921?" I asked. Madison reacted, surprised. "September twenty-first," I said. "It's your birthday. I always use mine, too."

"1027."

"October twenty-seventh, yeah," I said, also surprised she remembered. We looked at each other, both affected by the other caring enough to know our birthday.

Then Madison said, "I'm glad you know the combination, that way, if I'm killed, you'll be able to get the tape."

"Don't even say that!"

Madison crossed to the caviar, layered a spoonful onto a cracker. "I'm just saying." She took a bite. "God, this is good." She handed the other half of the cracker to me and I ate it.

"Incredible." I looked around the suite, taking it all in. "And not just the caviar, I mean, it's all so... opulent, is that the word? The size of the suite, the quality of the furniture, rugs, drapes. I've never been in a house this nice much less a hotel room."

"Cristal champagne, Gulfstream jets, designer clothes, limousines; I told you, Grace, this can be a very glamorous life. The men are rich, smart and attractive. I've traveled the world, stayed in the best hotels, been given scads of wonderful gifts and made a ton of money."

"But the men are just using you."

"And Jason wasn't using you? Or that creep you dated before him, Bret? He had you driving his kids all over town like you were his nanny."

"It's not the same thing."

"Isn't it? How many times did you have sex with them because *they* were horny? How many times did you just want to go to sleep but *they* wanted to get laid first? Men *always* use women. They'll say anything to get us into bed, but once they fuck us, they just want us to leave."

"What about love, marriage?"

"Yeah, let's talk about love and marriage. Sure, they'll fall in love, but for how long? Six months? A year? Two years? Ten years? Then they think we get too old, too fat or too boring and they dump us."

"That's just so cynical! My parents were happily married for twenty years before..." I trailed off as I realized Madison wasn't listening to me anymore. Instead she was staring at something over my shoulder with a shocked expression on her face. I turned around to see what she was looking at. It was the TV. There was some sort of press conference going on at the White House. The President shared the podium with a middle-aged woman. A banner headline read: ATTORNEY GENERAL RESIGNS.

"That's her," Madison said. "The woman from Chicago." Madison grabbed the remote control and turned up the sound.

"...Attorney General Chamberlain's resignation due to throat cancer has given us an opportunity to bring a passionate and dedicated woman to the job of America's number one law enforcement official. And so, I proudly nominate Margaret Cross to the office of the Attorney General of the United States."

"Oh, my God," Madison and I said in unison.

A loud knock on the door startled us. Madison opened it, Omar stood there. "Is everything to your satisfaction?"

"Yes, lovely," Madison said.

"Excellent. The Sheik would like to see you all in thirty minutes. Can you be ready?"

Panic seized me but Madison just gave Omar a provocative smile and said, "Ready, willing and able."

SIXTEEN

The sun set as Ryan steered his Chevy past Baker, California, just an hour and forty-five minutes from Las Vegas. Traffic was light and Ryan had the cruise control set to eighty-five.

Ryan had his cell phone to his ear listening to Grace Taylor's recorded voice. "Hey, this is Grace. Sorry I missed your call. At the beep, tell me your deepest secret."

"No answer," Ryan said to Sean. The phone beeped and Ryan said, "Grace, this is Special Agent Ryan Griffin. This is urgent. Your life is in danger. I can help you. I can save your life. Please call me." Ryan left his number and snapped the phone closed.

"Have you ever saved a life?" Sean asked.

"What?"

"As a cop, have you ever saved a life?"

"I've saved a few, both as a Chicago cop and an FBI agent."

"So you're a hero?"

"I don't think of myself as a hero."

"But to the people whose lives you've saved, I'm sure they think of you as a hero."

Images flashed through Ryan's brain. The hug he got from the terrified eight year old girl he'd rescued from a kidnapper, the tearful kiss on the cheek he got from the woman he pulled out of the burning car on the Eden Expressway, the grateful applause he got from the people in the bank when he shot the robber, ending a thirteen-hour hostage situation.

"Yeah, I guess they did," Ryan said.

"And did you always know, even as a little kid, that one day you'd be a hero?"

Ryan flashed on his past, not a pleasant vision. "No. Sean, what the hell are you talking about?"

"Destiny, fate, whatever you want to call it. See, when I was a kid, I was kind of a klutz. Whenever I did something with my dad -- "

"Your dad, the cop?"

Sean nodded. "My dad, the cop. Whenever we'd play catch, or go fishing, or build model airplanes, whatever, I'd do something to disappoint him. Drop the ball, get the hook stuck in my finger, get globs of glue all over the model. He'd yell, I'd cry and run to my room. My mom would come in and tell me not to worry. She told me I had a destiny. God put me on the earth to do something great and one day I would."

"And you believed her?"

"Well, sure."

Ryan looked at Sean and debated what to say next. Tell him the cynical truth or let the poor kid live in his comfortable delusion? Dempsey always said, *truth hurts, but as least it's the truth.* So, Ryan said, "Did it ever occur to you that she just said that to make you feel better? That she was deflecting your pain with a nebulous promise about the future so you'd stop crying? That telling you that one day you'd be a hero and your dad would love you was just a tonic to help you get through childhood?"

"Actually, it did. But not until I was much older, high school, I think, and by then the destiny thing was firmly planted in my psyche."

"Good, you had me worried there for a minute."

"But I still believe it. Sure, it became sort of a self-fulfilling thing, but it inspired me to be a cop. I didn't join the force just to impress my dad and uncles, though that's a side benefit. I joined the force because I truly believe I'm meant to do something great. Something heroic. And being a cop is all about being a hero. I mean, when terrified people run out of a building, cops go running in. The very essence of being a cop is to be willing to risk your life to save a complete stranger. How cool is that? So if my mother's tonic was what got me to where I am today, I say, thanks Mom. In fact, if you think about it, maybe my being a klutz was part of my destiny."

"How do you figure?"

"I had to be a klutz so my dad would yell, I would cry and my mom would fill my head with delusions of grandeur."

Once again, Ryan was impressed with Sean's passion. He was naïve, sure, but it was hard not to respect the kid's enthusiasm. And something else occurred to Ryan: Dempsey would have loved this kid.

"Have they checked in yet?" Eddie asked from thirty-two thousand feet above Milltown, Pennsylvania.

"About half hour ago," Vincenzo said. He was sitting at a blackjack table near the elevators so he would know if Madison and Grace came downstairs. The table was full, seven players crammed together, trying to beat the dealer. Vincenzo had won six straight hands, and parlayed his first fifty-dollar bet to a thousand dollars profit.

"Good," Eddie said. "Do you know what room they're in?"

Vincenzo stacked five one-hundred-dollar chips and slid them forward. "No, but I'm hooked up here. I can find out."

"Do it. There's been a change of plans. I'm still three hours away and time's become an issue. I need you to talk to Amber or Madison or whatever the fuck she's calling herself; she's got a videotape that belongs to me. Get it."

The dealer flipped a card in front of Vincenzo, king of clubs. "Will she want to give me the tape?"

"No fucking way. You'll have to convince her."

"How much latitude do I have?"

"Do whatever it takes."

That was music to Vincenzo's ears. He hadn't had the chance to hurt anybody in a long time. "Done and done." Vincenzo closed his phone as the dealer dropped an ace of diamonds on top of Vincenzo's king.

"Blackjack," the dealer said.

The other players cheered as the guy next to Vincenzo said, "Looks like it's your lucky day."

"You can say that again."

"Looks like it's your lucky day," the guy repeated and they both laughed.

SEVENTEEN

I looked hot. I mean, I know I'm cute and all, and that's what I usually get from guys, how cute I am, how adorable I am. Never, not once, has a guy said I was hot.

But I'd never had Madison dress me and do my make-up. She picked a white Chanel halter dress, white Salvatore Ferragamo sandals, wrapped a blood red sash around my waist then painted my fingernails and toenails red. She pulled my blonde hair straight back, added light blue eye shadow, a touch of rouge on my cheekbones and finished with bright red lipstick.

"Wow," I said.

"I'd fuck you," Madison said. She meant it as a joke, but as our eyes met in the mirror, I looked away, embarrassed.

"Sorry," she said, "I wasn't coming on to you."

"I know. My head's just spinning a bit. I can't believe I'm really doing this."

"Look, there're six of us and one Sheik. Odds are he'll pick another girl tonight."

"And if he picks me?"

"Damn it, Grace," Madison said, clearly exasperated. "We've been over this. You'll do what you have to do. We need to buy some time. For that, we need money, cash money, because if we use our credit cards, they'll catch us.

If we call anyone we know, they'll catch us. So we need cash, as much as we can make. You've slept with guys you didn't like, haven't you? Guys who wouldn't take no for an answer, so you screw them just to get rid of them. Boyfriends you're sick of but haven't dumped yet. This is no different. You're an actress for God's sake, *act* like he's the greatest lover in the world — and by the way, he's not half bad. *Act* like you've never been so turned on and fake an orgasm as if an Academy Award depended on it. And if he does pick you and you just can't do it, fine, run into the bathroom, pretend to puke and we'll tell him you have food poisoning."

There was a shave and a haircut knock on the door. Bang, badabang, bang... bang bang. Madison opened it to find Jade, Savannah, Cassandra and Tiffany. They looked spectacular, tasteful but provocative in brightly colored skirts and dresses. "Party time, girlfriends," Cassandra said.

"Great," Madison said. "Destiny," she said to me, "Shall we?"

Destiny, what was I thinking? "Ready, willing and able," I said in my best Madison impression and stepped into the hallway.

The Sheik's suite was at the end of the hall. As we walked toward it Savannah, Madison's occasional lover, fell in step with me. "Fabulous dress," she said, her hip brushing against mine. "Fabulous everything."

"Thank you," I said.

She took my hand. "Maybe you, Madison and I could get together later."

Right, a lesbian threesome, this was getting off to a great start. "Look, there's something I got to tell you, all of you."

Madison threw me a panicked look.

"This is my first time," I said.

"Dude, you're a virgin?" Cassandra asked.

"No, of course not," I said. "But I've never done a party scene like this before. I mean, I've never done it for money before. So I'm a little nervous."

"Terrified is more like it," Madison said.

"Don't worry," Jade said as we reached the Sheik's door. "You're in good hands. The Sheik is a class act. He'll take good care of you."

Savannah rang the doorbell to the Sheik's suite. The door swung open and two huge bodyguards stood there. They looked middle-eastern; one had a beard, the other a moustache, and they were dressed in blue business suits.

"Room service," Savannah said. "Six girls, served wet and wild."

"Hey, are you guys going to give us a cavity search?" Tiffany asked.

"No, silly," Jade said. "That's the Sheik's job."

The bodyguards laughed as they stepped aside and we entered. If I thought our room was nice, it was nothing compared with the palatial splendor of the Sheik's suite. We were in the living room, but I could see a formal dining room, a den, and full kitchen. A spiral staircase led to a second story where I assumed the bedrooms were.

Omar came down the stairs. "Excellent, I see you're all here." He turned to the bodyguards, spoke quickly in Arabic, and they disappeared into the den, closing the door behind them. Omar turned back to us. "And now ladies, I'd like to introduce you to his Excellency, Sheik Khalid.

A chubby-cheeked teenager came down the stairs wearing tan cargo shorts, a Los Angeles Lakers jersey, and flip-flops.

We were confused. Jade said, "That's not the Sheik."

"He's the Sheik's number one son," Omar said. Sheik Khalid, Jr."

"Dude, he's a kid," Cassandra said.

"Eighteen years old today, and you, ladies, are his birthday presents."

We were standing in a line at the bottom of the stairs. Young Khalid walked slowly past us, his eyes drinking us in. And though I'm sure all of the girls were disappointed the real Sheik Khalid wasn't here –- the generous Sheik Khalid who showered them with   gifts –- they all preened a little bit under young Khalid's stare. He was still the client and they were professionals.

"Nice assortment, Omar," young Khalid said, in perfect English. "Thank you." Omar made a slight bow, and then exited up the stairs. Young Khalid stopped in front of Jade. "I love Asian girls," he said. "What's your name?"

"Jade."

"Have you ever done porn, Jade? You look vaguely familiar."

"I've made a couple of movies for Vivid."

"*Rising Sun 2?* Weren't you the chick who did the two guys in the steam bath?"

Jade was pleased to be recognized. "That was me."

"You suck a great cock. Here," he said dropping his pants. "Blow me."

As crude as young Khalid was, Jade didn't miss a beat. She dropped to her knees took him in her mouth and went to work.

"Hey Blondie," he said looking at Tiffany. "Lick my balls."

Gross! But Tiffany dropped to her knees next to Jade, and started on the kid's balls.

"Is this the glamorous part?" I whispered to Madison.

"You two," he said, pointing at Cassandra and Savannah. "Start making out." Again, without missing a beat, Cassandra and Savannah folded into each other's arm and started kissing. "Tongue, girls, I want to see lots of tongue." Cassandra and Savannah responded, ramping up the passion.

"Now, you two," young Khalid said pointing at Madison and me. "Start kissing."

Oh, my God, I thought. I turned to Madison. She mouthed, "I'm sorry," then took my face in her hands and kissed me.

Let me tell you, I'd be embarrassed kissing a guy in front of a roomful of people much less another woman. I stiffened under Madison's touch and kept my mouth and eyes closed. I could feel Madison's tongue brush my lips, urging them to open, but I couldn't do it.

"Tongue, girls, let me see how much you love each other."

I opened my eyes and found myself looking into Madison's emerald green eyes. They were pleading with me: please don't fuck this up. Her tongue brushed my lips again. I opened my mouth and kissed her.

Now I'd love to tell you that fireworks went off and I heard the *Hallelujah* chorus, but I was so freaked out I could have been kissing Brad Pitt and not responded. Madison was a pretty darn good kisser, though, and she smelled wonderful.

"Oh, shit, I'm about to come, suck it baby, suck it!"

I opened one eye and watched him groan, thrust himself deeper into Jade's mouth, groan again and then it was over.

Cassandra and Savannah stopped kissing. Madison and I separated. Jade and Tiffany stepped back from young Khalid and we were back in line again.

I thought, is that it, can we go now? Oh, please let it be over.

"That was fabulous," young Khalid said. "And lucky for you girls, I'm only eighteen and took two Viagra. I'll be able to go all night."

My eyes dropped to his penis and damn if wasn't fully engorged and looking none the worse for wear.

"Strip naked, ladies," he said stepping out of his pants and taking off his Laker jersey. "Time to fuck."

Jade and Savannah shrugged out of their dresses, wore no underwear and were naked in seconds. Cassandra and Tiffany weren't far behind them.

Madison jabbed me in the ribs. "Please," she whispered as she kicked off her shoes, unbuttoned her dress and dropped it to the floor. She stood naked and looked incredible. Long legs, flat belly, perfect breasts. I also realized she had no pubic hair, she'd shaved it all off. Involuntarily, I glanced at the other girls, Savannah and Tiffany had thin landing strips, Cassandra and Jade were totally shaved.

"I thought looking at pussy was my job," young Khalid said to me. "And how come you're the only person in the room with their clothes on?"

"It's her first time," Jade said. "She's a little nervous."

"Really," the young Khalid said, intrigued. He walked up to me, studied my face. "You're very pretty."

"Thank you."

"Are your titties pretty?"

"I think so."

"Let me see."

It's now or never, I thought. A final desperate look from Madison pushed me over the edge. I pulled the straps off my shoulders and let the dress fall to my waist.

"Very nice indeed," young Khalid said. He leaned forward and kissed first the left breast, then the right. Yuck. "What's your name, princess?"

"Destiny," I said.

"Well, let's see what Destiny's pussy looks like. He pulled down my dress revealing my white panties. "Another layer," he said. "Who dressed you, your mother?"

"I did," Madison said. "Some things are worth waiting for." Her eyes went from young Khalid to me, her silent plea practically a scream.

"Indeed," young Khalid said. He dropped to his knees, took a hold on either side of my panties and pulled. I was now completely naked.

"Beautiful," he said, gently stroking my pubic hair, cut in a tasteful triangle, in case you're interested. "But it will be so much prettier once my fat cock's inside."

He lay back on the floor, his penis sticking straight up in the air. "Sit down, baby. I'm going to fuck your brains out."

I stared down at the pudgy teenager, at his drug-induced dick, then at Madison whose eyes begged me to do it. I stepped forward, centered myself over him and — panicked.

"No, wait, I just remembered, I forgot my... diaphragm." I grabbed my clothes. "I'll be right back."

I ran for the door. Madison grabbed her shoes and dress, called "Wait!" and chased after me.

I put on my dress as I raced down the corridor toward our suite, Madison slipped back into her dress beside me. "This isn't smart," she said.

"And letting that juvenile delinquent stick his thing in me is?"

"So you close your eyes and fantasize about George Clooney." She grabbed my arm, stopping me at our door. "It's not too late, let's turn around and go back to the Sheik's suite."

"I can't, Madison, I'm sorry. That kid is just too gross." I swiped my key and stormed into our suite, Madison behind me.

"But we need the money," she said.

"Then you go back and fuck him. I'm done."

"She's not going anywhere," a male voice said. We spun toward Madison's bedroom as a guy in sunglasses stepped out with a silenced automatic aimed at us.

Madison cocked her head as she looked at him. "I know you," she said.

"Vincenzo Sica. We met a couple years ago when Eddie brought you to Vegas."

"You were the guy who brought the two Chinese hookers to dinner."

"Good memory."

"They both hit on me."

"Can't say I blame them."

"Wait a minute," I said, turning to Madison. "How'd he find us?"

Madison turned to Vincenzo. "Yeah, how'd you find us?" Then it hit her. "Eric! It had to be. He's the only one who knew where we were going. That son of a bitch must've called Eddie."

"I like how you answer your own questions," Vincenzo said. "Now maybe you can answer mine. Where's the tape?"

Before Madison could answer, our suite door slammed open and the Sheik's two bodyguards burst into the room. "The Sheik demands you return to his suite," the one with the moustache said. "Immediately." Then the bodyguards noticed the gun-totting Vincenzo standing in the bedroom doorway.

If this was a movie, here is where it would all go slow motion. The Sheik's bodyguards threw back their jackets and reached for the guns in their shoulder holsters. Madison and I dove for cover behind the couch as Vincenzo calmly aimed his automatic and fired three muffled pops.

Three bullets ripped through the chest of the bodyguard with the moustache. He looked confused, then fell to the floor, dead.

The bodyguard with the beard had his gun out and snapped off a two quick shots at Vincenzo. The gun wasn't silenced and the blasts were deafening. The shots missed Vincenzo's head by inches, shattering a full-length mirror. Vincenzo stood his ground, calmly aimed and squeezed off two shots. The bullets snapped the bodyguard's head back, blowing out the back of his skull, and his lifeless body tumbled to the ground.

Meanwhile, Madison scrambled to her feet and grabbed the champagne bottle out of the ice bucket. As Vincenzo turned toward her she swung the bottle like a baseball bat. Vincenzo ducked and the bottle sailed over his head. Vincenzo yanked the bottle out of Madison's hands, then wacked her on the side of the head. Madison went down. "You, I need alive," he hissed, and then he stepped around the couch and stood over me. "You're just in the way." He aimed at my head. I reflectively threw my arms over my face and heard, Boom! Boom! Boom!

I waited for the white light and whatever eternity had in store for me, then realized that Vincenzo's gun was silenced, so if I heard the booms, someone else fired. I opened my eyes and saw three ragged bloodstained holes in Vincenzo's shirt. His eyes rolled back in his head, then he fell to the floor. A cascade of casino chips flew out of his jacket pocket.

I looked past his body to see Madison, her open purse at her feet, Officer Sean Harris's smoking gun in her hand.

"You saved my life," I said.

"Now we're even." Madison's eyes went to the chips. She scrambled for them, started picking them up. "Get your purse," she said. "We're going to need these." I grabbed my purse and we began stuffing the chips into the bag.

Suddenly, the suite door burst open as Omar and young Khalid ran in. "What's all the..." Omar trailed off as he saw the bodies sprawled on the floor and shock filled their faces.

Grace and I got to our feet. As I stood up my purse tipped over and Joey DeCarlo's mammoth gun fell out. "This isn't what it looks like," I said, sticking the gun back in my purse.

"There aren't three dead men on the floor?" Omar asked.

"Okay," I said. "That part is what it looks like. But we only killed one of them."

"You're not helping," Madison said, then aimed her gun at Omar and the young Sheik. "Put your hands behind your head and kneel down."

"You don't tell us what to do," young Khalid said. "We tell you what to do." He held out his hand. "Give me that gun now and I will see to it that your beheading will be quick and painless."

"Beheading?" I croaked.

"The punishment for murder in the Kingdom," young Khalid said.

"Nobody's getting beheaded," Madison said, cocking her gun. "But if you don't kneel down, I will shoot you."

"Your Excellency," Omar said, "perhaps we should do as she says. The woman is clearly deranged."

Young Khalid's eyes went from Madison to the gun, which was aimed at his forehead, then back to Madison. "You will live to regret this," he said and knelt down. Omar knelt next to him.

"There's not much about today I don't already regret," Madison said, searching one of the bodyguards. "And just for the record," she pointed at Vincenzo's body, "that son of a bitch shot your two men, then I shot the son of a bitch so he wouldn't shoot my friend." Madison pulled out a pair of plastic restraints. "Grace, go to the safe, get the tape."

I scurried into the bedroom as Madison searched the second bodyguard. She pulled out another set of plastic restraints as I punched in the combination and pulled out the tape.

Madison used the restraints to cuff Omar's hands and feet. "I would love to stick around and discuss the gory details with the police," Madison said. "But under the circumstances, that's just not possible." I rejoined Madison as she cuffed the young Sheik. "Sorry we couldn't stay for the ice cream and cake."

"Fuck you," he said.

Madison turned to Omar. "His daddy must be very proud."

I handed Madison the tape. She grabbed her purse, stuffed the tape and Officer Harris's gun inside.

"There is nowhere you can run," young Khalid said, in a dark threatening tone. "No place you can hide."

"Last chance to shoot him," I said.

"Don't tempt me," Madison said, "but we probably should gag them."

Wrong thing to say because they both realized they should probably be shouting for help, and they started screaming.

We grabbed two hand towels from the bathroom. I stuffed one in Omar's mouth. Madison stuffed hers in young Khalid's.

The shouts were sufficiently muffled so we ran out the door and I slipped a DO NOT DISTURB sign on the handle. As we raced for the elevators I asked, "You think anyone else heard the shots?"

One of the elevators opened and five uniformed security guards and one guy in a blue suit poured out. "Never mind," I mumbled.

"Oh, thank God," Madison screamed, pointing toward our suite. "There's a madman in there with a gun!"

The security guards pulled their weapons and sprinted for the suite as we stepped into the elevator, pressed the lobby button and gratefully watched the doors slide closed.

EIGHTEEN

The security guards flanked the suite door and pulled their weapons. They were all retired cops and knew what they were doing. The guy in the blue suit was their boss, Terry Conklin. Conklin, a black man who had grown up in poverty on Las Vegas's West side, pulled himself up with two tours in the army as an MP and then seventeen years as a Vegas detective before the Paradise Hotel wooed him away with a security job that paid twice the salary. He was smart and diplomatic and before long was named Paradise Hotel's Security Chief. Now he lived in a four-bedroom house with a hot tub and swimming pool with his wife and two kids. Life is what you make it, was his motto. Hard work was his mantra. He drilled his men relentlessly for any security eventuality, and a madman with a gun locked in a room was a well-rehearsed scenario.

Conklin pulled his electronic pass card, checked the eyes of his men to make sure they were ready, and then swiped his card. The light turned green and Conklin threw open the door, leading his men into the room. They came in high and low, eyes behind their weapons, and fanned out searching the suite. Conklin's eyes registered the three dead bodies and two gagged and handcuffed hostages, but he kept his mind focused on the search until he heard "Clear," called from all four rooms.

The hostages were screaming, indecipherable through their gags, but Conklin thought it sounded a lot like "Help, help."

"Uncuff them," Conklin told two of his men as he examined the dead bodies. He recognized the two bodyguards. They were part of Sheik Khalid's entourage and had to register with security to carry their weapons. The skinny dead guy with the sunglasses and three holes in his chest was a mystery.

Conklin turned to the hostages. He knew them both. Omar al-Domaini was Sheik Khalid's Charge d'Affaires and a frequent guest of the hotel. The kid he'd met this morning when the little punk propositioned the desk clerk, a keno runner and two cocktail waitresses.

"This is all your fault," the kid screamed at Omar once his gag was removed. "Wait until I tell my father."

Omar, a nice guy, was totally flummoxed. Clearly out of his element with all the blood and bodies, he stammered for a reply but came up empty.

"And you," young Khalid said, pointing his finger at Conklin. "You call this hotel security? I am holding you personally responsible."

Conklin wanted to grab the little prick's finger and break it off, but the customer always comes first, especially when their father was a whale the size of Sheik Khalid, who gambled millions of dollars at the hotel every year.

"Omar," Conklin said calmly. "Could you tell me what happened here."

Omar and young Khalid both started talking at the same time rendering them both, once again, indecipherable.

"Hold it," Conklin said. "Now, one at a time. Omar, go."

But the moment Omar started talking, so did young Khalid, result: verbal chaos. Conklin was about to silence them again when he heard a cell phone ring. He followed the sound to the dead guy with the sunglasses. He dug a blood stained phone out of his jacket pocket. Omar and the kid were still yammering away. Conklin called, "Quiet!" shutting them up, then answered the phone. "Hello."

Ninety-eight miles away at 23,000 feet of altitude, Eddie DeCarlo asked, "Vincenzo, is that you?"

"Vincenzo can't come to the phone right now," Conklin said.

"Why not? What the hell's he doing?"

"First, could I ask with whom I'm speaking?"

"Why don't you go first?"

"Terry Conklin, Paradise Hotel Chief of Security, who are you?"

"None of your fucking business. Now where's Vincenzo?"

"That depends on your theological bent."

"What?"

"He's dead. So he could be in heaven, hell, reborn as a bullfrog; all religions have different retirement plans."

"Dead? How the fuck can he be dead?"

"Looks like lead poisoning, three bullets to the heart."

"Are the women there, the blonde and the redhead? Did you catch them?"

"A blonde and a redhead," Conklin repeated.

"They're the murderers," screamed young Khalid to get Conklin's attention. "That's what we've been trying to tell you."

Omar pointed at Vincenzo. "The redhead told us that man killed my security agents, then she killed him."

Conklin flashed on the blonde and redhead they met at the elevator. "Son of a bitch," he said reaching for his radio. "Dispatch, red alert. Lock down the casino. Repeat, lock down the casino. Also, rewind the video for elevator

6, Central Tower, about two minutes ago. You'll see a blonde and a redhead. They are the targets. Consider them armed and dangerous. Repeat, armed and dangerous. Also, alert Las Vegas PD, we need SWAT in the casino, the coroner and Homicide detectives in Suite 2732. I'm on my way down."

"Conklin?" Eddie asked. "Are you still there?"

Conklin said, "Hold on," into the phone, then turned to his second in command, Sergeant Yacobian. "Secure the room, cops are on the way." Conklin turned to Omar and the kid. "You need a doctor or anything?"

"No," said Omar.

"I'll be back," Conklin said.

"When you capture them," young Khalid said, "I want them turned over to me for extradition to my country!"

Conklin ignored him as he hustled out the door and down the corridor. "Now," he said into the phone. "Are you going to tell me who you are?"

"Better than that," said Eddie. "I'm going to make you a very rich man."

Conklin got on an elevator, pressed the button for the second floor, home of the Paradise Hotel Security Center. "I'm listening."

"One of those women has a videotape. I'm willing pay you one hundred thousand dollars if that tape goes to me and not the police."

"I still don't know who I'm talking to."

"Eddie DeCarlo."

Conklin recognized the name. Though the mob was out of casino ownership and management, they certainly weren't out of Las Vegas. "One hundred thousand dollars," Conklin said. "That must be some tape."

"Let's just say it's got sentimental value. So, Mr. Conklin, we have a deal?"

"A hundred thousand dollars is a lot of money," Conklin said as the elevator arrived. "But I've spent my life trying to put scumbags like you behind bars. So, fuck your offer, Mr. DeCarlo and fuck you." Conklin disconnected.

"Shit," Eddie said, and then called up to the pilot. "How long before we land?"

"Twenty minutes."

"Well, step on it!"

Conklin walked into the Security Center. A bank of one hundred and twenty screens filled one wall. He walked directly to the central monitor, a sixty-inch plasma screen that could access any camera feed or the vast digital library of surveillance footage.

"We missed them," Conklin's right hand man, Barney Templeton, said. "Here, take a look."

Templeton's finger flew over the control panel creating a surveillance camera movie of Grace and Madison. Cut one showed them standing in the elevator. "Cute girls," Templeton said. "Hookers?"

"Oh, yeah." Something about them looked familiar, but Conklin couldn't place it.

Cut two showed them walking off the elevator, the blonde almost broke into a run but the redhead grabbed her dress, slowing her down. "Smart lady," Conklin said. "Running through the casino attracts attention."

Cut three showed them at the cashier cage turning in some chips. "How much money did they get?" Conklin asked.

"Eighteen hundred bucks."

Cut four showed them hurriedly crossing the casino. The blonde suddenly stopped in front of a roulette table.

The redhead stopped a couple of moments later and backtracked to the blonde. They started arguing.

"What's going on?" asked Conklin.

"Watch," Barney said. Reluctantly the redhead put cash down on the roulette table.

"How much was the bet?"

"Five hundred on number fifteen." A few moments later the blonde and redhead sagged, disappointed, as the dealer put the ball marker on number twenty-one and swept the money away. The girls started arguing again and hurried toward the exit.

The final camera angle showed the blonde and redhead exit the casino and get into a yellow cab. As the cab drove off Barney said, "Your lock-down call came eight seconds later."

"Fuck. Did you get the cab number?"

"No, it was blocked out by the back end of a van and the angle was wrong to see the license plate."

"So we missed them?"

Barney nodded. "They could be anywhere."

NINETEEN

"I can't believe I let you talk me into making that bet."

"Fifteen's my lucky number," I said. "If my lucky number is failing me, we really *are* in trouble."

We were in our third taxicab. That's right, third. When we got into the cab at the hotel, Madison told the driver to take us to the airport. But one block later she told the driver to pull over and we got out. "Casino security probably videotaped us getting into the cab so they know the cab number." We immediately hailed a second cab, jumped in, and Madison told him to take us to the Hard Rock Hotel. But after two blocks Madison had him pull over. "Just in case the first cab driver saw the number of the cab we got into." We waited until the second cab was long gone before flagging down cab number three. She told the driver to take us to The Plush Room; I had no idea what it was and didn't really care.

The cabby occasionally glanced at us in his rear view mirror, but he had his radio turned to a country western station loud enough so Madison and I could talk freely.

"What we need now," I said, "is one of your plans."

"I think I've got one." She took out her cell phone, turned it on. "Eddie wants the videotape of Margaret Cross and me. Why?"

"Because she's about to become U.S. Attorney General?"

"Exactly. Imagine the blackmail value of that tape. Eddie could hold it over her head so the Justice Department soft peddles Mafia investigations, or he can use it to force her to investigate one of his enemies. Or he could simply sell it to her for millions of dollars."

"Does she know you videotaped her?"

"Good question. I have no idea. As far as I know, only Eddie knows about the tape. But it doesn't really matter."

"So, your plan..."

Madison's answer was to dial 411 and hit send. "Yes, operator, I'd like the number for the White House. Yes, that White House."

"The White House, are you out of your mind?"

"No, just desperate. Oh, great," she said to the operator. "Yes, please connect me."

"There is no way Margaret Cross is going to want that tape in Eddie DeCarlo's hands. So we're going to use it to buy our freedom. Hello," Madison said into the phone. "I'm calling for the new Attorney General, Margaret Cross. Yes, I know her office isn't there, but she was with the President just a little while ago and, honestly, I don't know where else to call. You see, this is urgent; if you could just get a message to her, ask her to call 323-555-4593, tell her it's from her friend, Amber, in Chicago and it is urgent, a matter of life or death. Yes, I understand, no promises. Thank you." Madison hung up.

"So let me get this straight, we give Margaret Cross the tape and she gets the police to leave us alone."

"Sure. We haven't broken any laws. Everything we've done has been in self-defense."

"Except fleeing the scene of a crime, stealing a gun and the high speed chase stuff."

"All reasonable actions under the circumstances."

"Okay, so say she can get the cops to drop all charges, how is she going to get Eddie DeCarlo off our trail?"

"She won't be able to. If anything, Eddie's going to be even madder."

"Great. So we're still dead."

"No, no, she'll get us in the Witness Protection Program. That'll be part of our deal. We'll be relocated, get new identities, even have plastic surgery to change the way we look. We'll be perfectly safe."

"The Witness Protection Program?"

"It's our only way out."

"But what about our careers?"

"Over. We can never act again."

"And our family, our friends?"

"We may get to say goodbye, I'm not sure, but after that, no contact ever again."

Okay, my life wasn't great, but it was my life. I had issues with my mother, but she was my mother. I had a handful of close friends who meant the world to me. My career was in shambles but all it takes is one break, one job to turn a career around. And Madison was telling me I had to give it all up. "That's a terrible plan," I said. "I've spent my life building my life. Okay, that sounds weird, but it's true. I like my life, sort of. Well, not right now, so much, but in general. If you take away today, it's not a bad life. Anyway, I'm not ready to give it up and become someone else."

"You have a better idea?"

"No."

"Well, once you do, let me know. Because when Margaret Cross calls me back, I'm making a deal. And unless you've got a better plan, it's Witness Protection for me."

"And if I don't want to come with you?"

"Then you're on your own."

TWENTY

The cab driver glanced again at his two female passengers. Beautiful girls, no doubt about it, they had to be actresses or models or singers or something. He recognized them from somewhere, he was sure of it. His niece, Hillary, collected autographs, and Norman, the cab driver, decided to ask the girls for their autograph when he dropped them off.

The cab crawled along the Strip northbound, traffic jammed as usual. Southbound moved a little better, and as Ryan drove his Chevy past Grace and Madison's cab toward the Paradise Hotel, he had no idea he'd passed within fifty feet of his prey.

"Here comes another one," Sean said, as a Las Vegas patrol car, lights and sirens deployed, weaved in and out of the traffic, passing them.

"That makes two," Ryan said. "Plus that SWAT van we saw. All headed in the direction of the Paradise Hotel."

"You don't think..." Sean said.

Ryan's answer was to turn on the radio and find a news station, 970 am. "...Sources tell us that there are at least three victims from the shooting at the Paradise Hotel, but police haven't identified them yet."

"Are you thinking what I'm thinking?" Sean asked.

"Our girls, it's got to be."

The announcer continued. "We've got reporter Ron Morata on the way to the Paradise Hotel right now and we should be able to bring you more details momentarily."

"Shit," Sean said. "I hope we're not too late."

"We'll find out soon enough, kid. We're just two blocks away."

Much further away, two thousand four hundred and twenty-one miles to be exact, Alan Cross stood in the doorway of his Watergate Hotel suite bedroom and watched his wife sit on the edge of the bed and kick off her shoes. "God, I'm tired," she said.

They'd just returned from a celebratory dinner with some friends. Maggie had fun, enjoying the relative calm before the grueling round of lunches, meetings and dinners she had scheduled with the various members of Congress so she could charm and bedevil enough of them to ensure her confirmation.

Alan had a miserable time. Preoccupied with the Amber/Madison fiasco throughout dinner, he anxiously awaited the call that never came from Eddie telling him they had the tape. But a call did come, the message light was blinking when they returned to the suite and Cross had listened grimly to the message from the White House operator. Amber from Chicago needed to talk to Margaret Cross; it was urgent, a matter of life and death. Cross wrote down the number then crossed to the bedroom doorway.

"There's something you need to see before you go to bed," he said. Cross turned on the TV, flipped to CNN, they had a report on Afghanistan, switched to Fox News, and sure enough, they were showing clips of the high speed chase in Los Angeles, and the search for Grace Taylor and Madison Stone for the murder of Joey DeCarlo. As they flashed the girls' headshots on screen, Maggie stood up, shocked.

"Amber. I thought she was dead," Maggie said. "You told me she was killed in a car accident."

"I'm sorry, Maggie. I lied."

Maggie was smart and her analytical mind went to work. "But you didn't just lie so I'd stop seeing her, did you? There's something bigger at stake."

Cross nodded. "The last time you were together Amber videotaped you. Both of you, making love."

"Oh my God."

"She used the tape to blackmail Eddie DeCarlo into letting her go."

"Eddie DeCarlo, the gangster? You know him?"

"I told you, we went to college together."

"And you kept in touch?"

"Yes. We've done some favors for each other over the years."

"Like setting me up with Amber."

Eddie nodded. "You never asked me how I arranged for Amber. I assumed you didn't want to know."

Maggie wanted to get mad at Alan but couldn't. She'd brought this on herself. And it was true, she didn't ask Alan the details because the less she knew, the less she'd worry about exposure.

"Amber was Eddie's girlfriend," Alan said. "Eddie said she was completely trustworthy. Amber was never told your name or what you did. You met in a neutral city where no one knew either one of you. It seemed foolproof."

Maggie remembered Amber. She was certainly a skilled lover, and very nice, but something was wrong with her, deep down. She seemed sad, broken. Maggie was tempted to talk to Amber, ask what was wrong, but she didn't want to get emotionally involved again. This affair was about sex, nothing more. So Maggie uncharacteristically kept a wall between the two of them.

"What do you mean she used the tape so Eddie would let her go?" Maggie asked.

"Amber was a call girl before she met Eddie. He took her off the street, made her his mistress. She thought her hooking days were behind her."

"Eddie forced her to sleep with me?"

"Persuaded is probably a better word, but Eddie can be pretty intimidating."

"And once she realized she was nothing more than a whore to him, she wanted to leave him, but was afraid he'd hurt her. So she made the tape to guarantee her safety."

"Close enough. And for two years it's been fine. She disappeared, apparently never figured out who you were and everything was copacetic."

"Then I was appointed Attorney General."

"I had to assume she'd see the news coverage, see you on TV, realize who you were and how much that videotape of hers was suddenly worth. So I called Eddie, asked him to track her down and get the tape back. He sent his brother to L.A. but things seem to have gotten a little out of control."

"If that tape gets out, I'll be ruined."

"Well, there is some good news." Alan handed her the note. "Amber called, she wants to talk to you. I know she's in Las Vegas. Eddie should be there by now as well. If you can find out where she is, we'll tell Eddie and he'll get the tape back."

"And what about Amber?"

"What about Amber? Fuck Amber. This is all her fault. She's the one who made the goddamn tape. Eddie will take care of Amber, you just find out where she is and let me know."

Maggie thought about the woman she made love to in Chicago. Realized how heartbroken she must have been. Maggie picked up the phone. "Just for the record, this isn't all Amber's fault. It's all my fault. If I hadn't asked you to find me a woman, none of this would have happened."

TWENTY-ONE

The cab pulled to a stop. "Here you go ladies," the cab driver said with a slight Texas accent. "The Plush Room."

I opened the door and looked at the place. It had a Roman motif with marble columns, flashing lights over the door and a huge sign that said: THE PLUSH ROOM GENTEMEN'S CLUB.

"It's a strip joint?" I asked.

"I worked here for a couple of weeks on my way to L.A.," Madison said as she joined me on the curb.

"You ever had a normal job?"

Madison handed the driver twenty dollars. "Keep the change."

"Thank you, ma'am," he said. "Say, could I trouble you two ladies for an autograph, for my niece." He handed Madison a notebook and pen. "I know you're famous, I recognize you. But, sorry, I can't remember what from."

Madison and I exchanged a quick look, and then Madison signed the book, Scarlett Johansson. "We're actresses," she said handing me the notebook.

I almost never get asked for an autograph, though as a kid my mother used to make me practice in front of a mirror how to smile graciously as I signed my name. Well, this time I signed Reese Witherspoon, and handed the notebook back to the driver. "Give our love to your niece," I said and followed Madison inside.

It was a dark, sprawling strip club with two big stages where six girls pole danced to incredibly loud music. Another seventy-five, yes, I said seventy-five, or so girls in various stages of undress worked the crowd of several hundred men, serving drinks, flirting or giving them lap dances. A number of huge Samoan bouncers were scattered throughout the club, each wearing a headset, keeping an eye on the lascivious mob. Madison grabbed a waitress and asked, "Have you seen Caleb?"

"He should be in his office." She started to point but Madison stopped her.

"I know the way."

Every guy we walked by seemed to undress us with their eyes and I felt completely naked and gang-raped by the time we reached the office door. Madison knocked loudly, looked up at a video camera above the door. She blew a kiss. There was a loud buzz, the door clicked open and we entered.

The office was large, but crammed with furniture. A big desk was in the middle with a 27-inch iMac on it. A pool table was on one side of the room, two stuffed recliners sat in front of a large screen TV on the other. One of the walls was covered with pictures of Caleb and Hollywood celebrities. Another was filled with security monitors, at least twenty of them, showing what looked like every square inch of the club.

A handsome guy who looked a little like John Cusack stepped out from behind the desk and scooped Madison into his arms. "You are a sight for sore eyes," he said. He wore sneakers, designer jeans and a black silk T-shirt. As casual as that sounds, I bet he was in hundreds of dollars worth of clothes.

"Caleb," Madison said, "meet my friend, Grace."

Caleb shook my hand but his eyes did a quick inventory of my body. "Tell me you dance, Grace. Not all my customers love the silicone jungle out there; a select few crave small but perfect breasts."

"Thank you, I think. But when I dance, my clothes remain on and my perfect breasts covered up."

"She's a civilian," Madison said, and then turned to me. "Caleb's an old friend and just the kind of guy we can turn to in our moment of need."

"You in some kind of trouble?"

Madison waved at the wall of monitors. "All those TV screens and not a clue about what's happening in the world."

"We're wanted for murder and are being chased by the Mafia," I said.

"Very funny," Caleb said. "Look, I don't need the details, whatever you want, you've got."

"We can start with a place to crash," Madison said.

Caleb dug a keychain out of his pocket, slipped a key off, put it on the desk. "I've got a condo at Viewpoint Towers. Twenty-third floor, 2306, it's got an incredible view of the Strip and a guest bedroom that's all yours."

"See what I mean," Madison said to me.

"What else?" Caleb asked. "Money? A job?"

An intercom interrupted us. "Caleb, we got a problem on eighteen."

Caleb moved to the wall of monitors and checked the one marked 18. A drunken conventioneer in a funny hat was arguing with one of the dancers as two of his buddies were yelling at a security man. Caleb hit a button on the wall, leaned into a small microphone. "On my way." He turned to us. "I'll be right back." Caleb grabbed a headset off the desk and hurried out the door.

"Okay," I said. "He's like perfect. Did you guys ever hook up?"

"Sure. But Caleb's a sex machine. He's probably slept with every girl in that room."

"And?"

"And what?"

"Does practice make perfect?"

Madison smiled. "In his case, oh yeah."

I laughed, for the first time in a long time, I realized. "Look, about the Witness Protection thing, you're probably right, I'm just a little stressed and -- "

Madison's phone rang. "Oh, shit," she said. "This could be it." Madison dug her cell phone out of her purse and looked at the screen. "It's a 202 area code, that's D.C., it's got to be Margaret Cross." Madison answered the phone.

TWENTY-TWO

Margaret Cross sat on the bed. "Amber?"

"Actually, it's Madison, Mrs. Cross. My name is Madison."

"Please, call me Maggie. What was the name I used in Chicago?"

"Beth."

"Beth, yes. I thought you were dead, you know. I was told you were killed in a car crash."

"No such luck," Madison said.

"Yes, I guess we've got quite a mess on our hands."

"Do you know about the videotape?"

"I do now." Maggie shot Alan a look. "Just found out as a matter of fact."

Enough with the bullshit, Alan thought. Find out where she is.

"I never meant to hurt you. I just had to get away from somebody."

"Eddie DeCarlo."

"That's right. And I thought the tape was the only way. I would never have shown it to the press or used it to blackmail you. But now Eddie wants the tape back, he's sent men to kill me, twice. The police and FBI are after us and I've got nowhere else to turn."

"How can I help?"

"Everything that's happened, the men we've killed, it's all been in self-defense. Send someone to pick us up, bring us to you. I'll give you the tape and, in return, you get the police to drop all charges and you put us into the Witness Protection Program. You can do that, right, as Attorney General? Get us in the Witness Protection Program? It's the only way we'd ever be safe from Eddie."

"Yes, I think so." Maggie looked at her husband, could see the unasked question burning in his eyes. "Where are you, Madison? The Secret Service has an office in Las Vegas, I'll send some agents to pick you up and bring you here to Washington."

Oh, thank God, Madison thought. "A strip club, The Plush Room. We're in the manager's office."

"Sit tight," Maggie said. "Someone will be there shortly." Maggie hung up.

"Where is she?" Alan asked.

Maggie liked Madison. Just talking to her on the phone reminded her of the gentle soul she gotten to know in Chicago. "Why can't I do what I just said," she asked Alan. "Send the Secret Service to pick her up, bring her here. She'll give us the tape and problem solved."

"And what do you tell the President when he asks why you dispatched the Secret Service to pick up a couple of wanted fugitives in Las Vegas? What do you tell the press? How do you keep an army of reporters from digging into this story until the truth is served up on the front page of every newspaper? Eddie is our only chance, Maggie. Now, please, where are they?"

Maggie knew he was right. She'd never be able to explain rescuing Madison without revealing the truth. So her choice was clear: give up the chance to be the United States Attorney General and risk her whole sordid past coming out, or tell Eddie DeCarlo where Madison was. It took only moments for the rationalization gene to kick in, flooding her brain with all the good she'd be able to do the country as Attorney General; she'd get to help thousands, tens of thousands of people. The sacrifice of Madison and her friend seemed sad but inevitable. Besides, Madison was a hooker, she chose to live outside the law and that kind of dangerous behavior often leads to a tragic conclusion.

Maggie looked at her husband. "Ironic, isn't it, that one drunken night in Paris seventeen years ago has led us to this exact moment in time."

"Yes," Alan said. "I've often wondered what would have happened if we'd just gone to bed after dinner that night."

"Me, too," Maggie said and sighed. "She's in a strip club, in the manager's office, the Plush Room."

TWENTY-THREE

Eddie DeCarlo's chartered Cessna Citation taxied toward the Signature flight terminal, Las Vegas's biggest executive jet fixed-base operator. As they pulled to a stop and the pilot shut down the jet engines, Eddie looked out the window. A black Lincoln Town Car sat on the tarmac. Two guys in black leather jackets leaned against the car, smoking.

"That's Rico and Little Joe, two of Vincenzo's soldiers."

"I wonder if they know he's dead."

Frankie's cell phone rang. "Yeah," Frankie said. "Hold on." He handed the phone to Eddie.

"Hello," Eddie said.

"I found her," Alan said. "She's at The Plush Room, hiding in the manager's office."

"What, how?"

"Madison called Maggie for help."

Eddie barked a laugh. "I thought she was smarter than that. Great work, Alan, I'll call you when it's over." Eddie handed the phone back to Frankie. "We've got her."

There was a mob in the Paradise Hotel Security Center. People were crammed in front of the central monitor staring at the security camera version of Grace and Madison's escape. The image was frozen on the two women getting into the taxi.

Sean was shocked to see how Grace looked. She was heavily made up, her hair was back and the dress screamed sex. If there was ever a doubt whether she was a hooker, it was gone now.

"Their names are Grace Taylor and Madison Stone," Ryan said. "They're the women being sought in L.A. for Joey DeCarlo's homicide this afternoon." Ryan had flashed his FBI credentials to hotel security; they'd been led first to the crime scene then to the Security Center.

"I knew they looked familiar," Conklin said. "I saw them on the news earlier."

"I've seen them both naked," young Khalid said. "Very nice titties."

"Who is he?" Detective Leon Jackson asked Conklin. Detective Jackson was a six foot-five former Las Vegas High running back who looked and dodged tackles like OJ Simpson, but he blew out his knee senior year, went to community college then joined the Las Vegas Metropolitan Police Department. That's where he met the man who would become his best friend, Terry Conklin. They were Homicide detectives together, but when Conklin left to work at the Paradise Hotel, Jackson opted to stay a cop. "Guess I love my job more than money," he told Conklin. And that's why Conklin loved him.

Conklin looked at young Khalid standing next to Omar. He'd hoped to keep them out of the Security Center, but they insisted, and under the circumstances, Conklin didn't want to cause any more friction. "He's the son of one of our biggest whales. Two of the dead men worked for him." Conklin turned to young Khalid. "Sheik, maybe you'd like to go back to your suite and open the rest of your 'presents.'"

"A very good idea, Your Excellency," Omar said. "This is a police matter now."

"That redhead," young Khalid said pointing at the screen. "She stuck a gun in my face. That is attempted murder and I demand extradition to my country."

"We'll let the courts decided who gets who," Jackson said. "Our job's just to catch them."

"Got a name of the third victim?" Ryan asked.

Jackson picked up an evidence bag, inside was a blood stained driver's license. "Vincenzo Sica," Jackson said.

"He works for Eddie DeCarlo," Ryan said.

"The women told Omar and the kid that Sica killed the Sheik's men, then they shot Sica in self-defense."

"Just like L.A.," Sean said hopefully. He still clung to the hope that somehow this was all going to work out. "They killed Joey DeCarlo in self-defense."

"And just like L.A. they fled the scene of the crime," Ryan said. "Let's look at the exterior camera again, see if we get any clues about the cab."

The technician cued up the surveillance tape as Detective Jackson answered his cell phone. "Jackson... Right, got it, thanks." He snapped his phone closed. "A cab driver called 911. He dropped two girls off about a half hour ago; thought they were actresses, even got their autographs, then he stopped for dinner, saw their pictures on the news and realized why they looked familiar."

"Where'd he drop them?" Ryan asked.

"A strip club. The Plush Room."

TWENTY-FOUR

I stood in front of a mirror in Caleb's office staring at my face. "I'd like my old nose back."

"What?" Madison asked. She'd found a basket of snacks on Caleb's wet bar and was eating a bag of pretzels.

"I told you my mom changed my hair from brown to blonde. She also talked me into a nose job to take a bump out of my nose."

"How old were you?"

"Sixteen. So if Witness Protection's really going to give us new faces, maybe I could get my old one back. Brown hair. Bump in my nose. Even go back to my natural eye color."

"You don't have blue eyes?"

"Nope, blue contact lenses."

"God, it's almost like you're someone else playing the part of Grace Taylor."

"You're right," I said joining her at the wet bar, grabbing a handful of peanuts. "And I feel like I'm starring in a big budget action movie. Let me tell you, at this point, I'd much rather be playing a bit part like Sexy Babe. 'Course, I'll never get my mother off my back *unless* I'm the star."

"If you want to get your mother off your back, maybe you should work a little harder."

"What's that supposed to mean?"

"It doesn't matter anymore. Forget it."

"No, tell me."

"You'll just get mad."

"I won't. I promise."

"Okay. It's always amazed me how much you talk about acting and becoming a star, but how little passion you actually have for it. I mean, how many acting classes do you take? How many workshops?"

She was right, I was getting mad. "I've taken hundreds of classes, starting when I was only five years old!"

"Fine. But how many are you taking now?"

"That doesn't matter."

"Sure it does. The answer is none. How long do you work on a scene before an audition? Do you read the whole script or just your scenes?"

"They're crappy little roles in crappy little scenes, why would I waste my time reading the whole script?"

"Did you read the whole script when you first got to town?"

I thought back to that eager kid just five years ago. I was so happy, so honored to be auditioning I devoured every script they sent me. "Yes."

"Did you care how big the role was?"

"No."

"Did you go to classes? Workshops?"

Did I ever, three nights a week and every Saturday morning. "Yes."

"But not anymore?"

Not in almost a year. "No."

"So you bitch about crappy roles like Sexy Babe, yet you refuse to do the work necessary to become a serious actress."

"You know, you're right. I'm mad. Let's talk about something else."

"Too late now, sister, you've got me started. You hate what I do for a living; fine, so do I. But I'm trying to do something about it. I take acting classes. I'm enrolled in three workshops. I'm passionate about acting. What are you passionate about, Grace? I mean really passionate? Tell me."

I was rocked. Not just by Madison's attack, but by the terrifying realization she was right. I had soured on acting. The passion I felt when I first got to town was gone. In fact, I really wasn't passionate about anything. I was letting my life slip by one day at a time just going through the motions.

And then, right then, an epiphany of such gigantic proportions hit me that I actually felt dizzy. I *was* someone playing the part of Grace Taylor, in a script written by my mom and blindingly portrayed by me for twenty-eight years!

I had no idea who Grace Taylor really was. I'd been indoctrinated by my mother to become an actress. She put me on stage at nine weeks old, for Christ's sake! And I used to tell people that with pride. I should have said it with disgust.

Who was I, really? What would I have chosen to become given free will? I'd always liked animals, a vet maybe? Or a doctor. I played one once on *Person of Interest* and everyone told me I was very convincing. And that got me thinking. What roles had I played that I had a real affinity for? I was a lawyer on *Law and Order*, but was also the killer so that didn't bode well. I was an ad exec on *Two and Half Men*, and nailed it. Lord knows I watched enough commercials, maybe advertising was the answer. Or an architect, park ranger, fashion designer, teacher, psychologist? The list was endless. My head was spinning and I must've looked stricken because Madison asked, "Are you okay?"

"No, I'm anything but. You're right, Madison. I lost my passion for acting. I mean, my *mother's* passion for acting. I am playing the part of Grace Taylor, and, if you ask me, I'm not doing a very good job."

Suddenly, Madison looked stricken. She was staring at something behind me. "Oh shit."

I followed Madison's eyes to one of the security monitors. Four men were pushing their way through the club. A big guy was in front, fiftyish but handsome. A guy with thick glasses was just behind him, two guys in leather jackets trailed.

"That's Eddie," Madison said, pointing to the guy in front.

"Eddie? How'd he find us?"

The color drained from Madison's face as she realized. "Margaret Cross, she's the only one who knew. I'm so sorry, Grace, she betrayed us."

"We are so screwed."

Madison grabbed me by the hand, tugged me toward the door. "Come on."

"Wait," I said. "Caleb's key." I darted to the desk, grabbed Caleb's condo key. I was back by Madison's side as she opened the door. Eddie and his gang were standing there!

We all stared at each other for a shocked instant, then Madison slammed the door shut and threw the deadbolt. A millisecond later there was a stupendous crash and the door shook.

"They're trying to break it down," Madison said. Another crash and the wood frame splintered. Madison reached into her purse, pulled out Officer Harris's gun. "Stand back."

I jumped back and she fired into the middle of the door. Bang! Bang! Bang! "Don't just stand there," Madison said. "You've got a gun, use it."

I pulled Joey's gun out of my purse and looked at it. It was a revolver, big and heavy, the name Raging Bull was stamped into the side of the barrel. Six gigantic bullets bulged ready and waiting in the chamber.

Madison fired again. Bang! Bang! Bang!

I aimed at the center of the door and fired. Boom! The gun lurched in my hand and I almost dropped it.

"Don't stop," Madison called. "Keep shooting."

I did. Boom! And wow, what a feeling. I suddenly understood why people loved guns. That kick, that wonderful kick is pure power. You can feel it in every cell of your body. And you can smell it in the air and see the bullets demolish whatever they hit. It has a thrill for every sense.

I fired one more shot, and then searched the monitors for the security camera above the door, found it. I could see Eddie and his men hidden safely behind cover. Then Eddie yelled something I couldn't hear. The four men pulled guns and aimed at the door. I dove to the ground, screaming "Get down!"

Bullets ripped through the door, whizzing over our heads, pulverizing bottles on the wet bar, and drilling pictures of Caleb and celebrities.

Madison fired again. Bang! Bang! Bang!

I fired, Boom! Boom!

As loud as the gunshots were, the music was probably louder, so I was afraid no one knew how much trouble we were in. I spotted Caleb on monitor 18 still calming down the conventioneers. I scurried across the floor. Hit the button activating the microphone. "Help, Caleb, help!" Eddie and his men let loose another fusillade, which boomed in the office, and since the mike was still open, Caleb could hear. His head spun in our direction as he keyed his headset. "On my way!" he called. Then I saw him yell at his security men and they shoved their way through the crowd.

Wham! The office door shook. I glanced at the door monitor and saw the guy with the thick glasses rear back and plant a ferocious kick. Wham! The doorjamb fractured. He kicked again and the door flew open.

Eddie and his men charged through the door. Madison aimed and fired. Click! Click! Click! The gun was empty.

I tried to aim Joey's gun but Thick Glasses Guy ripped it out of my hands and tossed it out the door. It hit the wall and fell to the ground.

Eddie grabbed Madison by the throat, tore the gun out of her hand, hurled it into one of the monitors. It exploded as Eddie stuck his face inches from Madison's face and said, "Where's my tape?"

Before she could answer, Caleb and his Samoan bodyguards poured into the room. Chaos! A few wild shots were let loose but soon it was desperate hand-to-hand combat. Caleb and the Samoans used a combination of brute force and some kung fu moves while Eddie grabbed a pool cue, the guy with thick glasses pulled a knife, and guys in leather jackets settled for fisticuffs.

Madison and I were forgotten in the melee. We exchanged furtive glances then made a break for the door. I scurried into the hallway. Joey's gun lay on the floor. The chamber had popped open, but it looked otherwise unscathed. I scooped it up, slammed the chamber closed and dropped it into my purse.

I glanced back to see Madison dodge and weave her way through flying asses and elbows toward the door.

Behind her I saw Eddie jam the pool cue in Caleb's stomach, buckling him over. Then Eddie grabbed the eight ball, and smashed it into the side of Caleb's head. The club owner went down.

The Samoans weren't doing much better. Thick Glasses Guy had stabbed one who now knelt on the floor, hands on his stomach trying to stop the bleeding. One of the leather jacket guys pistol-whipped another bodyguard who toppled to the floor, unconscious.

Meanwhile, Eddie saw Madison trying to escape and he lunged after her. Madison was inches from the door when Eddie managed to grab her wrist. He yanked, pulling her back into the room and tossed her onto the desk. Madison crashed into the computer knocking it over as she tumbled to the floor.

I looked up from Madison in time to see Thick Glasses Guy duck a karate combination and plunge his knife into the side of another Samoan. The leather jacket guys teamed up on the last bodyguard, pummeling him until he dropped.

Madison was now surrounded in the office. I looked at her and saw the horrified look on her face. Madison realized she was trapped. Then I saw an idea ripple across her face. She reached into her purse and pulled out the videotape. "Grace," she called. "Catch." She threw the tape.

It was another one of those slow motion moments as the tape sailed across the office. All eyes were on the tape, even a groggy Caleb's. First Eddie, then Thick Glasses Guy and finally the leather jacket guys all reached for and missed the tape. I was a lousy catch in school, notorious for dropping baseballs, basketballs and Frisbees. But I knew this was one catch I had to make. I held out both hands and watched the tape all the way into my fingertips. I caught it.

And of course, that was the bad news. Because no sooner did I pull the tape to my chest then Eddie called out, "Get her!"

I threw a final regretful look at Madison and took off running.

TWENTY-FIVE

Eddie was on an emotional rollercoaster. He was thrilled by Alan's tip that Madison was at The Plush Room. And, as much as he hated to admit it, he was excited by the thought of seeing her again. On the drive from the airport to the strip club, all sorts of fantasies played out in his head. In one, she gave him the tape the moment she saw him, then dropped to her knees, terrified, apologized for killing Joey and begged him to spare her life. He shot her.

In another, she gave him the tape the moment she saw him, dropped to her knees, begged him to spare her life and he magnanimously spared her.

In a third, she rushed into his arms the moment she saw him telling him she was a fool for leaving, she loved him more than ever, please take her back and kissed him passionately. That was his favorite.

But in his wildest imagination, Eddie could never have imagined the cluster fuck he'd just witnessed: a gunfight through a locked door, a rumble with local heavies and an unrepentant bitch who threw the tape out the door to her blonde friend.

Well, that's why they call them fantasies. Eddie screamed, "Get her!" Frankie and the two local torpedoes sprinted after the blonde leaving Eddie alone with the beat-up and bleeding strip club bouncers and Madison. Eddie grabbed Madison by the hair and pulled her to her feet. "Long time no see."

"Blow me," Madison said.

Frankie led Rico and Little Joe into the club and after the blonde. They barreled through the crowd, pushing and shoving pissed-off customers out of their way. The music was deafening, huge subwoofers turned the bass notes into concussive blasts. There was no way anyone could have heard all the gunplay.

Frankie saw the blonde jump onto a stage, race past a pole dancer and vault over the first row of tables into the crowd. The audience loved it, giving her whistles of appreciation and applause.

Frankie and his boys leapt onto the stage after her. The blonde turned back to them, pointed and screamed, "Perverts, stop them!"

As Frankie, Rico and Little Joe started to leap off the stage, a wall of heroic patrons stood up, blocking the way. The three hoods pulled their guns. Frankie fired three shots into the ceiling. Dancers screamed, the not-as-heroic-as-they-thought customers scattered and Frankie, Rico and Little Joe resumed the chase.

However, the sight of three men with guns, screaming dancers and stampeding customers turned the club into pandemonium. Frankie and the boys fought through the melee, catching just fleeting images of the blonde as she dodged in and out of the panicked patrons surging for the exits.

Frankie saw the blonde squeeze out the door and he punched and kicked his way after her. He popped through the door to see the blonde run into the street. He ran after her.

The blonde looked unsure for a moment, and then stuck out her thumb. Three cars screeched to a stop. She got in a yellow Corvette, and they roared off just as Frankie got there.

"Shit," Frankie said, out of breath. Then the sound of sirens filled the air and four police cars came screaming toward the club. "Double shit," Frankie muttered as Rico and Little Joe joined him. The girl was gone and the cops had arrived. "Get the car and meet us behind the club," Frankie said. "I'll get Eddie."

Eddie, a gun hanging from his right hand, watched the bedlam on the security monitors. Unfuckingbelievable. Now they had a riot on their hands. His eyes moved from monitor to monitor, watching Frankie and the boys chase the blonde through the club. Occasionally a bodyguard would stir and Eddie would kick him in the head.

Madison lay on the floor, helpless. Eddie had tied her hands behind her back. Caleb was curled in a corner feigning unconsciousness. He would have liked to have helped Madison, but didn't think he could get to Eddie and his gun before getting shot, and he'd been heroic enough for one day.

"I'm sorry about Joey," Madison said.

"Shut up."

On one of the monitors Eddie saw the blonde slip out the front door. "She's getting away you, dickwads," Eddie screamed.

Go, Grace, go, thought Madison. It was all about survival now, Madison knew. Somehow she had to get Eddie to spare her life.

"You didn't have to send Joey, you know. If you'd just called and asked for the tape, I would have given it to you."

"Oh really," he said, not believing a word. "Then why didn't you just give the tape to Joey?"

"Because he didn't just want the tape, he tried to rape me, Eddie. That's why I fought back." A lie, sure, but knowing Joey's ladies' man rep and Eddie's jealousy, it might work.

Eddie looked at her, weighing her words. "Bullshit."

"It's true, Eddie. You remember the way Joey used to look at me when you and I were dating. He practically drooled." True enough, Madison thought. Of course, a lot of Eddie's guys looked at her that way. Eddie was famous for giving away ex-girlfriends to one of his crew, so the whole fucking gang used to stare at her, wishing and hoping.

"Just shut the fuck up."

On the monitors Eddie saw Frankie hurrying back toward the office without the blonde. What the hell, Eddie thought, a moment later Frankie entered. "Don't tell me she got away," Eddie said.

"Yeah, sorry."

"Woo hoo!" screamed Madison.

"But we got bigger problems. Cops, lots of them. I've got the car coming out back."

Eddie grabbed Madison, pulled her to her feet. "Don't celebrate just yet, baby," Eddie said. "The fun's just beginning." They slipped out the back door.

Sean had never seen anything like it. Scores of topless and scantily clad women stood outside the huge strip club, still flirting with the displaced customers. Two things amazed him: the size of the girls' breasts and well, the size of the girls' breasts.

Sean and Ryan rode up to The Plush Room with Detective Jackson. The trip from the Paradise Hotel to the Plush Room had been harrowing, Jackson squirting in and out of the gridlocked Strip traffic, his roof light and siren mostly ignored by the legion of taxi cabs and tourists.

When Jackson got to Industrial Boulevard, the traffic broke. He floored it, skidding around the corner, just missing a yellow Corvette.

Yeah, that yellow Corvette. Grace had closed her eyes, convinced they were about to crash. Ryan and Sean braced themselves for impact, never once glancing into the Corvette. So as Jackson's unmarked car slid by the yellow Corvette, missing it by just a few atoms, Ryan and Sean had no idea they'd come this close to finding Grace.

But as they piled out of Jackson's car, Sean was sure of one thing. "We're too late," he said.

"Again," Ryan said.

"Some guys were chasing a blonde through the club," one of the strippers told Jackson. The stripper was topless, wearing a g-string as thin as floss.

"What about a redhead?" Ryan asked. "She was with a redhead."

"Sorry, honey. Just saw the blonde."

Ryan ran into the club, Sean hot on his heels. They saw a tall guy in jeans and a black T-shirt, Caleb, talking to a couple of uniforms. He held an ice pack to the side of his head.

"We need paramedics," Caleb said. "I've got two men with stab wounds in the office."

One of the cops keyed his radio as Ryan asked, "What happened?"

"Let me tell you," Caleb said. "No good deed goes unpunished."

"Madison Stone and Grace Taylor," Ryan pressed. "Were they here?"

"Yeah. Madison's a friend. She worked here briefly a couple of years ago. She said they needed help. I didn't ask for details; guess I should have."

"So what happened?"

"These thugs came after them. They broke into my office, shot the shit out of the place. She called one of the guys Eddie."

"Eddie DeCarlo," Sean said.

"What?! Oh, shit," Caleb said. "Now I'm hot water with the fucking Mafia."

"Tell us what happened."

"Eddie and his thugs went after Madison and her friend, so my boys and I came to the rescue. Or tried to, they kicked our ass."

"Did they mention a tape?" Ryan asked.

"No, but Madison did throw something to her friend. And now that I think about it, it looked like a videotape. The blonde grabbed the tape and took off running. Eddie nabbed Madison and sent his guys after the blonde. They must've lost her in the club because Eddie's guy came back empty-handed. Then they took off out the back door."

"You have any idea where the blonde may be headed?" Sean asked.

Caleb hesitated for an instant before he lied and said, "No."

TWENTY-SIX

"How about a lap dance?"

"Excuse me?" I asked, distracted by the battle in Caleb's office, Madison's capture, the chase through the strip club, and the tire-screeching near miss with that police car. My head was spinning, I felt-light headed from anxiety and was scared out of my mind.

"A lap dance," the guy driving the Corvette said. He'd introduced himself as Larry. Larry looked like a movie character actor, you know the guys that are too short, too tall, too fat, too this or too that. Larry was short and fat and reminded me of a not-so-funny Danny Devito. "You're a stripper, right. I picked you up in front of the Plush Room. So when we get to Viewpoint Towers, could you give me a quick lap dance as a show of gratitude?"

Okay, another creep. But he did save me from the mobster with the thick glasses. An image of Madison giving the guy in the Bentley a blowjob flashed through my mind and I realized things could be worse.

"Or a quick hand job," he added.

Maybe not that much worse. "Look," I said. "I really appreciate you picking me up, but I'm not a stripper. I mean, look at me, my chest, who'd pay to see these puny things?"

His eyes went to my breasts, "They are kind of small."

"Exactly."

"So you're not a stripper?"

"No."

"Hooker?"

"No."

"Then what are you? I mean, you're dressed like a stripper or a hooker."

Oh, yeah, that. Madison remade me in that sexy Chanel dress, blood red nail polish and "fuck me" make-up.

"I'm an actress."

He studied my face. "Should I recognize you?"

"Probably not. The career hasn't exactly gone as planned."

"So you having a fight with your boyfriend or something? Looks like you were running away from someone."

"Boyfriend trouble is putting it mildly." I didn't want to get into any more detail than that so figured I'd redirect the conversation. "How about you, what do you do?"

"I'm a psychiatrist."

"A shrink? No kidding." A shrink, I thought. Interesting. With all the self-doubt I'd had lately, maybe a little professional advice would help. "Say, is there a name for a mid-life crisis when you're still in your twenties?"

"Are you having a crisis?"

"I think so."

"Well, since you won't bare your breasts, you might as well bare your soul." He laughed.

"Never mind, I'd feel silly."

"Have you ever been in therapy?"

"No. I never had a problem. Or I never thought I had a problem. But I'm beginning to realize I've been kidding myself. I've realized I have no idea who I really am, who I'm supposed to be and I don't know what to do about it."

"Authenticity," he said. "That's the key to self-realization. Live an authentic life."

"How do I do that?"

"By being true to yourself. But to do that, you have to understand your essence. Who the real 'you' is."

"And how do I do that?"

"Start stripping away everything about your life that's phony. That's a lie. That makes you unhappy. What's left is the authentic you."

What a bunch of gobbbedly gook, I thought. Then something occurred to me. "Wait a minute," I said. "I'm getting advice about being authentic from a guy who asked me for a lap dance and a hand job."

"That's right. I know exactly who am I. A nerdy guy who likes to sleep with beautiful women. The only way that's going to happen is if I pay them. So I moved to Las Vegas, a town crawling with beautiful hookers, and opened my practice. I'm a horny guy. I like to party. That's who I am. I'm living an authentic life." Viewpoint Towers loomed in front of us. He pulled into the portico. "There is no perfect blueprint for people," he said. "Everyone is different. The trick is to figure out who the hell you are and be unashamedly you." He handed me his card. "Call me if you'd like to talk."

"Thanks," I said getting out of the Corvette.

"Last chance for a handjob," he said, smiling.

"Goodbye, Larry," I said and he drove off.

I was working on autopilot now. I had no real plan. Just get to Caleb's condo and regroup. I walked through the automatic doors into a marble lobby and found myself staring at a security guard. He sat at a desk, three security cameras displayed behind him. No dusty old retired security guards at Viewpoint Towers, this guy looked like a marine. Hispanic, I think, and buff. Buzz cut, brown eyes, he had a real Benjamin Bratt thing going. "Can I help you?" he asked.

"Yes," I said pulling out Caleb's key, showing it to him. "Caleb gave me his key, said I should meet him here."

The guard checked me out and smiled. "Must be nice owning a strip club. Go on up."

"Thanks," I said and headed for the elevators. Having a security guard at the door reassured me. I desperately needed a safe place to hide until I figured out what to do next. Until I figured out how I could save poor Madison.

TWENTY-SEVEN

"I remember the first time I saw you. The first moment our eyes met. You remember that?"

Madison was bound to a chair in the middle of the Family's slot machine business on the outskirts of Las Vegas. Carcasses of disassembled slots sprouted like dead weeds in the dimly lit warehouse. Eddie circled Madison as he spoke, a Glock 9mm dangling from his right hand. Frankie, Rico and Little Joe stood back in the shadows.

"I remember," Madison said. She'd even told Grace about it just a few hours ago. Looking into his eyes that night was like looking into the eyes of an old friend. Someone who knew all your secrets. But now, looking into those same eyes, she saw only hatred.

"I had one thought that night," Eddie said. "To fuck your brains out. You just oozed sex. That's what made you such a good hooker. Sex came off you like perfume. You were so good at it. The best I ever had. I was consumed by you. Possessed. All I could think about was fucking you."

"We were in love, Eddie. That's what love feels like."

"Horseshit. They say there are some chemicals that affect your brain when you're in love. That's what you were for me, a chemical imbalance. Nothing more."

Madison realized Eddie was talking himself into hurting her. Distancing himself from their past. She had to fight back. "Well, just so you know, *I* loved you. You were the first man I ever truly loved, and judging by my circumstances right now," she added wryly, "probably the last."

Eddie looked at Madison. God, she was beautiful. Even more beautiful now, if that was possible. He had loved her. Too much, in fact, and that was the problem. Eddie was married, to Tito's daughter for Christ's sake. And he had two children, his precious twins, Christina and Lucy. He knew how important a stable home life was to kids. How divorce can fuck with a kid's head. But the more time he spent with Madison, the more time he wanted to spend with her. He brought her flowers, candy, jewelry. Two nights a week became five nights a week, and he actually considered divorce.

Then Alan Cross called. There were a lot of women Eddie could have sent to Chicago to sleep with Maggie. Women he could trust. But by sending Madison, he realized he could turn her from lover back to whore. And that was enough to break the spell. You fuck a whore, you live with a wife.

Of course, he hadn't counted on Madison's reaction. How heartbroken she would be. The image of her, pleading, "Eddie, a man doesn't share the woman he loves with his friends," still haunted him. He came so close that night to taking her in his arm, telling her never mind, he'd find someone else, she belonged to him for now and forever. But he steeled himself, knowing he had to put distance between them for the good of his wife and daughters, for the good of the Family. "He does when she's a hooker," he told her. Cold, brutal words meant to hurt her, meant to split them apart.

But she had done him one better. She made that tape, blackmailed him. At first, when she showed him the tape, he was furious. He almost killed her, in fact, sticking that kitchen knife under her chin. Unafraid, she stated her demands, "I'm leaving you and leaving New York. If anything happens to me, that tape goes to the press." She was so gutsy, so brave, he was almost proud of her. He'd fallen in love with Madison because she was sexy, sure, but she was also smart, and a survivor. And she'd used her brains and perseverance to figure out how to get away from him. So he let her go. She got the new life she wanted and he was free from a temptation he couldn't handle.

But now, Joey was dead, Vincenzo was dead and that fucking tape was still on the loose. The woman he loved wasn't the woman tied to the chair in front of him. She died the day she walked out on him. And it wasn't love anyway. Just a chemical imbalance. So as Eddie looked at Madison, beautiful or not, he was ready to do whatever it took to find that tape.

"Where's your friend?"

"I don't know."

Eddie raised the gun and fired. A chunk of concrete exploded inches from Madison's left ear.

"You will tell me," Eddie said. "It's just a matter of how much pain you're willing to take before the inevitable."

After her capture, the one promise Madison had made to herself was to never tell Eddie where Grace was. Grace was a true innocent in this whole mess; all she'd done was try to help her friend. Telling Eddie where Grace was would be signing her death warrant. She looked Eddie in the eye and said, "I. Don't. Know."

Eddie aimed the Glock at Madison's face, then shifted his aim to her right shoulder and fired. Blood exploded as the bullet tore into Madison's shoulder.

It felt like a punch at first, and then the pain came. White hot, searing agony. Madison fought back a scream as Eddie shoved his face in front of her. "Go ahead," he said. "Scream, because the pain is just beginning. Where is she?"

"Fuck you."

Eddie took a switchblade out of his pocket, touched the button. The razor sharp blade flipped into place. He placed the point of the knife over Madison's wounded shoulder. "Tell me."

Madison just looked at him, defiantly.

Eddie dug the blade into her shoulder. Madison screamed. Frankie the Fish cringed and looked away but Rico and Little Joe were enjoying the show.

Eddie pulled the blade out, looked at Madison. Tears streaked her face. Some of the defiance was gone. "Where?"

"Just kill me," she begged.

"Too easy," Eddie said, and jammed the blade back into her shoulder. Madison screamed, the pain excruciating, her will weakening.

Eddie pulled the knife out touched the point of the blade to Madison's left eye. Madison stared at the blood soaked knife then shifted focus to the man she once loved.

"The eyeball goes next," he said. "Now, where is she?"

TWENTY-EIGHT

Caleb's condo was fabulous. I gave myself a tour, starting with the gourmet kitchen that opened to the living room filled with designer furniture, a wet bar, huge patio and a drop-dead view of the strip. His den was an entertainment center with a wide screen projector TV and a massive collection of DVDs and videotapes, almost all of them porn. No surprise since he owned a strip club. The master bedroom featured a round bed and had a mirror on the ceiling. I stared at it trying to understand the appeal, then gave up and headed for the master bath. It was all white marble and chrome, with a Jacuzzi tub big enough for four. No mirror on the ceiling in there.

I went back to the living room, opened the balcony doors and stepped outside. It was a warm night, a full moon was rising and a gentle breeze tugged at my hair.

I still had an adrenaline buzz, not just from the fight and chase, but also from utter confusion. I had no idea what to do. I had to talk to someone. But who could I trust to help me? I pulled out my cell phone, turned it on while I tried to figure out who to call first. It buzzed letting me know I had three messages. I checked the first one.

"Babe, it's Jason, I think you took my toothbrush by mistake. And hey, did you really kill that guy?" BEEP.

"Grace, it's Mom. I'm sure you had a good reason to stab that man, but honestly, we have worked way too long and way too hard on your career for you to throw it all away like this. Of course, if it was self-defense and you don't end up in jail, this could be the break we've been waiting for. Call me." BEEP.

"Grace, this is Special Agent Ryan Griffin. I can help you. Please call me."

Okay, it didn't take a tactical genius to figure out who I should call. The FBI guy. But I really wanted to call my mother and tell her how she'd ruined my life by not giving me a chance to *choose* my life.

I wanted to live an authentic life, just like Larry. But unlike Larry, I had no idea what that was. And unless I survived the next few hours, I might never know. So as badly as I wanted to bitch out my mother, I went back into the living room, grabbed a pencil and piece of paper, replayed the messages and wrote down Ryan Griffin's number.

Suddenly the front door opened, startling me. I pulled Joey's gun out of my purse, spun to the door.

"Don't shoot," Caleb said, throwing his hands up. "It's only me."

"Oh, thank God," I said, dropping the gun back into my purse and putting the purse down on the couch. "Madison, where is she?"

"I don't know. They tied her up and took her out of my office."

"We've got to do something. We've got to save her!"

"I know, I know," Caleb said moving to the bar. He poured himself a healthy shot of Jack Daniels. "But we've got to be careful." He tossed back the drink, poured another. "You want something?"

Vodka martini, I thought. Or just hand me the bottle. But I remembered Madison's look when I had that drink on the plane, and the champagne in the limo. I was drinking a bit too much, lately, so although I would have loved to shut down a few synapses, I knew I couldn't take the chance. "No, thanks," I said. "A Coke, maybe if you've got one."

Caleb pulled a can of Coke out of the wet bar's fridge and poured. "Like I said, we've got to be very careful. Eddie DeCarlo has a lot of friends in this town. And though the mob's out of the casinos, they still control a lot of businesses; laundries, liquor distributors, people I deal with every day." As the ramifications of what Caleb said hit him, he paled, started pacing the floor. "This is bad," he said. "Real bad. Why the fuck didn't you tell me you were running from Eddie DeCarlo?"

"We did. I said we were wanted for murder and being chased by the Mafia. You thought we were kidding?"

"Well you should have made yourselves clear. Jesus Christ, I punched Eddie DeCarlo."

"Well, if it's any consolation, I don't think you hurt him, and he did knock you out with a cue stick; that's a good thing, right?"

"I hope so." I noticed him staring at my purse.

"Don't worry, I won't shoot you, I promise."

"What?" he asked, looking back at me. "Good. It's just that guns make me nervous."

"Tell me about it. So, how do we get Madison back?"

"I've got a few ideas, but to be honest, I'm famished. You had anything to eat?"

"Nothing all day except two crackers of caviar and a couple of cookies."

"I've got sandwich makings in the kitchen. Could you make us a couple of sandwiches while I try to figure this out?"

"Yeah, sure." I headed into the kitchen, not hungry but knowing I should eat. He had a bachelor's refrigerator, just the basics. Ball Park hot dogs, pack of Kraft American cheese, milk, four cans of Bud light, Dijon mustard, Best Foods mayonnaise, re-sealable package of sliced turkey, wilted lettuce, but I didn't see any bread. And there was no bread on the counter, either. I walked back into the living room. "Caleb, I can't find the… " I trailed off as I found him digging through my purse. "What're you doing?"

He pulled out Madison's videotape. "Guaranteeing my safety," he said.

"Give me that." I stepped toward him, he stepped back.

"Eddie wants this tape awfully bad," he said. "I figure if I give it back to him, all will be forgiven."

"It's not yours to give," I said, taking another step forward. Caleb backed onto balcony.

"What's on the tape?" he asked. "What's worth all the dead bodies?"

"None of your business," I said. "Now give it to me."

"No."

"Madison sacrificed herself so I could have that tape."

"Yeah, well, if it wasn't for Madison, I wouldn't be in trouble with the mob. The tape's mine."

"No, it's not," I said and jumped, grabbing the tape with both hands and trying to rip it out of his hands. Caleb tried to knee me in the stomach, but I twisted away so it was only a glancing blow. I remembered a move from Charlie Wang's class, stomped on his instep then kicked him in the balls.

He groaned and crumpled to his knees. I ripped the tape free and turned to run. I was almost through the balcony door when Caleb reached out and tripped me. As I hit the ground, the tape was jarred out of my hands and skittered across the balcony, almost sliding off the edge.

Caleb was back on his feet, running for the tape. I kicked out my foot, tripping him. He lost his balance, stumbled forward, hit the railing and, as I watched horrified, he flipped over the rail and tumbled off the twenty-third story balcony.

TWENTY-NINE

Frankie the Fish rode shotgun as Rico steered the Lincoln Town Car into Viewpoint Towers driveway. Frankie had to admire Madison's guts. She was stubborn. He'd been afraid she was going to let Eddie pluck out her eye before she finally burst into tears and told them where Grace was hiding.

Eddie had promised Madison he wouldn't kill Grace. Gave his word of honor. The same word of honor Eddie gave Salvatore Grisanti before he put two into the back of his skull. Why anyone would believe the word of honor from a man who makes his living breaking the law was beyond Frankie. But, it works every time.

Rico slowed as he approached the front door. Then, CRASH!

The roof of the car collapsed inward and the windows exploded as Rico and Frankie instinctively ducked. Rico jerked the car to a stop. Frankie and Rico leapt out of the car and stared at the dead body imbedded in the roof of the Town Car.

Frankie looked up, saw a blonde staring down. Grace. "There she is," Frankie said.

Rico looked up just as Grace disappeared back into the condo.

The security guard came running out to the car. "Jesus Christ," he said. "What happened?"

"He fell," Frankie said, then cold-cocked the security guard, knocking him out.

Frankie and Rico ran into the lobby and up to the bank of three elevators. Rico pointed to the floor display above the middle elevator. "That one's stopped on twenty-three."

"That's her floor," Frankie said.

The elevator started down, twenty-one, twenty, nineteen. Frankie and Rico pulled their guns and took up positions on each side of the elevator.

Twelve, eleven, ten.

This is too easy, Frankie thought. Talk about shooting ducks in a barrel.

Three, two, one. Ding. Frankie's finger tightened on the trigger as the door slid open. Then Frankie reacted, confused. The elevator was empty.

"What the fuck?" Rico said.

Then Frankie noticed something on the floor of the elevator. He picked it up. A videotape.

There was a loud bang behind them. Frankie and Rico spun to see Grace pop out of the stairway door and sprint across the lobby.

Frankie and Rico fired. They missed Grace, the bullets shattering the lobby windows. They raced after her, sprinting through the broken glass, leaping through the empty window frames just as Grace dove into the crumpled Town Car.

Grace dropped the car into gear, floored it. The tires squealed and the car spurted forward, and Caleb's dead body rolled off the roof and tumbled onto the driveway.

Frankie and Rico fired as she sped away. A couple of shots plunked into the back of the car, but Grace slid safely into traffic and disappeared.

"Fuck," Rico said.

"Forget it," Frankie said. "At least we got the tape."

The Plush Room was closed, the customers gone. The last of the strippers had finished changing and were walking out as Sean hustled outside, joining Ryan and Detective Jackson.

"Eddie and his three hoods got into a black Lincoln Town Car with a bound and gagged Madison Stone," Sean said. "The security camera didn't pick up the license plate."

"There are hundreds of black Town Cars in Vegas," Jackson said. "Every limo company in town drives them."

"Where they're going is more important than what they're driving," Ryan said, dialing Stubblefield and Cortez on his cell phone. "Jerome, its Ryan, I need a list of every one of Eddie DeCarlo's Las Vegas companies." Ryan's phone beeped. "Hold on a second, I've got another call." Ryan hit a button, said, "Ryan Griffin."

"I'm scared."

"Grace, is that you?"

"Grace?" Sean asked. "Is she okay?"

"I'm scared and I don't know who to trust," Grace said.

"Me. You can trust me."

"Me, too," Sean said.

A uniformed cop ran up to Detective Jackson. "We've got shots fired at Viewpoint Towers."

"Please tell me you're not at Viewpoint Towers," Ryan said to Grace.

"Not anymore."

"Tell me you haven't killed anyone else."

"Just one guy, but it was an accident, really. He fell off the balcony, after I tripped him, but it was self defense."

"Look, we need to meet."

"I don't know."

"Grace, I'm your only chance. Eddie's got Madison, maybe together we can get her back."

"You really think we can save her?"

"Yes. Now, where are you?"

"I'm driving, on Paradise Road. I see a casino up ahead. The Hard Rock."

Ryan turned to Jackson. "You know the Hard Rock?"

"Sure."

"Name one of the lobby bars."

"The Viva Las Vegas Lounge."

"The Viva Las Vegas Lounge," Ryan said to Grace. "I'll be there in twenty minutes."

There was a reluctant beat, and then Grace said, "Okay."

Ryan switched back to Stubblefield. "Anything?" Ryan asked.

"Yeah, we've got four businesses. Got a pen?"

Ryan took out a pen and his notepad. "Shoot."

Stubblefield rattled off the name of four businesses, "Desert Springs Liquor Distribution at 35905 West Carey Avenue, Clean Right Laundry Service at 18745 East Bonanza, Jackpot Manufacturing, this one's in Henderson, 3598 West Warm Springs Road, and a construction company, Desert Way Contractors, 23987 Sunrise Avenue."

Ryan handed the list to Detective Jackson.

"I'll send cars to all four."

Then Ryan had an idea. "Hey, Jerome, can Christy pull up employment records?"

Stubblefield and Christy were on speakerphone at the Newark stakeout location. "Sure can, handsome," Christy said. "What do you need?"

"Which company did Vincenzo Sica work for?"

Christy worked her keyboard. "Jackpot Manufacturing. It's a slot machine assembly plant."

Ryan pointed to Jackpot Manufacturing on the list in Jackson's hands. "This is where Sica worked."

"Got a hunch, bet a bunch," Jackson said. "I'll take that one myself."

"Good," Ryan said, and then turned to Sean. "Let's go meet your girlfriend."

Eddie bandaged Madison's shoulder himself. The shot had gone through the meat of her shoulder, missing the bone. Eddie had tended to gunshot wounds before. The sight of blood, pulverized flesh, even body organs had no effect on him; if anything, Eddie was fascinated by the human body.

The first gunshot wound Eddie cleaned up was when he was a freshman in college. It was two thirty in the morning and a loud knock on the door woke him up. It was Joey, shot in the side. He'd tried to carjack a Porsche in front of Elaine's restaurant, and the son of a bitch driving it pulled out a .32 and shot him. Joey knew he couldn't go to a hospital – they notify the police with any gunshot wound, so Joey ran around the corner, carjacked a Volkswagen Rabbit from a defenseless old lady, and drove to Eddie's apartment, one hand on the wheel, the other covering the bleeding hole in his side.

As Eddie cleaned out the wound, he gave Joey a load of shit about never carjacking in the first place –- it was too easy to get caught, and never working alone. Two soldiers minimum, there was strength in numbers.

"But it was a spur of the moment thing," Joey said. "I was just having a little fun."

And that asinine statement summarized Joey's journey through life. No matter how hard he focused on an assigned task, if a random idea pierced his consciousness, he was off in another direction.

The common term for someone like Joey was a fuckup. But Joey was loyal, loving, respectful and guileless. He was just a big goofy kid and everybody loved him.

Yes, death was a part of Eddie's life. Grieving was not. Dying is everyone's final destination, so pay your respects and move on. But from the moment Eddie heard Joey had been killed, he'd felt a hole in his heart. He'd lost his father, his mother, beloved aunts, uncles and friends but none of their deaths left a mark.

Why was Joey different, Eddie wondered as he worked on Madison? Because he was his brother? Maybe, but it was more than that. He pictured Joey's pockmarked face, crazed eyes, and booming laugh. The big lug loved life. And suddenly Eddie got it. Joey never took anything seriously. He had the heart and mind of a seven-year-old. The seven-year-old we all leave behind as we grow up, but often miss. And as much as Joey drove Eddie nuts, he envied the blissful way Joey lived his life.

"Ouch," Madison said as Eddie pulled the final tape tight. "That hurts."

"So does stabbing someone in the chest. Who did it, by the way, who actually killed Joey?"

Madison thought about lying, but it would be in the morning papers; Grace had told that cute cop that she'd done it, in self-defense. But she could try to deflect a bit. "Joey killed Joey. I told you, if he'd just asked me for the tape, I would have given it to him, but no, he has to play big bad Mafia man."

"And in the struggle someone killed him. You?"

Madison shook her head. "No, Grace. But it was an accident."

"Maybe, but dead is dead."

The door opened, Frankie the Fish and Rico blew into the room. Frankie held the tape over his head. "We got it!"

Oh shit, Madison thought. "What about Grace?" she asked.

"She got away," Frankie answered.

"Fuck," Eddie said. His back was to Madison so he couldn't see her relieved smile. "We got a VHS machine in this place?"

"Upstairs," Little Joe said. "In the office."

Eddie grabbed Madison by the arm, Madison yelped in pain as Eddie dragged her with him up the stairs and into the cramped office. As Eddie dropped Madison in a chair, Frankie shoved the tape into the machine and Rico turned on the TV. There was static for a moment, then a close-up of a blonde woman burying her face in another woman's shaved pussy, her tongue expertly working the clitoris.

"Nice," Rico said.

Eddie wasn't so sure, something didn't look right.

The angle changed as a naked guy came into the room and joined the women on the bed. One of the women started sucking his cock as the other kissed his balls.

"What the fuck is this?" Eddie asked.

Madison started laughing. "You got the wrong tape, fellas, Grace tricked you. That's a porno."

"She's right," Little Joe said. "I recognize the blonde, it's Jenna Jameson."

Eddie glared at Frankie. "Hey, a tape's a tape, how was I to know?"

"That's it, Eddie," Madison said. "Game over. Even I don't know where Grace is."

"No, but I bet she carries a cell phone." He pulled out his switchblade. "And I'll bet your left eye you know the number."

THIRTY

The Hard Rock Casino was loud. Not only was there the dingity dingity dingity of slot machines, but rock music also blared from hidden speakers all over the place. It had to be after midnight by now, but the place was packed.

I'd parked in the 7/11 lot across from the casino. I thought pulling up to the hotel valet with a crushed, bloodstained vehicle might have attracted the wrong kind of attention. I walked across the street and asked the doorman where the Viva Las Vegas Lounge was and he pointed to a far end of the casino. Why is it you have to walk through the casino in every hotel to get anywhere? Never mind, dumb question.

As I passed the people sitting at the blackjack tables, roulette tables, crap tables, and weird Asian dice games, I witnessed an amazing array of human emotions; joy, depression, confusion, frustration, anger. But most of the gamblers had one thing in common, concentration. They were taking it very seriously.

I never took gambling seriously. Granted, I only played number fifteen on the roulette table and plinked a few quarters into the odd slot machine, but it just wasn't important to me.

So I idly tried to make a list of the things that were important to me. Well, acting... I had to admit, mother be damned, that I used to love it. And I was good at it. But, honestly, it just wasn't that important to me anymore. And my family, I thought, but hey, that was only my mother and she was a major pain in the butt and number one on my shit list at the moment. I was suddenly between boyfriends, so no man made the list. Some great friends, sure, but somehow that didn't seem to count. I liked to read, chick lit and cooking books mostly, but it was hardly a priority. I didn't play tennis, or golf, or any other sport.

Oh, shit, another epiphany. There was *nothing* important to me. How did this happen? How did I get to be twenty-eight years old and become an emotional husk?

I walked into the Viva Las Vegas Lounge, looked around for Officer Harris, didn't spot him but it was hard to be sure because the bar was packed. I figured they'd be looking for me, too, so I stood in the entrance for a while, and when no one called out to me, I grabbed a stool at the bar.

"Cocktail?" The bartender asked. He was Asian, young and cute.

Fuck it, I thought. I deserved a drink. "Vodka martini, very dry, three olives."

"You got it," he said with a smile that I'm sure got him laid a lot.

And then it hit me. Something that was important to me. Drinking. I did it every day. I looked forward to it every day. When I first got to L.A., I hardly drank at all. Some white wine, occasionally, but that was it. Now I had a few drinks every night. Sometimes more.

But I wasn't an alcoholic. I mean, I never got that drunk, never did anything stupid like drink and drive or pass out or do things I regret in the morning.

It was just a nice way to finish off the day, sort of a demarcation; serious stuff like work on one side of the line, relaxation and a drink on the other. And admittedly, the booze did numb the frustrations of the day. It allowed me to brush off the day's busted auditions and get ready for tomorrow's shot at stardom.

The bartender slid the drink in front of me. "Thank you," I said and stared at it. To drink or not to drink, that was the question. I was talking myself into somehow believing that I'd reached some magical turning point. To drink the martini meant continuing down this miserable road of rejection and broken dreams that had led me to this pathetic moment in my life. To not drink the martini meant, well, nothing but a bullshit symbolic gesture about changing a life I had no control over at the moment anyway. So I picked up the martini and took a sip. It was ice cold going down but lit a gentle fire as it hit my stomach. I shivered that marvelous first-martini-sip shiver and sighed happily.

Then my cell phone rang. I looked at the caller ID, Madison. My heart leapt. Somehow she'd managed to escape. "Hello," I answered, thrilled.

"I've got your girlfriend," Eddie DeCarlo said.

"Oh, God, it's you," I blurted, heart sinking.

"I've got Madison and you've got my tape. Let's trade."

"Don't do it," I heard Madison scream in the background. Then I heard a sharp slap.

"Shut up," Eddie said to Madison.

"Let me talk to her," I said.

"No fucking way. She'll tell you I'm a lying, murdering cocksucker and she'd rather be dead than see me get the tape."

"Something like that," I heard Madison mumble.

"But I figure you'd rather get her back alive."

More than anything, I thought. "I would," I said.

"And I also figure you don't really give a shit about the tape."

I honestly didn't know what to do with the tape. If I gave it to the police, it wouldn't get Madison back. If I gave it to the FBI, still no Madison. Giving it to Margaret Cross wasn't an option since she'd betrayed us, so, all in all, the tape was pretty much worthless to me –– unless Eddie would trade it for Madison.

"I only care about Madison," I said. "I'm all for a trade."

"The tape for this traitorous bitch," Eddie said. "You've got a deal."

"Wait, how do I know you won't just kill me when I bring the tape?"

"You have my word. Few things are more valuable. Nothing is as sacrosanct."

Didn't this guy lie, cheat, steal and murder for a living? "Just your word?" I asked.

"I'm going to be honest with you, Grace. It's Grace, right?"

"Yeah..."

"As upset as I am with Madison, I used to love her. I don't want to hurt her. I don't want to hurt you. I just want the tape. Bring it to me and I promise, you'll both go free."

He sounded reasonable and sincere. And I wanted to believe him. "Okay," I said.

"There's an old drive-in theatre at the edge of town, where Paradise Road meets Route 40."

"Wait," I said, flagging down the cute waiter. "Could I borrow a pen?"

"Going to give me your phone number?" he asked with a wink, handing me the pen.

"Something like that," I said and wrote Paradise Road and Route 40 on the back of a napkin.

"Bonanza Drive-in. Be there in twenty minutes, and come alone. You do anything stupid, she dies. Got it?"

"Got it." He hung up. I sat there for a moment not sure what to do. That FBI guy would be arriving any second. If I told him about the Drive-in, he'd probably put together a SWAT team and try and take Eddie down. But Eddie said come alone, and if the FBI army showed up, I was sure he'd kill Madison.

I took another sip of the martini to clarify my thoughts. Madison's only chance was for me to come alone and pray that Eddie DeCarlo was a man of his word.

Another sip convinced me that the cute bartender really knew how to make a martini. And a final gulp gave me the courage I needed to face Eddie. I stood up and realized I had no money to pay for the drink. I may have killed one guy with a knife, helped another off a 23rd story balcony, fled the scene of a couple of crime scenes and stolen a car, but the thought of stiffing the bartender bugged me. Madison had warned me not to use my credit card; the cops could use it to track us. But since everyone and their brother knew we were in Las Vegas, I paid for the drink with my Visa and headed for the door.

That's when I saw L.A. police officer, Sean Harris. He was out of uniform, looking slightly uncomfortable in a blue suit, but I recognized him instantly. He still had that slightly shell-shocked look he had when I stole his pistol. He was hurrying across the casino with another guy in a suit. But this guy looked focused, determined and totally professional. Had to be the FBI guy, I thought, Ryan something or other. He was a little old for me, mid-thirties or so, but handsome in a Kevin Bacon sort of way.

I slipped out of sight behind a Wheel of Fortune and watched them walk into the Viva Las Vegas Lounge. Last chance, I thought. It would be so easy to run up to them and tell them where to find Eddie and Madison. But Eddie's words rang in my ear: come alone.

I hustled for the front door, weaving a path through a maze of gamblers. I burst through the front door onto the street, headed toward the crosswalk then stopped in my tracks. Two police cars were in the 7/11 parking lot and cops surrounded the blood soaked car.

Shit. I needed wheels. I thought about sticking out my thumb, but I didn't think even Madison could've talked someone into a trip to a deserted drive-in theatre at the edge of town.

I looked back at the Hard Rock's taxi line. Mobbed. So was the valet; cars were waiting bumper to bumper for the overwhelmed car parkers. In fact, I couldn't see a single valet anywhere. So I grabbed a parking ticket from the valet stand and trotted up to a yellow BMW convertible. I plastered on a big smile, opened the door, handed the driver the ticket and said, "Welcome to the Hard Rock!"

"Thanks," the driver said, a lawyer/stockbroker/too slick-for-his-own-good type. "You can park my car anytime."

"I get off at two," I said with a wink, then dropped into the driver's seat and floored it.

THIRTY-ONE

Ryan and Sean hurried through the casino. They looked like cops, or at least people on a mission, and the crowd parted for them.

Something flashed in the corner of Sean Harris's eye and he spun around glimpsing the retreating figure of a blonde dressed in a white dress hurrying away from him. The surveillance camera photograph Sean and Ryan had seen of Grace at the Paradise Hotel showed Grace with her hair pulled back wearing a white dress. Sean slowed, and then stopped. The more he thought about it the more he thought it was Grace.

"What the fuck are you doing?" Ryan asked appearing at Sean's shoulder, pointing to the far end of the casino. "The bar's this way."

"I thought I saw Grace, headed toward the front door."

"You sure? She agreed to meet us. Why would she be running away?"

"I'm not sure." Then Sean replayed the image in his mind; it was just a flash, a feeling more than a look. Never even saw the woman's face. "Never mind, it was probably nothing. Let's go."

So, once again, Sean and Ryan had come this close to finding Grace.

Sean followed Ryan into the Viva Las Vegas Lounge. His eyes scanned the crowd. "I don't see her," he said.

Ryan frowned, showed the printout of Grace's security camera picture to a couple of waitresses then finally to the bartender.

"Yeah, she was here," the bartender said, sizing Ryan up and the guy hovering behind him. They looked like cops but could've been PIs. "What's it to you?"

Ryan flashed his credentials, said, "FBI."

"Like I said, yeah, she was here. Left just a couple of minutes ago."

"Shit," Sean muttered. "I knew it."

"What happened before she left? Did someone meet her? Did she get a call?"

"She got a call. Didn't seem happy about it, then she finished her drink and left."

"You happen to overhear any of the conversation? You have any idea where she was going?"

"No, sorry."

"Call her," Sean said to Ryan. "I've got a bad feeling about this. Call her."

Ryan was worried, too. There was only one reason Grace would suddenly abandoned their meeting: Eddie DeCarlo.

Eddie walked out the back door of Jackpot Manufacturing with Frankie. Rico and Little Joe followed, Madison between them, her arms tied behind her back.

Eddie stopped and stared at the only car in the parking lot, a Dodge Caravan. "What the fuck is this?"

"That bitch stole our car," Rico said. "So we stole the van."

"Do I look like a fucking soccer mom to you? Next time, steal something nice."

"Sorry," Rico said, opening the back door and guiding Madison inside. Little Joe slid into the seat next to her.

The pain in Madison's shoulder flared as she hit the seat. But she hardly noticed. Her mind was spinning. She had to find a way to abort the meeting with Grace. No matter what Eddie said, Madison was sure that the moment Eddie got the tape he'd kill them both.

"The van's really not so bad, Eddie," Frankie said, getting in on the other side of Madison, behind the driver's seat. "It's got a DVD player and everything."

Eddie just shook his head and got into the front passenger seat. Rico got behind the wheel, started the engine and drove off. They turned right on Warm Springs Road and headed north.

Seconds later, Eddie heard the sound of approaching sirens and saw flashing police lights through the windshield. An unmarked car roared by, followed by two Las Vegas squad cars. Eddie spun around in his seat and watched them turn into the Jackpot Manufacturing parking lot.

Eddie smiled. "Looks the posse just arrived. Hope they like empty buildings."

Frankie and Rico laughed. Eddie looked at Madison. "Don't worry, honey. It'll be over soon."

That's exactly what Madison was afraid of.

THIRTY-TWO

I love driving convertibles. I love the way the wind blows your hair. The open roof seems to connect you to the road, the sky, and the whole wide world.

Okay, I was a little buzzed by the martini. And I probably shouldn't have been driving, but what choice did I have?

I took a corner a bit quick and my tires caught the dirt shoulder, sending me into a little skid. I over-corrected, slid across the center lane and in front of an approaching pickup truck. The startled driver honked his horn as he swerved away from me. I yanked the wheel to the right, just missing his front bumper and regained control of the car.

Something banged around inside the glove compartment every time I made a sharp turn. Once I had regained control of the car, I tried to open the glove box. But it was too far away for me to get at without pulling over, so I did my best to ignore it.

My cell phone rang. I fished it out of my purse and answered. "Hello," I said, knowing it had to be the FBI agent. "Don't yell at me."

"Where the hell are you?" Agent Griffin asked.

"On my way to meet Eddie."

"But we had a deal. You said you'd meet us."

"I said, don't yell."

"Grace, you can't meet Eddie DeCarlo alone. He'll kill you."

"No, he gave me his word. I'm going to trade the tape for Madison."

"So there is a tape."

"Yes, you were right all along. Madison had the tape, but she'd lied to me. So when I told you I didn't know anything about a tape I was telling the truth."

"Grace -- "

"In fact, I'm a very honest person," I said, on a roll now. "And though you may find it hard to believe, throughout this... escapade, I not only haven't murdered anyone in cold blood, I haven't even lied. Though to be perfectly honest, the car I'm driving was borrowed under less than honorable circumstances, but completely justified since I'm on a life or death rescue mission."

"Grace, you can't meet Eddie alone."

"He said he'd kill Madison if I brought anyone."

"He won't kill anyone until he gets that tape. That's what he really wants. Pull over. Let me meet you. Give me the tape and I'll trade it for Madison."

That actually made some sense to me. If all Eddie wanted was the tape, he really wouldn't care who delivered it to him, as long as he got it back.

"By the way, what's on the tape, Grace? What's on the tape that makes it so important to Eddie?"

Right. He didn't know what was on the tape. With all that'd happened, it seemed everyone knew what was on the tape. "Madison making love to a woman," I said. "But not just any woman; Margaret Cross."

"The new Attorney General?"

"Yep."

"Wow," Agent Griffin said.

"Yep."

"Okay, this is good. Now I know why Eddie is so desperate, and I'm more convinced than ever that Madison is safe as long as he doesn't have the tape. Let me trade the tape for Madison, then I'll put both of you in the Witness Protection Program where Eddie DeCarlo will never be able to find you."

"You know, my life's a real mess right now. I've realized I probably don't want to be an actress anymore, but I have no idea what I do want to do. So Witness Protection, and the chance to start over with a new name, new look, new profession, new everything is starting to sound pretty darn good."

"Good. Then pull over, Grace," Ryan pleaded. "Park your car. Tell me where you are and I'll come to you."

Then something occurred to me. "Tell me, Agent Griffin, why would you, an FBI guy, trade the tape for Madison and then let Eddie go? What's in it for you?"

There was a pause a little too long for my liking, then, "I'm just trying to keep anyone else from getting killed."

"Why don't I believe you?"

"I'm telling you the truth, Grace. Look, you are in serious trouble. You claim to be an innocent bystander but there is a trail of bodies wherever you go. The LAPD wants you. The Las Vegas PD wants you. The mob wants you. If any of them get you, your life is over. You'll spend years in jail if the cops catch you. You'll be killed if you meet Eddie. Your *only* chance is me. I've got the power of the federal government behind me. I can make your claim of self-defense stick. The cops will drop all charges. I can tuck you safely away in Witness Protection where Eddie can't get you. You can live a normal life. Trust me, Grace. I only want to help you."

"Trust you? So far today I've trusted and been betrayed by a long list of people including my boyfriend, my agent, Madison's manager, the creep who ran that strip club and the next Attorney General of the United States. So if you don't mind, the only person I'm going to trust from now on is me." I snapped off my cell phone and stepped on the gas. For better or worse, Eddie DeCarlo, here I come.

THIRTY-THREE

"Shit," Ryan said.

"What happened?" Sean asked.

"Grace has decided to commit suicide." Ryan was frustrated. Now that he knew what was on the tape, he wanted it more than ever. The future United States Attorney General, who also happened to be married to a fucking billionaire, caught on tape with a lesbian lover! That tape was worth a fortune if Ryan could get to Grace before Eddie did.

Ryan's cell phone rang. Be Grace calling to say you've changed you mind, he thought, and then answered. "Hello."

"I think I just missed him," Detective Jackson said. He was standing in the middle of the Jackpot Manufacturing warehouse. "There's blood on a pillar, cigarette butts on the floor and a porno playing in the office. Jenna Jameson, I think."

"I don't get the porno, but I know he's on the move. He's talked Grace into meeting him."

"Where?"

"No idea."

"So what's the plan?"

Indeed, Ryan thought. What's the fucking plan? "I'll call you when I have one." Ryan hung up, flagged down the bartender. "You sure you didn't hear where she was going? No clue at all?"

"No, sorry."

Sean stepped forward, inspired by an idea, excited. "Any chance she wrote the address down?" he asked.

The bartender nodded. "In fact she borrowed my pen."

"Not sure how that's going to help us," Ryan said. Sean pointed at the security camera above the bar. "Genius," Ryan said.

"It's almost over," Eddie said to Alan Cross on his cell phone. "I should have the tape back within the hour. Then I will hand deliver it to you."

"Thank God," Cross said from his Watergate Hotel suite. "I don't know how to thank you."

"Hopefully the new Attorney General will find a few ways."

Cross glanced into the bedroom. Maggie was in bed. But she wasn't used to betraying people so it took two Remys and an Ambien to get her to fall asleep. "I'm sure she will," Cross said. "Call me when it's over."

"Will do," Eddie said and hung up.

"So the Mafia's going to have a direct line to the United States Attorney General," Madison said. "How nice for you."

"It may help relieve some pressure."

"And don't forget to make a copy of the tape before you turn it over, just in case Ms. Cross develops a case of amnesia."

Eddie turned back to Madison, smiled. "That's what I liked so much about you, baby," he said. "You're smart."

"You really think so?"

"Absolutely."

"Good, because we're about to find out just how smart I am." And with that, Madison slipped down in her seat, flipped on her back sticking her legs above the headrests and kicked Rico, the driver, in the back of the head. Rico's head slammed into the driver's side window as he involuntarily jerked the steering wheel to the left, into the oncoming lane of traffic.

"Jesus fucking Christ," Eddie screamed as they drove right for a monstrous tractor-trailer. With an ear-shattering blast, the semi sounded its air horn. Eddie grabbed the wheel and yanked it back to the right. The van swerved, tipped, the tires shrieked, then the van flipped over.

Inside the van was a kaleidoscope of flying heads, legs and arms. Nobody was wearing seat belts, so now it was a matter of luck as to who would survive. Rico's luck ran out first as he was bounced off the air bag and was thrown halfway out the windshield on the first flip, then had his skull popped like a grape as the van flipped over the second time.

Frankie was luckier; he was pinballed between the front headrest and the roof of the car, escaping any serious damage.

Little Joe, an avid golfer who had three holes-in-one and a single digit handicap, broke his collarbone and right arm as the van hit the pavement the first time. And that's what went through his mind as he felt the bones snap: golf. This is going to ruin my game, he thought. Then the van flipped again, Little Joe's head slammed into the roof of the van, breaking his neck. If Little Joe had lived, his golf game would've really sucked. But he was dead before the van slid to a stop.

Eddie ricocheted off the dashboard airbag into the passenger side airbag into the driver's seat airbag, now available since Rico had left the building. Eddie split his upper lip and strained his left knee, but otherwise, escaped unscathed.

Madison welcomed death with open arms. It was a relief, actually, to finally surrender to the inevitable, to stop fighting the fates that had killed her parents and sent her on a rollercoaster ride of a perverted Uncle, drugged out rocker, stripping and cock-sucking.

As the van flipped, Madison closed her eyes and a family portrait came to mind, a picture taken of the three of them, Mom, Dad and little Madison, at Madison's First Communion. Madison wore the traditional white dress. The family smiled innocently at the camera. This had been Madison's favorite picture growing up. She used to stare at it endlessly in the bedroom of her Uncle's house. Sitting on the same bed her Uncle would come to every night for his "good night kiss." Madison would be crying, blaming her parents for getting on that plane without her, blaming them for dying without her.

When Madison ran away, she forgot the picture. She missed it so much she almost went back for it that first night but the thought of seeing her Uncle one more time terrified her so much, she couldn't do it.

A day hadn't gone by since that Madison hadn't thought about the picture. She missed the perfect family with their awkward smiles. She missed what might have been.

Madison's back was still on the seat when the van collided with the street the first time so it was her feet, not her head, that crashed into the roof of the van. If she had been sitting normally, she would have been killed instantly, but since it was just her feet taking the impact, a jammed left knee was the only damage. The second impact made her the meat in a Frankie and Little Joe sandwich, knocking the wind out of her. As the air was forced from her lungs,

Madison decided that was that and her last thought was of Grace and how happy Madison was to have sacrificed herself to save Grace's life.

The thought after Madison's last thought was that she wasn't dead. Then a cavalcade of thoughts buried her. I can't breathe. Fuck, my shoulder hurts. Breathe. Fuck, my knee hurts. Breathe, damn it, breathe.

She gasped, air refilling her lungs as the van screeched to a stop. Madison opened her eyes. She was staring into Little Joe's lifeless orbs. He was ugly when he was alive but he was totally gross dead.

Frankie the Fish was stirring beside her. She turned to him and he gave her a crooked smile. "Some ride, huh?" he asked. He looked weird, different somehow, and then Madison realized his glasses had come off in the crash.

Frankie blinked, feeling his face, as the blurred world refused to come into view. "Fuck," he said. "Where are my glasses?"

Madison turned to the front seat and found Eddie glaring at her, blood pouring from his split lip. "For a smart girl, that was pretty fucking stupid."

Frankie searched fruitlessly for his glasses then reacted, sniffing the air. "I smell gas."

"Shit," Eddie said as he tried to open his door. It was crushed, the frame bent, hopelessly jammed. Eddie used his elbow to punch out the window glass and crawled out.

Frankie fumbled for the latch, found it, pulled. The door slid open for a few inches then stopped. "Open, you mother fucker," he screamed then pulled with all his might. Madison could hear the screech of metal meeting metal as the door gave, millimeter by millimeter, until Frankie could squeeze out and tumble to the street.

That left Madison, hands tied behind her back, right shoulder and left knee volcanoes of pain, trying to slide across the seat and out the door.

The smell of gasoline was everywhere now, and Madison heard the whoosh of erupting fire.

Two hands suddenly shot through the door, grabbed her by the shoulders and pulled her into the street. Eddie. He dragged her across the street, away from the burning van.

Seconds later the van exploded. The concussion knocked an already unsteady Eddie to the ground. Madison fell on top of him. They both rolled over and looked at the conflagration as Frankie joined them.

"You saved my life," Madison said.

"Don't get the wrong idea," Eddie said. "I need to trade you for that tape. If it was up to me, I'd be cooking marshmallows on your melting flesh."

The semi that almost hit them had pulled over and the driver, a burly, grizzled veteran of millions of highway miles, Albert Kordecki, ran over. "Everyone all right?" he asked. Then he noticed Madison's hands tied behind her back. "Hey, what's going on?"

Eddie ignored the question, his eyes on the semi parked down the street. He turned to Frankie. "You know how to drive one of those things?"

"I got no glasses, Eddie. I can't see shit."

Eddie had hijacked enough trucks as a kid to handle it. "Fine, I'll drive it myself."

"Nobody drives my rig."

Eddie pulled his gun, leveled it at Kordecki. "Even if I say please?"

Kordecki had two teenage boys and a wife he still cherished after twenty-three years of marriage. But

Madison's bound hands and bleeding shoulder worried him. He looked at her, uncertain.

"Don't worry about me," Madison said, recognizing a guy with a hero complex and knowing if the driver did anything stupid, Eddie would shoot him dead. "I'll be fine."

Kordecki didn't like it but he tossed his keys to Eddie.

I want to be just like him, Sean thought as he watched Ryan commandeer the Hard Rock Security Center. Ryan was self-assured, confident, a real leader. How much was he born with, Sean wondered, and how much was beaten into him by the FBI?

There was a fire in Ryan's eyes as he directed Snuffy, the Hard Rock Security Chief, through the security cameras circling the Viva Las Vegas Lounge looking for one with a clear angle on Grace Taylor.

"Stop, there, that's her," Ryan said. "Zoom in, let's see if we can read what she's writing." The technician zoomed in, but Grace's shoulder blocked the piece of paper and you couldn't read anything.

"Shit," Ryan said. He pointed to the top right side of the screen. "We need an angle from there. Got a camera in that corner?"

As Snuffy went to work, Ryan wondered how he was going to get rid of Sean if they got a lead on Grace's location. The kid was a definite liability at this point. Ryan's goal was simple. Get to Grace before Eddie did and get his hands on the tape.

A new angle on Grace came up on the screen. You could clearly see the paper she was writing on. "Fantastic," Ryan said. "Now zoom in."

The image increased in size until they could read the paper over her shoulder.

"Bonanza Drive-In," Ryan said. "Where the hell is that?"

"About twenty miles north," Snuffy said. "Where Paradise Road meets Route 40."

"Thanks, guys," Ryan said to the security room crew. "You've been a big help." Then Ryan led Sean into the hallway and toward the front door. "This is where we part ways, kid."

"What?"

"You've been a big help, and I appreciate it. But I'm about to drive into a dangerous hostage situation. One I'm trained for and you're not. Grace and Madison's lives are hanging by a thread and if I'm worried about you fucking up, I won't be able to do my job, and someone may get killed."

Ryan was walking so quickly Sean was having trouble keeping up. "Eddie's got a whole crew with him. You can't face him alone."

The kid had a point. Ryan was so desperate to get the tape he hadn't taken the time to consider the odds. If shooting started, Sean's extra gun might come in handy.

"How'd you rank on the range?"

Sean smiled then proudly said, "Marksman."

Ryan was suddenly jolted by a memory of Dempsey asking him the same question. He had answered Dempsey the same way, with a smile and proud declaration, "Marksman."

Weird, Ryan thought. And for an instant he wondered how it was that Sean had stumbled into his life in the first place. A message from Dempsey? A heaven sent reminder to stay on the straight and narrow?

That's ridiculous, Ryan realized. Dempsey is dead, his life a ruin. And Ryan's life was one videotape away from financial freedom.

But unless he beat Eddie DeCarlo to the Bonanza Drive-In, he might have to fight to get that tape, and like it or not, Sean's firepower would come in handy.

"Okay," Ryan said as they burst through the front door and up to Ryan's rental. "But you've got to promise me you'll do exactly as I say."

Sean's face exploded in a grin. "You've got my word."

THIRTY-FOUR

Did you ever wonder what I'd look like if you hadn't made me get that nose job?"

"What? Grace, is that you?"

"Or what I would have become if you hadn't made me become an actress?"

"Grace, it's four o'clock in the morning."

"It's four o'clock in the morning, do you know *who* your daughter is?"

"Honey, you sound drunk. Are you drunk?"

Actually, I was. Well, not drunk, but let's just say I was keeping the high from the martini going. I'd found out what was rattling around inside the glove compartment, a pint of Absolut vodka. I'd had a few swigs waiting for Eddie and Madison to show up. I knew it wasn't a good idea as I took my first drink, but I was scared shitless and I figured a little liquid courage couldn't hurt.

And if meeting a mobster under a full moon in the middle of the night wasn't bad enough, the abandoned drive-in was spooky as hell. The painted plywood screen was falling apart and the rusted-out speaker stands stood like tombstones in the weed-infested parking lot.

"I may have had a couple of drinks," I said. "But my mind is crystal clear. Okay, forget what I'd look like, forget what I might've been doing, how about this: how old would my baby be? Would I have had a boy or girl? What would I have called the baby? How happy would I have been if you didn't talk me into that abortion?"

Okay, now you know. I *never* talk about it, but I think about it every day. Remember when I told you about the college professor I was in love with, Paul, the one who said he was separated, but then his wife returned from a sabbatical?

Well, as Madison would say, I wasn't completely honest with you.

That's the story I always tell; the son of a bitch was still married and I dumped him.

But here's the truth: He wasn't separated, he'd never been married. We were madly in love. I got pregnant and he wanted to marry me. I wanted to marry him. I'd stay with him at the University of Florida, he'd teach, I'd do local theater or get my teaching certificate, and we'd have a passel of kids and live happily ever after.

And that was the starry-eyed plan until I called my mother. She didn't try to talk me out of it on the phone. No, she hung up without saying a word, got in her car and drove from Tampa to Gainesville, pulled me out of my Psychology of Shakespeare class and onto the quad.

"Are you out of your mind?" she practically screeched. "Grace, you've been given a gift from God. Pure talent. Do you have any idea how few people on earth are blessed with your natural ability? We have spent your whole life preparing for your career in Hollywood. We've honed your craft, your look, and your image. We talked about this, no serious relationships until you've established your career. You can't honestly be thinking about throwing it all away for a schoolgirl crush on your teacher!"

"I love him, Mom."

"Oh, please. By my count you've already been in love three times, not counting your lesbian fling with what's her name."

"Ellen, her name is Ellen."

"And you'll be in love four or five or fifteen more times before it's all over, so please, I beg you, never mention marrying this man again."

"But, Mom, I'm pregnant."

"About that... I thought you were on the pill." My mother's greatest fear was that I'd get pregnant in high school and ruin my life so she actually put me on the pill when I was sixteen, before I'd ever had sex.

"I am. I mean, I was, but I started breaking out so I switched to a diaphragm, and I guess I forgot one night."

"I honestly think you might stand a small chance of still making it in Hollywood if you were married when you got there –– small, mind you, but you'll stand no chance if you're raising a child. You are going to spend twelve hours a day in your car, driving to auditions, meeting producers and directors, going to the right nightclubs, the A-list premieres. You won't have time to raise a child."

"Maybe I don't have to go to Hollywood. I could stay here. There are plenty of small theater companies. I'll still be acting."

"Thank God your father isn't alive to see this. He wanted you to be a star more than anything."

Yep, she even played the dead father card. And as much as I hate to admit it, it started to work. She kept after me all afternoon, manipulating me as she had for my entire life, finally convincing me that I had twenty years ahead of me to have children; marry Paul, if I had to, but make him promise to move to L.A. and for god's sake, without a baby in tow.

First thing the next morning, Mom took me to the clinic and I had an abortion. Don't hate me. I hate myself enough for both of us.

I didn't tell Paul before having the procedure because I was afraid he'd talk me out of it. And I really hoped that he would understand. He didn't. He couldn't believe I'd chosen my career over him. He couldn't believe I'd chosen my mother over him. He couldn't believe I'd aborted his child.

He never spoke to me again.

Funny how the mind works; ever since then, I've sabotaged every relationship I've been in when they get too serious, and never trusted myself when having sex to reach orgasm.

So, there I stood in the middle of the Bonanza Drive-In, bitching out my mother for a decision I made. A decision only I'm ultimately responsible for. But hey, we all blame someone.

"Grace, why are you talking about the abortion, you haven't mentioned it in years?"

Instead of answering, I took another swig from the bottle of Absolute, and then tensed as a huge semi trailer pulled into the parking lot. What the hell, I thought as the semi turned, centering me in the blinding headlights. Then the headlights clicked off, the driver door opened and Eddie DeCarlo climbed out.

"Got to go, Mom," I said. "If you never hear from me again, it's because I'm dead, in Witness Protection or just sick of your shit."

THIRTY-FIVE

"Why did you become a cop?"

Here he goes again, Ryan thought. Doesn't he ever shut up? "Sean, we're driving one hundred and five miles-an-hour to a potentially deadly rendezvous with one of the most dangerous men in the country. Now is not the time for chit chat, it is the time for silent reflection and perhaps a prayer to the Almighty to bless and protect the righteous."

"Right, sorry, I'll shut up."

And he did shut up, but the damage was done. At least it was from Ryan's point of view. He hated thinking about why he had become a cop, now more than ever.

He was seven years old. It was that horrible summer when his father abandoned Ryan and his mother, that horrible summer when the young man, feeling alone and betrayed, was lured into the battered, pale blue Volkswagen bus by the chubby guy with the cute dog and two tickets to the Cubs baseball game. That horrible summer when Ryan was kidnapped by that perverted son of a bitch, held in the basement of his Highland Park house for three months, given up for dead by his mother, the media and ninety-nine percent of the Chicago police department. But one cop, a woman named Michelle O'Flannagan, had lost a niece, Kristin, a few years earlier, stolen from the food court at the Woodfield Shopping Mall. She was kidnapped, and for five days the city searched for her. Michelle's sister begged her to help her search for the girl, but Michelle was in Homicide, not Missing Persons, and she was swamped, in the weeds on three active investigations. Besides, literally thousands of people were looking for Kristin, what difference could Michelle have made?

Kristin's body was found after three days, dismembered and discarded in a Jewel Tea Grocery Store dumpster. After the funeral, Michelle's distraught sister slit her wrists and bled to death in her bathroom.

Grief and guilt ridden, Michelle transferred to Missing Persons. She would never be too busy to help a young boy or girl again.

As the weeks turned to months and young Ryan's kidnapping moved from page one to page to ten to no page at all, Michelle kept at it. Following every lead, every tip, then rechecking them. And that's what broke the case.

She re-interviewed the few people on the street that afternoon; three gardeners, a postal worker, a UPS delivery guy and a Roto-Rooter plumber. When the UPS driver mentioned to the cop doing the interview that he saw a kid get into a blue van with a guy and a dog, the cop fucked up. The cop was a young father with a wife and three kids. The cop had to jam his wife and kids into a ten-year-old Chevy wagon, and he was dreaming about buying a Dodge Caravan. So when the UPS guy said van, the cop personalized it and mistakenly wrote down minivan. And that's what kind of vehicle the cops were looking for – a minivan.

But when Michelle talked to the UPS guy, an immigrant from Cambodia who spoke broken English, he said van, not minivan.

Michelle pressed, showed him pictures of all sorts of vans, until the Cambodian's eyes lit up when he saw a picture of a Volkswagen bus.

That changed everything. There were one hundred and fifty-nine Volkswagen buses registered in the Chicago area, but only twelve blue ones. She tracked down every one, and when she knocked on her eighth door, she knew she hit pay dirt. Albert Ridgeway, an overweight, baby-faced twenty-nine-year old man flushed a guilty red when she flashed her badge. He started crying, blubbering, "I'm sorry, I'm so sorry. I didn't hurt him, I promise."

Michelle swept her Colt out of its holster and stuck it in his face. "Where is he?"

"Downstairs," Albert sobbed. "In the basement."

Michelle cuffed him, called for backup and an ambulance, found the basement door and hurried downstairs. Ryan was ankle chained to a stake in the floor. He looked healthy, clean and well fed, but he had the thousand-yard stare of a POW.

Albert Ridgeway confessed to the kidnapping, claimed he never had sex with Ryan. Michelle found that hard to believe, but when she gently questioned Ryan, he confirmed it. Ridgeway would feed him three times a day, talk to him about baseball and comics, and was trying to become Ryan's friend.

And it was slowly working. Stockholm Syndrome is an effective tool of kidnappers, and Albert Ridgeway was a patient man.

Ryan was reunited with his mother, who yelled at him for getting in the Volkswagen bus in the first place. And despite the rescue being on front pages everywhere and the lead story on every morning news show in America, Ryan never did hear from his father.

But Ryan read all the newspaper and magazine articles about the tenacious cop who wouldn't give up looking for him. "I've got a job to do, just like everyone else. But I'm lucky, sometimes I get to solve a crime, right a wrong, and save a life."

Those words stuck with Ryan. He read more about cops, learned about courage, duty and honor. Before Ryan turned eight years old, he knew what he wanted to do with his life. Be a cop like Michelle O'Flannagan. Solve crimes, right wrongs and if he was lucky enough, save a life or two.

But reality has a funny way of putting things in perspective. Michelle O'Flannagan never got to see Ryan follow in her footsteps. She was killed in a car accident on her way to her youngest daughter's high school graduation.

Not as catastrophic an end as Dempsey, but still, where was the justice in that?

Ryan glanced over at Sean. The young cop was full of the same unbridled enthusiasm that Ryan had when he first joined the force. There were plenty of bitter old-timers around bitching and moaning, but Ryan had no trouble ignoring them. *He* would be different. He'd never burn out, crust over or give up.

Until now.

Now he wanted to grab Sean by the collar and tell him to throw his badge away and run as far and as fast as he can. This world doesn't deserve his kind of dedication. The world is unfair. The game is fixed. We are nothing but cannon fodder for the gods.

Sean, in the meantime, was awash in optimism. This was it, he thought. His moment. His destiny. Riding shotgun with an FBI agent to a dangerous hostage situation. He wasn't sure he'd be eligible for a LAPD Medal of Valor for action taken in Las Vegas, but he'd trade the medal for admission into the FBI Academy in a heartbeat.

"I just want to thank you," Sean said suddenly. "This is going to sound, well, stupid, but I'm loving this. Being with you, driving over a hundred miles-an-hour to an uncertain future. Risking our lives to rescue someone we hardly know. This is as cool as it gets. This is why I became a cop."

"Oddly enough," Ryan said, a bittersweet smile on his face. "It's why I became a cop, too. I wanted to solve crimes, right wrongs, and maybe get to save a life."

"And you've done all that, right? And not just once, but a bunch of times. Do you realize how lucky you are? I mean, you're living the dream."

Okay, that was it. Ryan couldn't keep his mouth shut any longer. "Look, Sean, there are some things you should know."

Sean turned to him, eager, all ears, ready to ingest Ryan's inspirational words of wisdom.

"It's all a bunch of crap," Ryan said. "You want to be a cop because you were brainwashed by your father and your uncles. You never stood a chance. You were shitting blue straight out of the womb. And let me tell you what you get after a lifetime of selfless service — zilch."

Sean was confused, not sure if Ryan was kidding or serious. "What're you talking about?"

"Tell me about your dad. He still married to your mom?"

"Well, no. They're divorced."

"He drink?"

"Yeah."

"A lot?"

"Kind of."

"And your uncles, they divorced? Drink too much? Do they all seem to spend all their time complaining about the fucked-up world we live in and that we're all going to hell in a hand-basket?"

Sean didn't answer. His silence was confirmation enough.

"That's what you've got to look forward to, kid."

"No, I know cops, veterans, who still love what they do."

"Or that's what they keep telling themselves, too afraid to admit the truth. Let me tell you about a guy who did love his work, who wasn't cynical, who couldn't wait to get to work each day to defend the rights and liberties of complete strangers. My partner, Dempsey Magee. He turned me from a good cop into a great cop. He inspired me every day with his work ethic, his crystal clear vision of right and wrong, crime and punishment, God and country. And he had a wonderful marriage to a woman he adored.

"And what was his reward for almost thirty years of selfless service for the 'greater good'? His beloved wife got cancer, died a horrible death. His lifetime of sacrifice didn't save her. The God he worshipped didn't save her. And Dempsey, his entire belief system now bankrupt, killed himself."

"I'm so sorry."

Ryan waved it off. "I don't need your sympathy, just your attention. Don't believe all the bullshit. Don't think you've got a destiny because your daddy didn't love you. Don't throw your life away just because he did. Because your uncles did. You're young, smart, you've got your whole life ahead of you. I've got a feeling you can be anything you set your mind to, so I beg you, don't be a cop."

Ryan's words buzzed in Sean's head like a swarm of angry bees. Sean wanted to argue with Ryan, tell him how wrong he was. But a lot of what Ryan said rang true. He'd nailed his father and uncles perfectly. Could he be right about everything?

"Look," Ryan said, pointing. The Bonanza Drive-in hovered on the horizon. Ryan pressed the accelerator to the floor. "I just hope we're not too late."

THIRTY-SIX

Eddie looked scary, and mad. Then I realized something was wrong. His face was bloody, his lip bleeding and he was limping. "Where's Madison?" I asked, suddenly worried.

Eddie turned to the semi. "Bring her out." The passenger door opened and a guy I didn't recognize got out dragging Madison with him. Then I realized it was Thick Glasses Guy, without his glasses. Madison's hands were tied behind her back, she had a bloody wound in her shoulder and was limping.

"What did you do to her?" I demanded.

"What did I do to her? That bitch tried to kill me! She did kill two of my men."

"Get your hands off me," Madison said, pulling free from Thick Glasses Guy. "I told you not to come, Grace. Why didn't you listen to me?"

"Because I'm not leaving here without you." I turned to Eddie. "So, I give you the tape and you give me Madison. That's our deal, right?"

"Right," Eddie said.

"Run, Grace, now. He's never going to let us live."

"I gave you my word, Grace," Eddie said. "I won't hurt you, I promise."

"Even if he lets us go tonight, he'll come after us tomorrow or the next day."

"Then we'll worry about it tomorrow or the next day. Tonight, let's worry about you." I reached into my purse. "Here's your tape."

But instead of the tape I pulled out Joey's gun and leveled it at Eddie.

Madison was right. Eddie was going to kill us. If not tonight, then tomorrow or the day after. We'd killed his brother, other members of his gang. I've seen enough mob movies, read enough books. There was no way he could let us live.

Witness Protection was an option if we could talk Special Agent Griffin into hiding us there. But that meant starting a new life. I didn't want to start a new life, I wanted to *fix* this one. It was time to finally stop playing the part of Grace Madison and find out who I really was. Figure out what I wanted to be. Only one thing stood in my way, Eddie DeCarlo. So I was going to do to him what he wanted to do to me. Kill him.

I pulled the trigger.

THIRTY-SEVEN

Click. The hammer fell on a spent cartridge. Grace pulled the trigger again. Click. Click. Click. Joey DeCarlo's humongous Tarus Model 416 Raging Bull .41 caliber magnum was empty.

Eddie stared, stunned, at the pistol. How could he be so stupid as to let this dumb cooze get the drop on him? Then he reached for his gun.

Madison stared, shocked, at Grace. Pride filled her at Grace's brave, albeit failed, attempt at heroism. Things were about to get really ugly really fast, but at least Grace hadn't been naïve enough to trust Eddie.

Frankie the Fish stared, confused, because it was all a blur to him and he couldn't see shit.

Grace stared, horrified, at Eddie. There was no hole in him. No blood gushed out and, not only was he alive, he was pulling out a gun of his own.

But there should have been a hole. The gun held six shots and Grace was sure she'd only fired five times during the battle in Caleb's office. She must've miscounted and now it would cost her her life.

Then, a memory engulfed her. Thick Glasses Guy tearing the gun out of her hands and throwing it into the hallway. The gun hitting the wall, the chamber flying open as it thudded to the ground. Grace picking it up, snapping the chamber closed, dropping it into her purse.

If the chamber turned when she closed it, the final bullet could have shifted from the next chamber to the last chamber.

As Eddie unfurled his arm, centering Grace's chest in his front sight, Grace pulled the trigger again.

Boom!

For Eddie DeCarlo, the next few seconds ramped into slow motion. He saw the bullet leave Joey's gun, saw the surprised look on the blonde's face, heard Frankie the Fish scream a warning, watched the bullet hit the front of his shirt, felt it rip through his flesh, bone and heart, saw his gun drop, unfired, from his hand.

Then he was in the air, knocked off his feet by the .41 caliber magnum. He saw the moon hanging above him surrounded by a million stars; so beautiful, he thought as he hit the ground.

Eddie was ready to die. He'd lived his life the way he wanted. He was an honored and respected man. His wife and children loved him.

Every day he walked out of his house he knew he might never come home. Getting killed was an occupational hazard. But he expected an honorable death, assassinated in a restaurant, shot down on the courthouse steps, garroted by a torpedo flown in from Palermo. Instead, he's killed with his brother's gun in the middle of the desert by a fucking broad.

How embarrassing, Eddie thought, and then died.

"Is he dead?" Grace asked.

Madison leaned over, looked into Eddie's lifeless eyes. "Very," she said, surprised by the rush of emotion she felt.

He looked so calm, just like he looked all those nights she slept next to him. She should be thrilled he was dead, it served him right; hell, he'd just shot a bullet into her shoulder, stabbed her with a knife. He was planning to kill her, for Christ's sake. But looking down at the man she once loved, the *only* man she'd ever loved, she was overcome with regret. Oh, what might have been if he'd never asked her to sleep with Margaret Cross. What might have been if they'd stayed together?

Frankie the Fish was feeling a different emotion. Rage. Somehow, this cunt had killed Eddie and, glasses or no glasses, tape or no tape, he was going to kill her. "You bitch," he said, his eyes flicking from Eddie's corpse to the blurred image of Grace. She wasn't in focus, but he could see well enough to aim at body mass. He reached for his gun.

Grace watched Frankie unholster a howitzer-sized automatic and turn in her direction. "Oh, shit," she mumbled, then looked at the gun Eddie dropped. It was fifty feet away, but her only chance. She dropped her purse and started running.

Madison saw Frankie level his gun at Grace. She lowered her head and charged him. But Madison was hobbled by her hands tied behind her back and the sprained knee, so Frankie easily sidestepped Madison and kicked her to the ground.

Suddenly a pair of headlights raked over him. A Ford Chevy roared through the drive-in's entrance and headed right for them. Frankie ignored it and turned back to Grace.

Ryan and Sean saw the tableau through the windshield. A dead body on the desert floor, Madison writhing on the ground, Grace, exposed, running across the parking lot, Frankie tracking her with a huge fucking automatic.

"She's not going to make it," Ryan muttered.

Sean couldn't believe it. They'd come so far, gotten so close. He couldn't accept that Grace was about to be gunned down in front of him. And he wouldn't accept it.

Ryan's tirade was forgotten as Sean pulled out his gun, aimed at Frankie *through* his own windshield and opened fire.

"Jesus Fucking Christ," Ryan screamed as flying glass peppered his face. But he kept the car aimed at Frankie.

Frankie fired the same instant as Sean. Luckily, Grace dived for the gun just as Frankie pulled the trigger. She heard the shots whiz over her as she hit the ground.

Sean's first three shots missed, all high, but he kept pulling the trigger, and God bless the thirteen shot Glock magazine, because shots four through eight stitched a path down Frankie's body; neck, shoulder, stomach, thigh.

Staggered, but not down, Frankie turned toward the charging vehicle. He tried to aim at the Ford, but Sean put two more in the center of Frankie's chest and the mobster went down.

Ryan hit the brakes and they slid to a stop. "That was incredibly stupid," Ryan snapped, then softened his tone. "And the only possible way you could've save her life. Nice going, kid."

Sean's heart almost burst with pride at the compliment.

THIRTY-EIGHT

It all happened so fast. I dove for Eddie's gun, Thick Glasses Guy shot at me, a car thundered toward us with someone firing shots through the windshield. At me? At Thick Glasses Guy?

I scooped up Eddie's gun, rolled over and got my answer. Frankie did a funny stagger step as four shots thunked into him. He was so pissed he forgot about me and turned to the car. Not a good idea. He took two more in the chest, and crumpled to the ground.

The car skidded to a stop and I leveled my gun, ready for anything at this point, and then relaxed when the car doors opened and I recognized the cute cop, Sean. He leapt out of the car and bent over Frankie's body, checking for a pulse.

I have to admit, Sean looked pretty hot, a gun hanging from his right hand, silhouetted by the neon effervescence of the Las Vegas skyline.

The other guy had run to Eddie, checking to make sure he was dead. Special Agent Ryan Griffin, I presumed.

But I had no time for introductions, I ran to Madison, knelt down, started untying her hands. "You all right, sweetie?"

"I've been punched, kicked, stabbed and shot. How the hell could I be all right?"

That made me laugh as Sean joined us and we helped Madison to her feet.

Sean turned to me. "Hello again," he said, smiling shyly.

"Was that you shooting through the windshield, saving my life?" I asked.

"Yeah."

"Thanks," I said, feeling idiotically self-conscious. What was this, high school?

"Who shot Eddie?" Special Agent Griffin asked. He was standing over the mobster's dead body.

"That would be me," I said. "But it was -- "

"Self defense, I know," Special Agent said with a grin. "Like all the others. Nice to finally meet you, Grace."

"You, too. But it was only sorta kinda self defense. I tried to kill him in cold blood -- "

"Grace," Madison interrupted. "Just shut up."

"No, I want them to know the truth," I said to Madison. I turned to Sean. "I especially want you to know the truth. When I pulled a gun on Eddie and tried to shoot him in cold blood, it was still self-defense since it was only a matter of time until he tried to kill me. But then my gun didn't fire, and Eddie was pulling his gun so when my gun finally did go off, it was absolutely, positively self-defense."

"Works for me," Sean said.

"And where is the tape that started this whole mess?" Special Agent Griffin asked.

I pointed, "In my purse."

Special Agent Griffin crossed to my purse, pulled out the tape. He looked at it with grim satisfaction. "Well, Eddie can't use this tape anymore. But I can."

Those words hung in the air for a moment, and then registered.

"What do you mean?" Madison asked.

"It means Agent Griffin's going to take the tape," Sean said. "Blackmail the new Attorney General, or her husband."

"Or the President," Special Agent Griffin said. "Someone, anyone. What I'm not going to do is end up like Dempsey."

"Who?" Madison asked.

"His old partner," Sean answered.

"He sacrificed his whole life for nothing but heartache. Well, forget that, I've learned my lesson. Give me a choice between being a cop or being rich, I'll take rich."

"Don't do this, Ryan," Sean said. "You resort to blackmail and you're no better than Eddie DeCarlo."

"Eddie lived in a ten thousand square foot house, flew in private jets and had millions in offshore accounts. Yeah, I can live with that. Look, Sean, everyone wins here. Eddie DeCarlo's dead, the world's a better place. The girls' names will be cleared, but with this adventure in their resume, their place in the celebrity firmament is guaranteed. Watch out Paparazzi, here they come. And you, Sean, got to live out your destiny, you saved a life and will be hailed as a hero. You'll be redeemed in your daddy's eyes and be well on your way to a gold detective's shield."

We heard the sound of approaching sirens. Sean raised his gun, pointed it at Ryan. "I can't let you do this."

Ryan raised his gun, pointed it at Sean. "Are you willing to die trying to stop me?"

"Enough already," Madison said. "Just shoot each other so Grace can get me to a hospital."

"I have a better idea," I said, stepping between them. Shoot me. Put me out of my misery. End this miserable day of days."

"Grace, move," Sean said.

"No." I turned to Agent Griffin. "You want to do a presto change-o from good guy to bad guy, fine, it's your conscience." I turned to Sean. "You want to die a hero? Fine, but pick something worth dying for, neither that videotape nor Agent Griffin's integrity are it." Then to both of them I said, "So, on the count of three, either shoot me or lower your guns. Three."

They both hesitated a moment, then both guns went down.

The sirens were getting louder.

"If you're leaving," I said to Agent Griffin. "You better get while you still can."

Ryan ran to his car, hopped inside. "Hey Grace," he called back. "For someone who's not sure she wants to be an actress, that was a pretty good performance."

And with a spray of sand, he drove off.

THIRTY-NINE

And so ended the worst day of my life, but, of course, it wasn't the end of the story.

Special Agent Griffin worked fast. He drove from the Bonanza Drive-in directly to the airport. On the way, he contacted Alan Cross, told him that Eddie DeCarlo was dead, but a certain videotape had come into Agent Griffin's possession and he'd be willing to sell it to Mr. Cross for ten million dollars.

To a man worth more than a billion dollars, ten million was a small price to pay to protect his wife's secret, so by the time Agent Griffin arrived in Washington D.C. to deliver the tape, ten million dollars was already deposited in a numbered Swiss bank account.

Agent Griffin got his money, emailed a resignation letter to the FBI and got on a plane to Geneva.

Alan Cross destroyed the tape immediately. He didn't want anything to threaten his wife's ascension to the Cabinet.

But Cross should have talked to his wife first. Horrified by her husband's relationship with the mobster and disgusted with herself for betraying Madison to Eddie DeCarlo, Margaret Cross appeared on CNN that night, ostensibly to introduce herself to the American people. Instead she announced that for personal reasons, she'd decided to withdraw her name from consideration as Attorney General of the United States and, in fact, was resigning as the Georgia Attorney General.

She also decided to withdraw as Alan Cross's wife and a few days later filed for divorce.

Meantime, things got pretty crazy at the Bonanza Drive-in once the cops arrived. After all, there were two dead bodies — Eddie DeCarlo and Thick Glasses Guy; two wanted felons – Madison and yours truly. And a rookie L.A. cop sort of masquerading as an FBI agent.

Luckily, Sean knew the Las Vegas cop in charge. His name was Detective Jackson and Sean had met him earlier that night.

FBI Agent Griffin must have really made an impression on Sean because he totally protected him. Sean never mentioned the videotape. He said Special Agent Griffin had left Sean in charge of the crime scene at the drive-in so the FBI man could get back to his New York office as soon as possible.

Sean explained how everything Madison and I had done was in self-defense. Again, Sean never mentioned the videotape, he just said that Madison had been an old girlfriend of Eddie DeCarlo and the gangster didn't take kindly to getting dumped.

I think Detective Jackson suspected there was more to the story, but since Madison and I had been a nexus for murder and mayhem since we got to Las Vegas, he was more than happy to put us on a plane back to Los Angeles.

And as predicted by Agent Griffin, the media went gaga for both Madison and me. Madison didn't try to hide the fact she was an escort, in fact, it made her even more of a celebrity.

It's only been two months since our adventure and she's been besieged with offers to guest star on TV shows, she's got a couple of movie offers, two publishers want her life story and Victoria's Secret wants her to design a line of lingerie.

But Madison is taking it slow. She's waited a long time for the chance to become a legitimate actress and she wants to use her fifteen minutes of fame wisely. No rash decisions, no quick buck schemes. Madison is going to do this right.

Speaking of right, Agent Griffin was so right about Sean. He was hailed as a hero in the L.A. press. His father and uncles couldn't have been prouder. Though only a rookie, the LAPD has put him on the fast track to get his gold shield.

But Sean has been haunted by the advice he got from Agent Griffin. Like Griffin's former partner, Sean believed in God and country, right versus wrong, making a difference. And he doesn't want to end up as, well, his own father and uncles, Dempsey Magee or Agent Griffin. So Sean is holding on to his dream, but taking nothing for granted.

And that leaves me. Well, needless to say, I have a few issues with my mother. She flew out to see me as soon as I got back to L.A. I thought it was to console me, help me deal with any trauma I might be feeling.

Nope. She came out to manage what she was sure would become the Grace Taylor Express Train to Fame. She wanted to capitalize on all the media and finally see me become a star. Only one problem, I'm not sure I want to act anymore. Like Madison, the offers are rolling in. But I'm not ready to commit to anything yet.

First I want to find out who Grace Taylor really is. Start living what Larry, that creepy shrink I met in Vegas, called an authentic life. But it isn't easy. Luckily, I've got a new boyfriend I can talk to, someone who knows what it's like to be brainwashed by your parents when you're growing up. But in his case, they filled his head with dreams of LAPD blue. That's right, I'm dating Sean, and I've never been happier.

Oh, and just in case you're wondering, the answer is yes. A toe curling, fingernails digging into the back, I never knew it could be so good, yes.

So, I'm making progress already. Grace Taylor, here I come.

THE END

BUT WAIT!

Before you go, thanks to Camel Press, we've included an excerpt from another novel by James L. Conway – a Hollywood thriller full of mystery, murder, mayhem, and humor – *Dead and Not So Buried*...

Here's what the critics have said about *Dead and Not So Buried:*

"Screenwriter Conway hits the ground running with this entertaining, debut Hollywood potboiler with a likable PI and tongue-in-cheek humor. It's a clever mystery with one more satisfying twist at the very end. Great fun."

-- Library Journal

"His characters breathe on the page and are enlivened with emotions and desires that are nearly palpable. Add frequent plot twists that are capped by a satisfying ending, and you have a mystery novel of the hardboiled school that is sure to keep even the most ardent reader guessing."

--New York Journal of Books

"A fast paced thriller mystery... An unusual plot that sprawls all throughout Hollywood, *Dead and Not So Buried* is an excellent pick for community library suspense and thriller collections."

--Midwest Book Review

"This mystery has all the markings of a bestseller. James L. Conway proves with his first novel that he knows how to write a great mystery with a likeable lead character that leaves his readers wanting a sequel or maybe a series."

--Suspense Magazine

And now here's your preview of *Dead and Not So Buried…*

Prologue

Lightning ripped the sky like a knife through flesh.

Okay, that's a little much. Fact is, there was no lightning. Hell, there wasn't a cloud in the sky. But kidnapping is a heinous crime, heinous enough for a little atmosphere. So even if there was no lightning, there should have been.

The Kidnapper broke in through the rear gate. A crowbar snapped the rusted chain. His size eleven boots left a clear path across the dew-sodden grass, past the flowers, through the statues, to her chamber.

Having long since vacated her body, she couldn't hear the scratching and scraping as he broke into her sanctuary. Couldn't see him as he entered her cold, white room. Never felt him sweep her into his arms.

The Kidnapper shuddered. She looked terrible, much worse than expected. Her white gown was streaked with dirt and mildew. That shock of blond hair was reduced to just a few sparse, wispy patches. And her face was a mess. At least she didn't smell.

She fit easily inside the oversized burlap bag. He pulled the cord. Outside once more, he scanned the grounds with his sharp green eyes. Nothing. He cocked an ear. Just a solitary siren destroying someone's peace a few miles away.

He placed the ransom note in the doorway then tossed the bag over his shoulder and retraced his steps toward the rear gate. Except for stealing Marvel comic books from Harmon's Drug Store when he was a kid and doing a little coke when he first got to Hollywood, this was the first time he'd ever broken the law. He'd expected the anxiety buzz, but the hard-on was a complete surprise.

His car was parked a block away. The top was down on his black SL 550. He placed her carefully on the back seat. He didn't bother buckling her in, though; after all, his victim had been dead for almost forty years.

He slipped behind the wheel of the convertible. Once he got the ransom he'd pay off the leasing company. He was getting sick of their repo threats. Everybody's repo threats.

The car purred to life. The kidnapper smiled as he put the car into gear and drove away from the cemetery. Unbelievable. He'd actually pulled it off. He'd kidnapped one of Hollywood's greatest icons.

And now everyone would have to pay.

The Beginning

I was in my office when the call came. Sitting at my desk admiring the front cover of a paperback novel. My paperback novel. *Rear Entry*, by Gideon Kincaid. That's me. Ex L.A. cop turned private detective turned novelist. The Joe Wambaugh of the PI set.

I should be so lucky. The book had only been out for two weeks. Too soon to tell if anyone would buy it. Dreams of fancy cars and private planes were on hold as I continued to earn a living poking through other peoples' lives.

Hillary came in from the outer office. "I'm sorry, Gideon," she said, her features twisted in compassion.

My own features were twisted in confusion. "Sorry about what?"

"I understand if you don't want to talk about it."

Hillary's my secretary, a smart twenty-five-year-old with all the good stuff—blond hair, blue eyes, great body. But there's a sweetness to Hillary, an endearing naivety that makes me look upon her as a little sister. All my thoughts about Hillary are pure. Well, almost all of them.

"I'll be happy to talk about it," I said. "If I had any idea what we were talking about."

"Death."

"If you're asking me to take a stand, I'm definitely against it."

I've known Hillary since she was ten years old. Her father, Jerry, was my partner for a couple of years when I was driving a black and white out of the West Valley Division. A couple of years ago she showed up looking for a job. I'd just lost my secretary, and Hillary needed the job, so I said sure. She didn't just want to be a secretary, she told me, she wanted to be a PI like me. I told her I'd show her the ropes but never really got around to it. Truth is, she's so good in the office I'd hate to lose her.

"Okay," she said. "I didn't think you'd want to talk about it. But it won't do you any good to, like, keep all that grief inside. It'll fester and feed on itself. Eat away at your insides until your soul dies and you become one of the walking dead. A spiritless zombie going through life like a blind man in a garden." She did that from time to time—rattled on in New Age nonsense. Something to do with her being a native Californian. "Anyway," she said. "Alex Snyder's on line two."

"Alex Snyder?"

"From the mortuary ..." She said it like only an idiot wouldn't know what she was talking about.

"Of course, the mortuary ..." I said, as if I knew what the hell she was talking about. It's never a good idea to let your secretary think you're an idiot. I picked up the phone. "Gideon Kincaid."

"This is Alex Snyder, from Westside Cemetery. I wonder if we could meet."

"Look, if this is some kind of sales call, I—"

"No, Mr. Kincaid. This is business. Important business. Please, I need to see you right away."

Somebody must've stolen a headstone, I thought. Or maybe his teenage daughter had run away. It didn't really matter. He needed help, and that's what I did for a living. "All right, Mr. Snyder. I'm on my way."

My office is in Sherman Oaks, in a strip mall on Ventura Boulevard. Above a pet store called The Bunny Hop. My romantic soul felt I should have an office in one of the funky old buildings on Hollywood Boulevard—much more Chandleresque. But I get the creeps in Hollywood. Frankly it scares the shit out of me. Not the weirdos, the gangs, or the homeless. But the decay. If society can let the Boulevard of Dreams turn into an urban nightmare, what chance does the rest of the city have?

Westside Cemetery is in Brentwood, about twenty minutes from Sherman Oaks, so I used the time in my car to catch up on my literary career.

"Bad news."

"Sales are slow?"

"Slow would be good. They're nonexistent. The publisher's decided the title's the problem. *Rear Entry* sounds like a sex manual for gay men."

I was talking to my agent, Elliot. He's got a boutique agency for writers on their way up. Or down. I wasn't sure which category I belonged in. "Elliot, the title was their idea."

"Everybody makes mistakes."

"Let them make mistakes with Grisham's next book."

"Almost nobody writes a bestseller their first time up. Not even Grisham."

"It took me three years to write *Rear Entry,* and now you're saying I have to write another book?"

"You told me you wrote for the pure joy of it."

"I was lying."

"I warned you writing was a tough way to get rich."

"I thought *you* were lying."

"Never fear, Bubele. It's not over until the buyer for Barnes and Noble sings. If they give us a doorway display, hell, who knows ..."

"Anything I can do to help? Interviews? Book signings?"

"Reality check, Gidman. You're nobody. James Patterson does interviews because he's famous. People will watch a show to see him. Ratings go up, he sells more books. It's a help you/help me kind of simpatico. Stephen King does a book signing because he's famous. People come to a bookstore just to see him. More people in the store mean sales go up. We've got that help you/help me thing going again."

"But they got famous writing books."

"Correctamundo, but they wrote bestsellers. Writing bestsellers made them famous. And fame is the ultimate passkey. Before you can hit the interview/book signing trail, *Rear Entry* needs to become a bestseller."

"But how will it become a bestseller if I can't do any interviews or book signings?"

"Welcome to Catch 22 Land—chicken and the egg and all that."

"So that's it? There's nothing I can do?"

"You could get famous first. Break a big murder case. Solve a million dollar diamond heist. Marry Lindsey Lohan. You need something to single you out, something to make people sit up and take notice."

Yeah, right, I thought. *Who's going to notice a two bit PI?* "All right, Elliot," I said. "Thanks for the advice."

"Wait, I've got one more piece of bread to throw upon the waters."

"What?"

"Don't give up your day job."

Dead and Not So Buried

There's something very soothing about cemeteries—all that grass, the flowers, the fountains, the birds. It's a shame they're wasted on the dead.

The Westside Cemetery is in the heart of Brentwood. It's small—only about two acres—but some of Hollywood's biggest stars are buried there.

I was shown into Alex Snyder's office by his secretary—a middle-aged woman who oozed warmth and compassion. Alex Snyder also oozed warmth and compassion. He was the kindly grandfather type—late sixties, thick gray hair, natty moustache, reassuringly plump. He smiled as I entered, shook my hand. "Mr. Kincaid, a pleasure to meet you."

"Please, call me Gideon."

"Gideon," he said, smiling.

"Will there be anything else?" the secretary asked.

"No, Bernice, thank you."

She closed the door. Snyder pulled a .45 Smith and Wesson out of his desk and shoved it in my face. "Where is she?"

"Get that gun out of my face before I make you eat it," I said. It's tough to talk tough with a gun an inch from your nose, but I didn't think he'd really pull the trigger.

He pulled the trigger. The bullet blew a hole in the wall a micro millimeter from my left ear.

There was a scream from outside the door then a fearful Bernice asked, "Alex, are you okay?"

"Just dandy, Bernice," he said, his eyes never leaving mine. To me he said, "The next one is between your eyes. Now, where is she?!"

"Who?"

"Christine."

"Christine who?"

His eyes nearly bored holes in mine before he said, "You don't know, do you?"

"No."

A little more cornea drilling, then: "I believe you." He lowered the gun, backed away and sagged into his desk chair. "I'm sorry, Mr. Kincaid. I hate violence, but this kidnapping's got me a little crazy."

"Maybe you should start at the beginning."

"I got a call this morning at five-fifteen. One of the gardeners found Christine Cole's crypt open and her body missing."

Holy shit. "Christine Cole?"

Christine Cole was one of the biggest movie stars of the sixties. A model turned actress, she vaulted to fame the year after Marilyn Monroe died and took her place as Hollywood's "it" girl. A sultry blonde with a killer body, Christine oozed sex. And she used it. To the gossip columnists' delight, Christine unabashedly slept her way through the rich and famous. And she battled some personal demons with drugs and alcohol. But Christine also had talent, and she made a string of hit movies. Four, to be exact, and only four. Because, on a foggy April morning, a drunk Christine lost control of her silver Jaguar XKE on the Pacific Coast Highway and plunged to her death. She was thirty-three years old.

Her death had shocked the world. And, like that of Bogart and Monroe, Christine's fame had only increased since her passing. Her image was on everything from tee shirts and coffee mugs to perfume and push-up bras. A true Hollywood icon.

Someone had robbed her grave. Stolen her corpse.

Who steals a corpse?

I said, "There can't be much of her left after forty years. Just bones, right?"

"Bones. The gown she was buried in. And some jewelry. She was buried wearing a bracelet, necklace and diamond ring."

"Valuable?"

"On another body, no. But these were on Christine Cole."

"How much is the kidnapper asking?"

"Two million dollars."

It suddenly hit me. "Wait a minute … why'd you think I knew where the body was?"

"Your business card was attached to the ransom note."

"What?"

"The kidnapper says you have to deliver the money." He handed me the note. The words looked like they were cut out of a variety of magazine articles.

IF YOU WANT TO SEE CHRISTINE AGAIN, HAVE GIDEON BRING $2,000,000 IN USED $100 BILLS TO THE NORTHWEST CORNER OF HOLLYWOOD AND VINE AT 3 P.M. TODAY, OR I'LL SELL THE BODY, BONE BY BONE.

My business card was paper-clipped to the top of the page. In the six years I'd been a PI, I must've given out hundreds of business cards. Was this guy an ex-client? Someone I'd interviewed? Someone who'd picked up my card from a desk? No way of knowing. "I'll be happy to deliver this ransom free of charge." I wanted to find out who this son of a bitch was.

"I appreciate that, but I'll pay for your time—as long as you promise me you won't do anything to jeopardize the safe return of Ms. Cole's remains."

In other words, don't let it get too personal. "I won't." Something was nagging at the back of my brain. There was a familiar aspect about all this, but I couldn't get it to bubble to the surface. "I'd like to see her crypt."

"The funeral itself was small, only thirty-five guests. But outside the gates stood hundreds of reporters, photographers, police officers and fans."

We were standing in front of the open crypt. The marble facing had been pried off, the bronze casket slid open. The only thing inside was the dried remains of a few roses.

"I played the organ," Alex Snyder said. "You know what they requested? 'Yesterday.' Christine loved the Beatles."

A set of footprints in the still-wet grass led to a rear gate. The chain had been broken, snapped by a crowbar, from the looks of it. Probably used the same crowbar on the crypt. "I could talk to a few neighbors," I said. "See if anyone saw anything last night."

"Absolutely not! Don't talk to the neighbors. Or the police. Anyone. We'll be ruined if the tabloids find out we lost Christine Cole's body. I just want to pay the money and get her back."

"You realize the kidnapper might take the money and not return the body."

"I'll take that chance. Will you help me?"

I fingered the ransom note and my business card. "I don't think I have a choice."

WE HOPE YOU'VE ENJOYED THIS EXCERPT FROM *DEAD AND NOT SO BURIED*. IT'S AVAILABLE NOW AT AMAZON.COM.